NOBLE CONFLICT

NOBLE CONFLICT

A VIETNAM WAR NOVEL

*A Soldier Reflects on His Struggle With
Issues of Morality and Integrity
In a War Zone*

Norman S. Pratt

iUniverse, Inc.
New York Lincoln Shanghai

NOBLE CONFLICT
A VIETNAM WAR NOVEL

iUniverse books may be ordered through booksellers or by contacting:

iUniverse
2021 Pine Lake Road, Suite 100
Lincoln, NE 68512
www.iuniverse.com
1-800-Authors (1-800-288-4677)

First Edition
Publisher's Draft

All characters in this book have no existence outside the imagination of the author and have no relation whatsoever to anyone bearing the same name or names. They are not even distinctly inspired by any known or unknown author, and all incidents are pure invention.

ISBN: 0-595-33294-3 (Pbk)
ISBN: 0-595-66825-9 (Cloth)

Printed in the United States of America

To Pamela,

For Her Loyal and Enduring Support

CHINA

Hanoi

LAOS

HAINAN

SOUTH CHINA SEA

THAILAND

The DMZ

Hue

Pleiku

An Khe

Qui Nhon

CAMBODIA

Cheo Reo

Cam Ranh Bay

Saigon

Vung Tau

VIETNAM

NEJuliano04

FOREWORD

The first draft of this novel was written as a nonfiction memoir in 1967, the year after I returned from Vietnam. I wrote it in longhand and my wife, Pamela, typed it on an old carriage typewriter. It was never published. Several times I almost threw it away.

Then, thirty-five years later, I looked at it as an unearthed manuscript—a first-hand recreation of life during a time of war, and rewrote it as general fiction.

Noble Conflict is not intended to be a standard military book, nor is it an action adventure. It is the story of a group of army engineers—an interpersonal study with a military backdrop. I have attempted to tell this story in a straight-ahead story-telling style. The Introduction is written in the third person. The rest of the novel is in the first person with a simple clear theme: *We can only choose how we act, not under what circumstances we must act.* Words in italics are by others and are meant for those who seek a more intellectual approach and deeper purpose than the narrative implies.

I sincerely thank iUniverse for the valuable editorial comments provided by their professional staff, and I am particularly grateful to Judy and Bob Williams for copyediting the final draft. Enjoy.

INTRODUCTION

"God help us," Lieutenant David Jeffries whispered in the early morning coolness at the Richmond Airport.

God help us to help each other, he thought as he panned the two hundred officers and men standing in columns of two, waiting to board the 707 for San Francisco.

"God help us to help each other to attain the best of which we are capable."

Jeffries knew they were capable of the best, collectively. Individually, however, he had doubts, especially of himself. Maybe it was because he was tired. At 0300 hours, they were all tired—fatigued from the rigors of moving equipment by rail and truck convoy to the Port of Norfolk, bewildered by the training and inspections and the processing of new replacements. Jeffries, as three out of every four men in the Company, had been uprooted from his old unit and transferred to the 362nd Engineer Equipment Company for duty in Vietnam.

An air of excitement grasped his tired but anxious body as the line of troops, dressed in starched army fatigue uniforms, streamed upward on the boarding ramp. Halfway up the ramp, he tripped. His steel helmet fell from his head. He stabbed blindly to keep it from falling. The helmet bounced from his outstretched hand onto the ramp where he stood. Slowing the line of troops, he knelt to pick it up and cursed silently, knowing others had seen him falter.

David Jeffries thought of himself as a perfectionist. He didn't like mistakes. He wanted to be a good soldier. He expected to be a good soldier. He thought he knew how to be a good soldier.

Swallowing his pride, the thin young six-foot-tall army lieutenant placed the helmet back onto his head and continued up the loading ramp and into the plane. The officers were seated in first class. First class was to his liking.

He stopped at the first vacant aisle seat, lifted the M14 from his shoulder, reached up overhead and laid it into an overhead storage compartment. He removed his helmet and placed it next to his rifle, and then he sat down next to Lieutenant Joe Goodrich and across the aisle from Captain John Slaughter, the company commander.

He didn't know either of them very well. What he did know was that they didn't like each other very much. Slaughter liked to yell. Goodrich liked to preach. Neither liked to listen.

John Slaughter was a six-foot, two-inch tall muscular airborne ranger. He had brown eyes and black hair. He was married and had two children. He was a former enlisted man who got his commission through OCS. David Jeffries liked John Slaughter. Slaughter's directness and decisiveness made Jeffries feel comfortable.

He wasn't so sure about Joe Goodrich.

Joe Goodrich was a green-eyed redhead, five-feet, ten-inches tall. He was thin. He was a graduate of a small liberal arts college where he had majored in forestry. He was single. Smart and with a great intellect, he was quick-witted, and he enjoyed putting others down. Politically liberal, he sought to reform the military to be socially sensitive. He was a self-declared peacenik.

Jeffries thought he could get along with both of them. He knew he could. He could find the common ground.

They sat quietly during the four-hour flight to San Francisco. Slaughter and Goodrich turned their thoughts off and went to sleep. Jeffries couldn't sleep, unable to turn his thoughts off. Jeffries thought too much. He was an emotionally sensitive man who had outwardly learned to endure and disguise the introverted tendencies of meekness that were intolerable in an army officer. Inwardly, however, it was the opinions of others that were of concern to him—that and what others thought of him as a soldier. Jeffries wanted to be a good soldier. He expected to be a good soldier. He thought he knew how to be a good soldier.

The plane landed in San Francisco, where the troops were loaded onto military buses and transported to Oakland Army Terminal and the troop ship USNS Gordon.

In the port area there were long slow-moving lines of troops waiting to board the ship. The lines stretched around the dock area and up the boarding ramp. Red Cross women handed out cookies and coffee. It was like a World War II deployment, all very professional and businesslike. It seemed like the right thing to do. They were going to war.

Once aboard the troop ship, the officers were separated from the men. Jeffries was berthed with other junior grade officers in a first-class stateroom which had been gutted and equipped with six bunk beds. There were no chairs. The room reeked with the sickening odor of vomit. They opened the portholes, but there was little air. The vomit-stenched room was unbearable—as close to hell as they thought they could ever get.

That night the men were confined to the ship, but the officers were given a six-hour evening pass to San Francisco. Jeffries, Goodrich and Slaughter changed into khaki uniforms and black dress shoes. They caught a taxi to the downtown area, where they found several glitzy topless bars. They picked one. It seemed like the right thing to do. They were going to war.

Once inside, they were seated at aisle seats where endless lines of the topless waitresses carried trays of drinks past them. They were seated close enough to reach out and touch the girls, but they didn't. When they ordered drinks, the girls would lean over and gently touch the men's shoulders with their bare breasts. For entertainment there was a rock band on stage and several birdcages near the ceiling with topless and bottomless dancing girls. It was as close to heaven as they thought they could ever get.

But heaven didn't last long. By midnight they were back aboard ship. By morning they had sailed beneath the Golden Gate Bridge and by noon they were seasick.

Jeffries was moderately seasick for seventeen days: the entire trip. He spent much of his time trying to ignore it, but there wasn't much else to think about besides seasickness. Some of the time he spent in the mess hall, listening to John Slaughter lecture about small unit tactics. Other times he spent lying in his bunk, listening to Joe Goodrich quote Buddhist proverbs and lecture about the duty to get to know each other and to treat each other kindly. He hated that. He eventually learned better. He learned it was best to get up and move around and get away from people.

Daylight hours during good weather he spent outside on the upper deck. He would lie down in the sun against the steel bulkhead and read. He only had two books, *All Quiet on the Western Front* and *Aristotle's Nicomachean Ethics*, and he kept reading them over and over again. He liked that. That gave him an excuse to delude about his own training and moral virtues. Lieutenant David Jeffries was at peace with himself. He was going to war. He wanted to be a good soldier. He expected to be a good soldier. He thought he knew how to be a good soldier.

But all of that had passed now. The seventeen-day voyage had ended. It was time to stop thinking and start doing.

CHAPTER 1

We are crammed shoulder to shoulder aboard a landing craft approaching Qui Nhon. The butts of our slung rifles warm the hip, but our helmets are heavy and our stomachs ache from seasickness as we peer across the last mile of the South China Sea toward desolate green mountains that ring the coastal town like a giant horseshoe. No one speaks. The only sound is the roaring of engines until the landing ramp is lowered with a muffled thud onto the sandy beach where sampans bob in the water and children play in the yards between white masonry buildings and rusty tin shacks.

The beach is narrow and crowded with construction equipment—ours—equipment we had loaded onto the freighter in Norfolk: bulldozers, graders, scrapers, cranes, several dozen trucks, and a gigantic rock crusher. It is an awesome sight. And there are natives here—Oriental people standing on the beach, old men and children mostly. They watch us scurry about over the equipment. They point. They wave. They smile.

The captain has ordered us to move inland, find and secure a bivouac site, and await his instructions. I walk quickly toward my jeep, wondering if it will start. It does, and I see that it is full of gas.

PFC Hayman is my jeep driver. He is a skinny young black man, about my height. An inner city high school dropout, he is loveable but annoyingly incompetent. "Where are we going, sir?" he asks as he tosses his rifle into the back of the jeep and climbs into the driver's seat.

To be perfectly honest, I haven't the slightest idea where we are going. All I know is that we are going someplace else because we have to clear the beach for

1

the 1st Air Cavalry Division. I don't know where we are going, but I'm sure it is in the right direction. Our cause is moral. Our cause is virtuous. And *moral virtue is the right aim and direction.*

I had carefully studied maps of this area aboard the ship while crossing the Pacific, but now I find the actual terrain looks nothing like what I expected. To begin with, gigantic jungle-covered mountains lie just beyond the outskirts of the town, and they are so proportioned and so close that the beach seems like a stage. In addition, the town is much larger and cleaner than I expected, and it has paved roads.

Hayman pulls the jeep onto a dirt road, heading out of town. Several bull-dozers are loaded onto tractor-trailers which fall in behind in convoy formation. "Where are we going, Lieutenant?" Hayman asks again.

"I have to see the captain," I reply. "This road isn't on the map." We are supposed to go five miles inland. I assumed that we would follow the road, which showed on my map as a solid red line, but the paved road went right through the center of the town of Qui Nhon, and it was quite obvious that we could not move our construction equipment through the narrow streets without knocking down several buildings.

The road on which the convoy now forms is an unmarked dirt road leading south, directly out of town toward what shows on my map as a leper colony.

While I study the map, Hayman studies the terrain. He sits behind the driver's wheel and lifts the steel pot from his head and stares intently down the dirt road into the jungle. He is young, maybe nineteen, about six feet tall, with a flawless dark complexion and short black hair. Hayman is a radio operator who just happened to be assigned to an engineer company. He could have just as easily been assigned to the infantry. Instead of driving my jeep, he could be hustling around the jungle, carrying a battery pack on his back and waving an antenna for snipers to fire at.

"Hayman," I say to him again, "my map says there is a leper colony down this road."

"There are people in black uniforms up ahead," Hayman says, lifting a pair of field glasses to his eyes. "I can see them walking along the road."

"Give me the glasses," I tell him. "You're only a private, I'm the officer."

I take the field glasses from Hayman, prop my foot up onto the jeep, and cocking my helmet back, lift the binoculars to my eyes. The people in black uniforms look harmless enough. They are walking slowly toward us along the road. I can see now that the road forks to the right, away from the leper colony. I conclude it must be a military bypass around the town.

This road must lead somewhere acceptable. I personally instruct each of the drivers to turn on their headlights and to keep two hundred yards between vehicles. I haven't the slightest idea where we are going, but we are going somewhere else because we are under orders to clear the beach for the twenty thousand men of the 1st Air Cavalry Division.

As the convoy pulls out, some of the men put their headlights on, while some do not. Nobody maintains proper distance between vehicles. The trucks move along this unmapped dirt road not as a disciplined military convoy, but huddled bumper-to-bumper. The dirt road is dry. It obviously hasn't rained here in several weeks. Dust quickly envelopes the slow-moving convoy as we approach the right fork.

Just after making the turn, we enter a wooded area and spot a group of armed Vietnamese men in black uniforms coming straight toward us.

"Sir, what's a Viet Cong look like?" Hayman coughs as the convoy comes to a halt in a cloud of dust.

"I don't know," I cough back, "but it doesn't seem like they would be walking down this road in broad daylight."

Upon closer inspection, the men in black uniforms appear to be harmless new army recruits. The group is disorganized and obviously undisciplined. Some wear hats, some do not. One is dragging the butt of his rifle along the ground. They are all laughing and joking. I am struck by their physical size. None of them are over about five-feet four-inches tall. They are thin, with hollow faces and recessed eyes. They appear frail, but not weak. Their muscles are taut. And they smile. They wave to us as we pass by. I wonder what they must be thinking about us, our strapping six-foot frames, our starched fatigue uniforms, our staring eyes. We are of larger stature. We are tall and reeking, with a wealth of high-tech equipment.

There is a Vietnamese army sergeant with them, dressed in green. The sergeant speaks a little English. He motions for the convoy to stop. He walks up to me and announces that we have entered a South Vietnamese Army Training Camp and that we may not proceed because there is an overhead communication wire ahead, which the bulldozer atop the lead truck cannot clear. He motions for us to turn around.

While we are talking, machine gun fire opens up on the left flank. Instinctively, the drivers exit the vehicles and take cover in the wooded areas. It is a bit embarrassing. The machine gun fire is being generated by a group of recruits on a rifle range. It is also a bit fortunate. We have not yet opened the ammunition.

We climb back into our vehicles and prepare to proceed. The only thing in our way is a single strand of overhead communication wire. The wire is propped up on two wooden poles—one on each side of the road. The Vietnamese sergeant begs us not to destroy the wire. I want to oblige and try to explain that with adequate time we might work something out. I don't think he understands what I am trying to say, and I don't have time to try and explain it to him. We don't speak the same language. We will never speak the same language. It is an unfortunate situation. I salute the sergeant and wave my arm forward. The line of communications is torn from the uprights by a bulldozer high in the air atop the lead lowboy, and broken with a violent snap.

We follow the bumpy dirt road through a heavily wooded area for about a mile until we reach a narrow two-lane bituminous paved road, which runs north and south and is known locally as Route 1.

Route 1 follows the coastline the full length of the country. We are about halfway between North Vietnam and Saigon—about 400 miles south of the border with North Vietnam, and 400 miles north of Saigon. We have to turn right or left. There are Vietnamese villages to the right, and military encampments to the left. We turn left and drive about two miles into Canh Van Valley.

Canh Van Valley is a charming little river valley nestled between high steep mountains and covered with heavy green vegetation. Between the mountains there flows a narrow slow-moving tidal stream, partially dammed up to accommodate a few small rice paddies. Many low areas along the stream have been taken over by wetlands vegetation. The stream is paralleled on the west side by Route 1.

Military support installations lie west of Route 1. There is a transportation unit, a quartermaster unit, and a marine detachment. There is nobody else. The next site should be ours, but there is no contiguous site available. Instead, the road narrows. We then pass though a small village where several people wave to us. In the middle of the village is a store with a small colorful hand-painted sign advertising Coca Cola and Beer Lareau.

Ahead on the right is a clear spot of land above the flood plain with several thatched huts along the side of the road and a narrow opening through which our equipment can be maneuvered. It looks like a perfect location for our camp—a bit small, but big enough to accommodate all of our equipment. We pull off the road, squeezing in between two huts, and drive into the site where we park in random fashion. Directly behind us, to the west, are huge, steep hills, covered with thick green vegetation.

Fallon is the platoon sergeant. It is in the heat of midday that the tall burly man waddles toward me, his firm muscles swelling, carrying a sweat-soaked handkerchief in one hand and a bottle of Beer Lareau in the other.

"Sir, you want a swig?" Fallon rasps.

"Where did you get it?" I reply enviously.

"Bunch of kids over there sellin' it," he says. "Fifty cents a beer, twenty-five cents a coke." Fallon laughs. He has a nasty laugh, like *don't mess with the man.*

As far as I am concerned, "Fallon is the man." First of all, he is physically imposing. He is six-feet, four-inches tall, heavyset, with black hair and black eyes. Second, he is experienced. A middle-aged man nearing retirement, he is a decorated Korean War Veteran and the only one in the company with any combat experience. I have great respect for Sergeant Fallon. I have great respect for him, even though his insignia of rank indicates only three stripes. Fallon is the lowest grade non-commissioned officer: a buck sergeant.

He had recently been busted from first sergeant to buck sergeant because of an altercation. Rumor has it he caught a man in bed with his wife, rammed a revolver down the fink's throat, but never pulled the trigger.

"Sir," Fallon says to me, "don't you think we should set up security? You're the ranking officer 'til the captain gets here."

"Yes," I reply. "We better set up security. I don't like the looks of that hill. There could be snipers up there." I was thinking we could be attacked any minute, but that seemed rather absurd, because by this time several dozen women and children are roaming the area selling beer and trinkets. I tell Fallon to place an armed guard every fifty feet around the perimeter. Then I sit down under a shady bush, wondering what to do next. It seems incredulous that civilians have already infiltrated our position. I know Slaughter will be furious when he arrives.

A small, dignified-looking man with a gray beard, long flowing white hair, and wearing a white Nehru jacket, shuffles up the trail by which we had entered. He looks like somebody important, so I rise and walk to greet him. There is a woman by his side, wearing baggy pants rolled to the knee, an over-size silken shirt and a thatched cone-shaped hat. When she is close enough to see the polished second lieutenant bars on my shirt collar, she runs toward me.

The old man stands quietly by while the woman shoves a basket of trinkets in my face. "You buy?" she begs with a modest smile. Her teeth are black and nearly rotted off at the gums. She is the ugliest woman I have ever seen. If I could speak Vietnamese I would ask her if she had ever heard tell of tooth-paste. Nobody else in the company can speak Vietnamese, either. I shake my head to indicate no. After a while she gets the message and goes off, trying to sell her goods to Fallon.

The old man is still standing nearby. He has what I consider a serious look on his face. I smile; he smiles back. I think maybe he is not so serious after all, but he is. He starts yelling and flailing his arms and pointing in all directions about the camp. I listen intently and try to figure out what he is talking about.

Fallon motions me away from the old man and to the perimeter of the site. He points to a thatched bamboo hut a short distance from our position and lying near a knee-high rice field ready for harvest. "We got a problem with that hut over there." Fallon roars. "We'll have to burn it down. Somebody could sneak right up there alongside of us and lob a hand grenade. If anything happens, we'll be firing right into that hut. Tell Slaughter to burn it down."

Fallon and I walk the perimeter. The old man follows us, screaming emphatically. I try to push the old man away, but he will not leave.

The old man is either trying to convey a message of extreme importance, or he is crazy. I am quickly coming to the opinion that he is probably crazy and that we had better get him out of here. I motion for him to leave.

The old man becomes silent. He takes the old woman by the hand and leads her toward the trail we had entered by. On the way he stops and picks up a handful of sticks. He looks at me with a frown of despair and points to several earthen mounds. He walks to the mounds, one at a time, and places an upright stick on each one. We have moved into a graveyard.

That doesn't bother me. That doesn't bother anybody else either, except Lieutenant Joe Goodrich, who is adamant that we do not disturb any grave sites. He is insistent to the point that his actions are disruptive.

Captain Slaughter soon arrives. Slaughter is furious to see civilians freely roaming the area. "This is ridiculous," he yells at Joe Goodrich. "Get these civilians out of here."

"Sir," Joe replies, "we can't set up here. This is a graveyard. This place is sacred to these people."

Joe Goodrich is an independent thinker and has his own philosophy about things. However, he also cares about what other people think. He expects others to see things his way, even though many of us do not, especially John Slaughter.

Slaughter is outraged over the disorganization, indecision, and lack of cooperation. He warns everybody to move in the same direction. He ostracizes Goodrich for his meekness and orders him to clear the fields of fire, distribute the ammunition, and set up fifty-caliber machine guns.

He is also upset because Engineer Headquarters at Qui Nhon has refused to release any more equipment until the base camp is secure and Slaughter has a plan drawn up showing exactly where he will park each and every vehicle.

He even yells at me. "How do you expect us to move the Big Deuce into a little site like this?"

"Sir, I don't know," I reply.

"I'll tell you how, Lieutenant. You are moving out."

John Slaughter is committed to discipline. John knows how to take orders. He may not like the orders he is given, but he always follows them. And John Slaughter loves to yell orders, and always expects his orders to be followed.

Slaughter calls a meeting—right now—right where we are standing. He gathers the platoon leaders and platoon sergeants around him. There are eight of us all together: four second lieutenant platoon leaders, three four-stripe staff sergeants and one three-stripe buck sergeant.

Slaughter places one hand on his hip and points with the other, first at me, then at Sergeant Fallon. "You two are taking a detachment forty miles inland to An Khe to support the First Cavalry Division, not because I have any confidence in you, but because you are the only ones in this whole company with any equipment."

We are all taken by surprise. Fallon seems particularly upset. He nervously tugs at his cap. "I don't want to go," he says. "I'm too old." He then removes his cap and uses it to slap the nearest man to him—Sergeant Roscoe. "Roscoe wants to go."

Roscoe lifts his head and pushes out his chin. Newly promoted to Staff Sergeant, the tall lanky young man with blue eyes and brown hair now outranks Fallon. He exudes inexperienced optimism. "What do you know, Fallon? Huh? What do you know?" The cocky young Sergeant Roscoe pulls a switchblade from his pocket and presses it into the back of Fallon's neck.

"Roscoe, you put that thing away before I show you how to use it," Fallon warns.

Roscoe snaps the knife closed and flips it into the air, making a one-handed catch before coolly sliding it into his starched fatigue pocket. He looks at me and says, "Sir, your platoon sergeant won't last one week with the 1st Cav."

"Oh yeah," Fallon's cheeks shake furiously, "you ninety-day wonder. You aren't old enough for Boy Scout camp," he says as he waves his clenched fist under Roscoe's broad chin. "How the hell did you ever make platoon sergeant?"

Slaughter ignores them both. He is upset over the fact that he cannot go to An Khe himself. But he cannot go to An Khe. He has been ordered to retain the rest of the Company in Canh Van Valley. Slaughter is not happy.

Slaughter advises us that I am to lead an advanced party to An Khe and report back to him exactly what is needed there. Slaughter desperately wants the whole company in An Khe with the First Cav, but Engineer Group Headquarters in Qui Nhon needs a contingent nearby to justify their existence. Slaughter's fate, at least for the foreseeable future, is to make peace with the civilians.

After the meeting breaks up, Slaughter and I walk together around the campsite, which overlooks the surrounding rice paddies and nearby shacks. I show him the thatched hut that Fallon recommended we burn down. We both agree that it would probably be in our field of fire, but it is also probably some-body's home and to destroy it at this time might be a mistake, since it could serve to alienate the very people we are supposed to train for peaceful coexis-tence. We decide to let it stand, at least until tomorrow.

"I wonder if any of these little bastards are Viet Cong," Slaughter says as he watches the lanterns come on in several shacks nearby. "I'll bet this place is crawling with them." Slaughter places his hand on the forty-five automatic strapped to his waist and storms off to inspect the guard.

I fear Slaughter is right. Some of these people are Viet Cong—or if they are not, they soon will be. In any event, it is not my problem and there is absolutely nothing I can do about it.

We have canned C-rations for supper and call it a day. It is somewhat crowded in the small bivouac area, but I manage to find a place to lie near my jeep. Officers are authorized one pup tent for their own private use. Unfortunately, I discover I have been issued two right sides and no left side. So while most of the men pitch two man pup tents, I unroll my sleeping bag onto the ground and pray that it won't rain.

We arise at dawn to the sounds of birds chirping, the smell of buffalo dung, and have a breakfast of canned eggs. The dew is still fresh. The view is beautiful. I marvel at the freshness of the countryside, at the valley covered with lush light green carpets of rice paddies, and at the dark green jungle-covered mountains that surround us.

In the early morning hours we watch a convoy of South Vietnamese infantry drive into the countryside. It looks like a group of recruits starting on a training mission. They are headed south, but there is no danger to the south. The danger is to the north and to the west.

An Khe is west. That is where I am going: An Khe. That is where Slaughter wants to go: An Khe. But Slaughter doesn't yet have all of his equipment.

While Slaughter tries to move the rest of his equipment from the beach, Fallon and I take off for Engineer Group Headquarters in Qui Nhon to find someone to give us a briefing on how we get to An Khe and what to do there.

Engineer Group Headquarters in Qui Nhon is located in an old French Villa, an impressive looking three-story building with double-pane windows and jalousie doors. Around the perimeter of the building is strung a double row of concertina wire.

The open windows are easy targets for hand grenades. The headquarters building is rapidly being fortified by two Spec 4s who are stretching chicken wire across the windows, while a PFC stands guard behind a fifty-five gallon oil drum full of sand. Fallon taps one of the workers on the shoulder and asks if he knows where we can find the 1st Cav Liaison Officer. The man spits out a mouthful of staples and tells us that he can't right now because they are going to get bombed.

Fallon asks him if he thinks they are going to get bombed right away, because if they are, we are going to get out of here. The specialist says he is just following orders. He points to the main entrance of the building, where a major is standing in the doorway.

Standing with his hands on his hips, the major looks around disapprovingly. He is a mature man, short of stature, about five-foot-eight, with a crew cut and a mustache. The nametag on his shirt reads "Powers."

His rank and demeanor intimidate me. Why is that? What is it about an authority figure that is naturally repulsive to some people? Why do majors intimidate lieutenants? Why do lieutenants intimidate sergeants? Why does this major look so disconcerted?

I think for a moment that he is staring at me, but he is not. He is staring across the street at a soldier who is slouched in a jeep. The man wears no rank. He has obviously removed his insignia of rank and he wears no shoulder patch. He wears starched fatigues, a steel pot on his head, and carries a submachine gun in his lap.

The man is about the same size as the major, but he is a bit thinner, and clean-shaven. He sways back and forth in the jeep, waving his machine gun at the major. I can't read the nametag on his shirt, and I get the impression the major can't either.

The major points his finger at the man, directing him to come forward into the headquarters building.

The man grins, and then he lifts his machine gun overhead and fires a burst into the air.

We all jump for cover, except for the major. Fallon and I fall to the ground. The PFC ducks behind a fifty-five gallon drum. The Spec 4s jump through the windows into headquarters. But the major never flinches.

The major stomps down the front steps and across the street. He approaches the soldier and brazenly reaches for his weapon. "Sonny-boy, I'll take that until you learn how to use it," he says.

The soldier sits up militarily, places the machine gun on his hip and swings to the right. "Sir," the man says in a southern drawl, "if you think you're man enough, go ahead and try."

His challenge takes the major by surprise. The major backs down and storms back into headquarters. Fallon and I stand up and brush the dust from our fatigues, keeping an eye on the soldier. We can now read his nametag. It reads "Perry."

Perry is not a young man. He is, I estimate, in his mid-thirties—a career soldier—old enough to know he will probably be killed over here, and old enough to have made up his mind to do it his way. Perry impresses me. His bold actions give me confidence.

Fallon and I walk up the front steps and enter the main foyer of the headquarters building. The rooms inside are large, with high ceilings. The reception room is to the left. There are two civilian secretaries in the reception room—young girls, well dressed in native Vietnamese dresses, English-speaking and polite.

I introduce myself and ask to see the 1st Cav Liaison Officer. The girls smile. One of them rises and escorts us into a back room where she introduces me to the major.

The major shakes my hand and tells the girl to leave.

He takes us over to a large wall-mounted map. Pointing to the map, he speaks knowledgeably. "Elements of the 101st Airborne landed near An Khe yesterday partially secured the area and are now conducting sweeping operations within a twenty-mile radius. One battalion is dug in along the An Khe Pass." He points to a position of increasing relief ten miles east of An Khe. "Six bridges along Route 19 have been blown and Baileyed. The road is secure as far as the Pass until 1700 hours. Don't travel the road after 1700."

"It doesn't sound too safe before 1700," I comment.

"It isn't. Intelligence reports an entire NVA Battalion crossed the road two nights ago and is operating somewhere near An Khe, but you shouldn't have any trouble during daylight hours."

He reminds us that an aircraft carrier loaded with the First Cav is approaching Qui Nhon Harbor. Combat helicopters are available now and the combat troops expect to disembark over the next few days. They will be going directly to An Khe. The Cav has its own Battalion of Combat Engineers but needs additional construction equipment to prepare its base camp. That is our mission at An Khe, base camp construction.

Major Powers suggests I take an advanced party as far as An Khe Pass and report back to him when ready for the full detachment. That sounds all right to me.

I leave the headquarters building with mixed emotions. I am optimistically excited, but Perry, who has fortunately left, leaves me unnerved. I hope I never see him again. Life is too short to deal with the Perry's of this world. Perry's way is the hard way.

An Khe holds promise for me. I am excited. Fallon, on the other hand, is totally unhappy. The Korean War Veteran doesn't like the sounds of a mission at An Khe. He drives recklessly through a crowded commercial district of shops and bars, and then to a nearby residential area. The residential area is a clean area of French-style masonry architecture where I feel safe. There are small, single-family homes, a small apartment building, and an elementary school. We pass in front of a two-story white masonry building with a small black and white sign, which reads, "Southern Baptist Alliance." I tell Fallon they must be kidding.

Fallon parks in front of the elementary school and asks me to wait in the jeep while he runs an errand. I let him go.

While I am sitting in the jeep, a small Vietnamese boy stops by and asks me if I want to buy some *piasters*—Vietnamese currency—one hundred *piasters* per dollar. He speaks clear English with a slight accent. I tell the boy I want some, but all I have is a ten. With that he reaches into his pocket, pulls out a wad of bills, gives me one thousand *piasters* and asks if I want any more. Unbeknownst to me, the exchange rate has jumped twenty percent since yesterday.

A group of children are playing nearby. One of the children, another little boy, seeing the money change hands, comes over and steps up onto the running board of the jeep. We are eye to eye—me sitting and him standing. "You lieutenant. You have very much money." The boy is extremely well-dressed in light blue shorts, white shirt, and a navy blue sport coat. He carries three books under his arm.

"You speak English?" I say.

"Yes, I speak English very good."

"What are you carrying?"

"These are my school books." He cocks his head and smiles and points to the lieutenant bar on my baseball cap. "Lieutenant have *beaucoup* money. I be lieutenant someday."

I tell him if he studies enough books he could be a general someday. He is extremely well-spoken and understands every word I say. He pushes a book under my face. "I study English." The little boy turns to the middle of the book and begins reading.

He is a good reader. He reads slowly and with emotion. He is a very nice little boy. But he has competition.

He has competition from a slightly older boy, a poorly dressed dirty little bully who pushes his way onto the jeep and shoves a bundle of postcard size glossy pornographic photographs in my face. "Hey, you number one GI, you buy dirty pictures."

It is embarrassing. I push the smut peddler back and let the clean little boy up onto my lap. "How old is that kid?" I ask.

The clean little boy doesn't answer. Instead he asks, "Lieutenant, you buy coke? I get you coke. You buy." Then he jumps off of my lap and runs down the street.

"No. I don't want a coke," I yell.

The little smut peddler hops back in the jeep and persists. "Lieutenant, you buy dirty pictures, yes. Twenty pictures five dollars. You number one GI. You buy."

Where did this kid come from? Why is he so bold? Who taught him to do this? Where did he get his merchandise? Will he sell many pornographic pictures? Yes, he will. I buy a packet of pictures and then push the smut peddler away.

The other little boy soon returns. He reaches up and hands me a cold coke. "You buy dirty book. You give me 50 *pi*."

I pay him, watch him put the money in his pocket and let him back into the jeep. He watches me take a drink of coke and stares at the hair on my arm. It suddenly occurs to me that most Vietnamese have no hair on their arms and legs—not that it matters to me—but he seems intrigued with my body hair. "You buy dirty book, you give me five *pi*," he begs, while craftily pulling the hair on my arm.

"You like hair. You like the hair on my arm, don't you?"

"What is hair? Why do you have it and I don't?"

I like this kid. He is a nice kid. "What does you father do?" I ask.

"My father is a school teacher."

"Do you have any brothers or sisters?"

"I have," he raises three fingers, "one brother and two sisters."

"What does you brother do?"

"My brother goes to school."

"What do your sisters do?" I ask.

"I don't know," he replies.

"Do they go to school?"

"No. They too old." The little boy continues pulling the hair on my arm. "They make *beaucoup* money while I go to school, read books. I no have *beaucoup* money. Lieutenant have *beaucoup* money. You give me five *pi*."

I want to give him five hundred *pi*, for I fear he will need it. There will soon be several thousand American troops here and the ramifications of that inflation will be hard-felt among the civilian population in their struggle for the necessities of life. The prices of food, clothing and shelter are sure to rise.

I look lovingly at the little boy and then decide to buy another coke. I look disdainfully at the little smut peddler, thinking how different he is. Then I turn and watch the other children playing in the nearby school yard. These kids here aren't much different than the kids I grew up with. There are good kids. There are bad kids. How they behave mostly has to do with upbringing. *People are the same the world over. They do what they are trained and conditioned to do.*

Fallon returns with a case of booze under his arm, an assorted collection of bourbon, gin, and vodka. He says he's buying one-third interest in the Hong Cong Bar. Fallon is kidding, I think. Fallon enjoys kidding. He explains the opportunities of war and asks if I want in. He predicts five thousand dollars a month income from his investment and proudly declares it is perfectly legal for military personnel to operate as private entrepreneurs in a foreign country as long as they pay taxes. He is quite persuasive, like a stockbroker. Fallon jokes that he is particularly bullish on bars and brothels.

We return to Canh Van Valley, where I spend the rest of the day preparing for An Khe. I want to take Fallon with me, but Slaughter decides I should go alone. Fallon will remain behind to help prepare more equipment. Slaughter wants to try to move the entire company to An Khe, and to do it as soon as possible.

At night I lay under the stars, unable to sleep, thinking about what happened today, and then wondering what tomorrow holds. Today we reacted to conditions and did the best we could. Tomorrow we will react to conditions and do the best we can, just the same as it has always been. There will be winners. There will be losers. There will be the weak. There will be the strong. Some of us will try to excel. Most of us will just try to survive. That's the way it has always been—reacting to conditions, reacting to conditions over which we have little or no control.

CHAPTER 2

Three miles north of Qui Nhon, Route 19 branches west as a narrow two-lane paved road and follows the Dak Krong River toward the central highlands. Green rice paddies lining either side of the road flow peacefully through the valley from steep, wooded mountains beyond. Occasional small villages— Cum Lam, Phu Phong, and Nhon Ngai—dot the countryside along the way.

Hayman and I ride the lonely road alone. Our jeep seems to hit every pothole in the road and our jeep trailer, stacked high with supplies, bounces like a little wagon on a bed of stones. We travel swiftly, fifty to sixty miles an hour, through the lowlands, slowing to forty through the scattered villages, crawling over Bailey bridges hastily constructed over dropped spans of concrete and steel.

"Hayman, do you know how to work the radio?" I ask.

"Yes sir," he replies.

"If anything should happen out here, we might need it in a hurry."

"It's broke," he says calmly.

As the jeep hits a pothole I stabilize myself against the front windshield. "What the hell do you mean, 'It's broke'?"

"The wire's broke off the microphone." Hayman laughs. "We can receive, but we can't transmit. But right now we can't even receive because we are out of range."

I should have taken more time to learn about the radio, but I had never used it. And I don't want Hayman to know that I don't know the effective range. "That's no excuse for not maintaining the radio. I ought to have you court-martialed. We'll need that radio at An Khe."

"No we won't," Hayman says sarcastically. "This is an AM radio. The infantry uses FM."

I lean back on my seat, curse softly, and gaze apprehensively toward the mountainous ridgeline ahead, and then I look down to study my map. On the map I can see the terrain. I can see contours. I can see vegetative areas. I can see villages. But on the map I can't see the people. I cannot communicate with a map. And we have no radio communications.

Straight ahead about a quarter of a mile is a lone civilian bicyclist, an old man in white pajamas wearing a white cone-shaped hat. I don't know who he is or if he is to be trusted. If we could speak his language we could stop and talk to him, but we don't know the language. We are completely unknowing and untrained to deal with Vietnamese civilians. The only training I received was a twelve-hour course in escape and evasion and an eight-hour course in guerilla warfare. During the escape and evasion course I was captured and thrown into a ten-foot-deep pit where I was beaten with a folded newspaper by an airborne ranger. During the course in guerilla warfare I was taught how to avoid pungy sticks and Viet Cong ambushes. Basically, we were trained to trust no one and to take care of ourselves.

Maybe Joe Goodrich is right. Maybe we have to get to know the people. But we don't speak the language.

We drive by the lone bicyclist. He is not a part of our agenda. We must do what we are trained to do. That is our practical wisdom. And *practical wisdom is the right means of attainment.*

I sit back and gaze apprehensively toward the mountainous ridgeline ahead. What is up there? Am I adequately prepared to deal with what lies ahead? Do I have practical wisdom?

I recall the passage, "Yeah, though I walk through the valley…" from Bible reading in school. It was often read in high school homeroom during early morning opening exercises. I could spot the kids in school who never went to church because when it was their turn to read the Bible they would often pick the 23rd Psalm. I always listened, but I often didn't pay much attention. There was this looker named June who sat right alongside of me in homeroom. I couldn't forget her. After Bible reading and the Pledge of Allegiance I'd whisper "June is busting out all over." She'd smile. Bible reading didn't seem very important then. The important thing was to prove that to go from the outside of a circle to the inside of a circle you have to pass through the circle.

An algebra teacher taught me that in tenth grade. I remember sitting through weeks in high school, proving seemingly useless theorems. In college it was a chemistry teacher. One day he put a match to a large balloon full of hydrogen after telling us we wouldn't understand the significance of this until years later. It exploded with a loud jarring "bang." Then there was a drafting teacher who went to the blackboard with a piece of chalk and announced he could draw a perfect circle. And he did.

Looking back, I think the drafting teacher may have cheated. It would have been easy for him to cheat by simply inscribing a faint tracing line on the blackboard visible only to him. The rest of us couldn't see it. We didn't know he cheated. We thought he was naturally gifted. That's not cheating.

The 101st Airborne is in concealment somewhere along the foothills of the An Khe Pass at the location where Route 19 begins its climb from the valley to the central highlands. An entire battalion is there, well camouflaged and concealed by the jungle. Hayman and I cannot see them as we approach. We see only one man, a PFC holding an M16 and wearing the white screaming eagle shoulder patch of the 101st Airborne.

He waves us off the road. A rifle shot rings off in the far distance. "They're up there again. The little bastards are back up there." The PFC's eyes, burning with the intensity of lasers, look up the narrow winding road, which rises gracefully between two ridgelines. "Our mess sergeant got it up there yesterday." The young soldier pulls a handkerchief from his pocket, lifts his steel helmet and wipes his eyes. "He told the old man he was tired of watching the rest of us go on patrol and he wanted to see some action. Now he is dead."

Hayman and I look at each other, first in disbelief, then in absolute fear. I fumble for words, but I am unable to speak. Finally, I turn to the PFC and say something. "You must be a career soldier."

"No, sir," he answers. "I have seventy-four days left. I volunteered airborne because I thought it would be fun to jump out of an airplane. I never dreamed I'd be in a mess like this. None of us did." He tightens the grip on his M16. "I'm a short-timer. I want to go home."

Don't we all? I trust this man. He is a model soldier. He will attack with vengeance at the slightest provocation and he will do it with great proficiency. But he will not attack without cause.

I tell him I am supposed to go to An Khe. He tells me I can't get there without an armed escort and that I may proceed only as far as the top of the Pass. The 101st is dug in along the Pass with a command post near the top, about three miles ahead.

The Pass is a steep and winding incline through thick woods, interspersed with small, clear areas of high brown grass. The grade is so steep that Hayman must put the jeep in low gear just to drive up the narrow, winding two-lane bituminous paved road. It is a lonely drive, with nothing in sight except for thick green vegetation and intermittent fields of grass.

I chamber a round in my M14, not that it will do any good, just to make me feel better. We round a sharp bend where the thick, wooded area on the left side of the road opens onto a broad field of knee-high brown grass. We can see several hundred yards up and across the undulating steep sloping field. On the other side of the open field are more trees. The mountains are covered with thick, beautiful green trees. It is quiet. It is peaceful.

Suddenly, another rifle shot rings off in the distance. Just as suddenly, several hundred soldiers rise up from the field of grass, each carrying an M16 held at the ready. They stand in mass, spaced uniformly apart, each staring at me. Shortly, they disappear back into the field of grass.

A short way further up the Pass there is a bivouac area located to the side of the road. There are three general-purpose tents, a few pup tents, and a field mess area with tables, gas stoves and fifty-five gallon drums for washing silverware. Cooks are preparing a hot lunch of K-Rations. Several soldiers are standing in line with their mess gear.

Hayman pulls the jeep up and parks in front of one of the tents. I hop from the jeep, walk to the tent and look inside. There is one person inside, standing over a table map. He wears no rank or shoulder patches. He carries a submachine gun. I immediately recognize him from the confrontation with Major Powers in Qui Nhon. It is Perry.

"Who are you?" I ask.

"I'm your liaison with the First Cav."

Well, that is just wonderful. I am taking orders from a boldly aggressive man of undesignated rank and unknown training or qualifications. Maybe he is a fraud, or maybe not. Maybe he went to Yale, Harvard or Princeton. Whoever he is, he seems to be a leader who knows what he is doing. That deserves my attention.

He points on the map to a position along Route 19. "This is where we are now." Then he points to a location ten miles west of our position along Route 19. "This is the town of An Khe." He picks up a black grease pencil and draws a large X in the middle of a broad plain about two miles north of An Khe. "This is where we will park the helicopters." Then he points to an area of high relief to the southwest. "This is Hong Cong Hill. That's where the Viet Cong are. That is where you are going tomorrow."

My patience is about to run out. "Who's in charge here?" I ask him.

Perry is a little man with an impressive athletic body. "I'm in charge," he says. He is square-jawed, stands erect, and looks a little like Robert McNamara. "Just do what I tell you."

Apparently there are only a few VC on Hong Cong Hill. They will be removed tomorrow by the 101st Airborne, one day before 1st Cav arrives. According to Perry, tomorrow's mission is simple. Hong Cong Hill will be taken by helicopter assault of the 101st Airborne. Perry and I will fly in with the assault troops to analyze what is needed in the way of construction equipment. He will remain there. I am to fly back to bring up what equipment is needed.

I emphatically tell Perry I don't need to go with him. We need all the equipment and I have to return to Qui Nhon to get it. He tells me I don't have to go to Qui Nhon. He tells me to send Hayman with a message. He needs me with him on Hong Cong Hill to scout out an acceptable location for a borrow pit. Reluctantly, I agree and write a note to Slaughter, requesting that he bring the entire company to An Khe tomorrow. I suspect Major Powers won't let him leave the safety of Canh Van Valley, but I figure it is worth a try anyway.

Hayman leaves for Qui Nhon in the late afternoon, accompanied by a machine gun jeep escort. That will make Slaughter happy. I spend a restless night and arise at 0400 hours.

At sunrise, ten Huey helicopters land, one behind the other, in formation on Route 19. The 101st Airborne loads aboard armed with M16's, thirty-caliber machine guns, grenade launchers and ammunition belts.

I have been assigned to the last chopper. I climb aboard and sit down between two PFCs loaded for bear. Perry climbs in and happily sits down on the opposite side, next to a door gunner. The door gunner leans out the side of the chopper onto a thirty-caliber machine gun, which shakes as the chopper blades roar overhead.

The engines rev to a whistle and the choppers lift off, one behind another. My stomach muscles tighten. I tighten the grip on my M14. We rise and circle over the Pass to an elevation just above the mountaintops and then head west. The choppers barely clear the tree line at the top of the mountains, and then fly close to the ground, proceeding swiftly over the highlands brush country on a straight line for Hong Cong Hill.

It takes ten minutes to reach Hong Cong Hill. It is a big hill. The closer we get, the bigger it looks. It is high, steep, and covered with trees.

The choppers head for a clear landing area near the bottom of the hill where a small campfire burns. People are running away from the campfire towards the wooded area at the base of the hill. They are dressed in innocent-looking peasant clothing, but they carry weapons. They are Viet Cong. We have caught them by surprise, with their breakfast fires burning.

Our machine gunner rams an ammo belt into his thirty-caliber machine gun and swings into a position to fire forward. The lead helicopter slows to land and the shooting starts. Bullets whistle through the air. One rips through the tail rotor of a nearby chopper, causing it to go into a tailspin and crash to the ground.

Our pilot slows the craft to a hover and then swings sharply in a turning movement, which permits us a clear view of the landing site. Three choppers are already on the ground—one disembarking, one lifting off, and the other in flames. Bullets fly everywhere. The VC have taken up concealed positions and fire at the incoming choppers. Men jump from the choppers and fall face down on the ground to return fire.

The machine gunner next to me opens fire into a tree line. That should make me feel good, but it doesn't. We are sitting ducks, virtually helpless, without cover and at the mercy of incoming fire. There is no place to hide. Several bullets soon tear through the thin hull of our ship, but no one is injured.

Our chopper touches down. Everyone jumps out except the chopper crew and me. Perry motions for me to jump, but I can't move. I am paralyzed by fear.

I can't remember anything that happened for the next several moments. I must have blacked out. The next thing I remember is lying on the ground, searching for my weapon while the 101st pursues the retreating VC.

I shake uncontrollably. Damn it! I am ashamed. I look around to see if anyone is watching. No one is. No one cares. They are all busy chasing the VC.

After regaining my composure, things don't seem so bad. I haven't let anybody down. I haven't embarrassed myself. Nobody has indicated their displeasure at my actions. Things aren't so bad. Things have been much worse.

High School football was much worse. We lost a lot. Out of twenty-four games over a three-year period, we lost every game except two. We won one game; it was wonderful! We drove all over town blowing car horns. We tied one game; that was a religious experience. We lost twenty-two games; that may have been great for the other teams, but it was terrible for us. I didn't mind losing so much. It wasn't the losing. It was the embarrassment of disappointing the fans, and particularly the cheerleaders. They must have hated us. Nothing is learned, nothing is gained, and no good comes from losing.

After locating my weapon on the ground nearby, I stumble to my knees in time to see Perry lift his machine gun and fire at retreating VC. The volley clips one man just above the shoulders, decapitating him and tossing his head into the air. Perry turns and waves his arm overhead for me to come forward. I begin to crawl slowly on my knees, pulling myself along by the elbows. Perry motions again this time, pumping his hand up and down for me to get up and run.

No way am I going to get up and run anyplace. To the right, a breakfast fire burns with the smell of pork, alongside two dead VC in a pool of bloody entrails. To the left, a chopper burns with the smell of gasoline and several dying soldiers. To the rear, an open field invites sniper fire. And to the front, the infantry fires up into the woods at the retreating VC.

Finally, more out of confusion than courage I stand up and run forward toward Perry, hoping he can provide me with some sense of security, which he does. Even amidst all of the confusion of battle, Perry projects resolute purpose to demand success and achieve victory. His bold decisive actions instill confidence, drawing me like a magnet to his side. Not wanting to let go of the only security blanket I have, I fall at his side and point my M14 up toward the steep slopes of Hong Cong Hill, hoping to convince him I am a worthy comrade. I grab my M14 firmly, flip the safety and fire off a round. The recoil against my shoulder feels good. I fire another round, then another, then another. Squeezing the trigger, absorbing the recoil and taking aim has an unexpected calming effect. My hands stop trembling. My heart rate slows. I feel more in control of my emotions, my actions, and my reactions.

It is a short, but bloody encounter, with lots of VC casualties. The heaviest American causalities are from the helicopter crash. The American casualties are placed into rubber body bags and stacked up alongside the road. Most of the VC casualties are thrown into an open hole and covered with dirt.

Several machine gun jeeps soon arrive. One jeep is designated for psychological warfare. Two severed VC heads are tied to the headlights and that jeep is driven through the town of An Khe.

Perry commandeers another jeep to reconnoiter the area where the base camp will be located and a potential borrow-pit site, where we will obtain gravel fill to construct the necessary roads. Apparently there will be one main road, Perimeter Road, to be built around gently undulating open fields for the helicopters, as well as several interior roads connecting units. Engineer Group Headquarters has already identified a potential borrow-pit site. Perry drives me there to take a look. To my dismay, the site is located on the far side of Hong Cong Hill, meaning we must work outside of what will eventually become a secure perimeter. That does not sound good. In fact, it sounds terrible. I express my concern to Perry and advise him that we will need infantry to protect us, or we need to find a suitable site inside the secure perimeter. Perry advises that neither is available.

In the early afternoon I board a helicopter and return to the Pass. Troop convoys line Route 19—the 101st Airborne pulling out and the 1st Air Cav moving in. To the west, the 101st Airborne heads toward Pleiku with many two and one-half-ton trucks, some pulling 105-howitzers. To the east, a convoy of 6-inch self-propelled guns crawls up the Pass—big guns, twenty-mile range. Behind that stretch many troop transport trucks loaded with 1st Cav troops.

Near the bottom of the Pass, parked alongside of the road, is one-half mile of construction equipment—the Big Deuce: bulldozers, graders and front-end loaders loaded onto lowboy trailers, and lots of dump trucks. It looks like Slaughter has sent much of the Company. Maybe he came himself.

Our chopper touches down in front of the lead jeep. Hoping to see Slaughter and Fallon, I wave excitedly, but neither of them is there. Roscoe leads the convoy.

"Where's Fallon?" I yell.

"Fallon's sick, Lieutenant," Roscoe yells back.

"Where's Slaughter?"

"Slaughter's back in Canh Van Valley, setting security and preparing to be attacked. He sent you half the equipment and one platoon of men, and Lieutenant Goodrich. Lieutenant Goodrich is here."

Of all the officers Slaughter could have sent, Joe Goodrich is the last person I hoped for. Joe and I had entered active duty together in the same engineer basic class at Ft. Belvoir. I had arrived and signed in one day ahead of Joe, which means I outrank him. He resents that and won't let me forget it. Also, Joe is a peacenik. He is not actively anti-war; he has never carried a sign or marched in any anti-war demonstrations or made any public display of his feelings. He has never delivered a public speech or written to his congress-man—nothing that bold. He uses one annoying tactic. He constantly com-plains that our approach to the war effort is wrong; we should be making peace, not war.

"Where's Hayman?" I ask Roscoe. "Where's my jeep?"

Sergeant Roscoe steps to the side of the road, turns back toward the body of the convoy and motions for Hayman to bring my jeep forward. "I don't know who is leading this convoy, you or Lieutenant Goodrich," Roscoe says. "You better drive back and discuss that with my platoon leader."

I hop into the jeep beside Hayman and ride along, looking for Joe Goodrich. It is a bit perplexing that I have to look for Joe. As convoy com-mander, Joe belongs at the front of the column, or at least somewhere near the front. The further we drive along the column without seeing Joe, the more per-plexed I become.

Joe is all the way at the rear of the convoy, in the very last vehicle. That is upsetting, but not surprising. Joe Goodrich marches to his own drummer.

Joe sits, leaning back, with his feet cocked up on the dashboard and his arms behind his head. "You been shot at yet?" he asks sarcastically.

"There's one hell of a battle up there," I say, expecting Joe to say something complementary. But he won't. For some reason, Joe will not give me the satisfaction of feeling pride of accomplishment unless the accomplishment is to his liking and of his making. That is just the way Joe is. I don't understand why a man of such admirable intellect insists on putting me down. Physically, Joe wouldn't hurt a fly. Psychologically, however, he is boldly aggressive.

"Just don't involve my platoon in anything dangerous. We're here to build, not to fight," Joe says.

I am really not in the mood for a confrontation with Joe Goodrich. This is not the time, nor the place. Even if it were, I couldn't win. Joe is smarter, more aggressive, and less sensitive. I don't have a prayer against Joe Goodrich intellectually. But that doesn't matter now. I outrank Joe. I signed up for active duty one day before Joe signed up. I'm the ranking officer and I am in charge here.

I slide into the rear seat of Joe's jeep and whisper into his ear, saying in no uncertain terms, "Joe, you are going to do exactly what I tell you."

"Yes, sir," Joe says aloud, sarcastically. "What do you want me to do first?"

"Joe, I just want you to do what I tell you," I say quietly.

"Sure. You're the ranking officer and I will take orders from you."

"Good," I emphatically respond.

"I will take your orders," Joe says, "but my platoon sergeant and my men will not."

"Are you crazy?" I yell at Joe.

"No," Joe replies, "but you might be."

"Look Joe," I say, "I really don't have time to get into this right now. There's a war up this road and we're headed right into it."

"You're headed into it, not me. I'm a lover, not a fighter. I'm going to help you build whatever it is you want to build and then I'm going back to Qui Nhon."

"As far as I'm concerned, you can turn around and go back to Qui Nhon right now. Roscoe and I can handle this."

"You stay away from Roscoe," Joe insists. "I am the second-platoon leader. The chain of command goes through me. You tell me what to do and I will tell Roscoe."

I am disappointed. I had not expected this from Joe and am surprised by his belligerent attitude, if not his big mouth. Joe was never one to avoid confrontation, even with Slaughter. Joe would often speak up, not necessarily saying what he exactly meant, but always making his point, and his point here, I believe, is one of principle. He knows full well the significance of the effort at An Khe as opposed to Canh Van Valley. He understands the potential repercussions, if not the eventual outcome of a combat effort in the highlands.

Joe may be smarter than I am, but I signed on for active duty one day ahead of Joe. I am the ranking officer. *For everything done there are benefits received and prices paid.* One extra day of active duty wasn't much of a price to pay for the benefit received. That was a bargain.

I return to the head of the column and tell Roscoe I am in charge. I tell him Goodrich is unfamiliar with what lies ahead and would find it difficult to lead a contingent into an area where he is unfamiliar. That's what I tell Roscoe. He understands, and motions for the convoy to follow me up the Pass.

Follow me. I'm first. That's great. I love it. That is what junior officers are trained for—to be followed, to be first. Besides that, it feels good. There is nothing quite as exhilarating as being first: first chair, first in the class, first in the race. Nothing is better than being first. But being first also carries with it responsibilities. You have to know what you are doing; you must be skilled in what you do in order to instill confidence in others. You must succeed, and you must win. You must win. Sometimes winning is assured. That is the right time to lead. That is easy. Sometimes, however, winning is not assured. Sometimes we have to bet on the percentages. Leading in such times as these may not be so easy, and it takes courage. I have decided to lead. I take a deep breath and motion back for the convoy to follow me up the An Khe Pass.

The Pass is steep and winding. Our convoy can move ahead only in low gear because we have so much heavy equipment. Each prime mover strains to lift the construction machinery upward and around the many sharp bends in the road. The climb takes us about twenty minutes, straining all the way until we finally reach the top.

The top of the Pass is relatively flat, open terrain—a highlands plateau with very few people where the vegetation is low, the open fields are broad and the view unobstructed. Hong Cong Hill is clearly visible, about ten miles away. We drive west toward the Hill at moderate speed. The trucks spread out and no longer scream as they did climbing the Pass. The engines now purr. We have arrived in the central highlands, where civilian life is less dense and moves at a slower pace.

We drive about eight miles toward the town of An Khe without seeing a soul. Route 19 bypasses the town so we will not get to see the results of this morning's jeep run with severed heads. I suspect that the town is nearly empty of people. We continue along Route 19 until just west of An Khe, where a small narrow dirt road branches north toward Hong Cong Hill. It is a narrow dirt road covered with deep ruts.

We turn onto the dirt road, driving slowly toward the hill, looking for stable, open areas to park the huge trucks before they get stuck. And from what I see, they could get stuck very easily. Nevertheless, we drive on, down the muddy road, toward a narrow opening in the heavily-wooded tree line near the base of Hong Cong Hill. I am about to conclude that we have hit a dead end when I look ahead to see a machine gun jeep. There, alongside the jeep, stands Perry. Alongside of Perry is a pile of body bags, stacked up like cordwood.

Perry motions for us to pull off the road and start unloading equipment. "Let's get started!" he yells.

Joe Goodrich climbs out of the jeep and approaches the body bags. Joe kneels down, bows his head and starts to pray. After a few moments he whispers, "They were too young to die."

They had died in a helicopter crash twelve thousand miles from home. They had died of no fault of their own, doing their duty. They gave all they had, all they might have had: wife, family, children, education, career, home, joy, happiness. They gave it all. That was the price they paid for benefits received by others.

That infuriates Joe Goodrich. "These young boys died uselessly for a bunch of crooked, lying politicians."

Maybe Joe is right. Maybe the only ones to benefit from these deaths are a bunch of crooked, lying politicians. Politicians are the decision makers. Politicians get where they get by being aggressive, by defeating other people, by hurting other people. Or maybe it's the stockholders of the corporation that manufactured the helicopters that crashed. Or maybe it's the responsible employees of the helicopter company that manufactured the helicopters. Or maybe it's the civilian contractors who make their living by working overseas. Or maybe it's the overzealous career military officer. Or maybe it's the journalist trained at our finest universities. They are, for the most part, smart people, people of intellect, doing what they were trained to do.

"Let's get started," Perry yells again.

"Who is that idiot?" Joe asks.

"I'm not sure," I reply. "He says he is our liaison with the 1st Cav." I then turn to Perry and ask, "What do you want us to do?"

Joe Goodrich is furious. "What do you want us to do?" Joe yells. "Well, I'll tell you what to do. The first thing to do is to build a sign here at the main entrance with the name of this base painted on it in big bold letters. We could name it after the first poor dumb bastard to get killed here so the rest of us will feel an obligation to die next."

Joe has made a mistake. He has talked down to Perry, and Perry doesn't like it.

"Your wisdom astounds me," Perry says in a low tone.

With bulldozers now unloaded, Perry calls the officers and noncoms to gather around him. He points in a northeasterly direction toward a hedgerow. "Start right there," he directs, "and follow the stakes."

We look for construction stakes, but there are none.

"Pardon me," I say, "but we don't see any stakes."

"So drive some, Lieutenant. You have a road to build."

"We understand that, but somebody should tell us where to build this road."

"The main thing," Perry says, "is to end up with a circle big enough to put a heliport in the middle and twenty thousand men around the perimeter."

Sergeant Roscoe calls for several equipment operators to follow him to the hedgerow. Roscoe gathers the men around him, and with his outstretched hand makes a big circle. "We are going to start right here," he says. "Go all the way around there in a big circle and when we get done we'll end up right here in the same place where we started. Roscoe smiles at his men with a triumphant grin. "Now, who wants to go first?"

Every one of the equipment operators raises their hand. That pleases me. The common man believes in what he is doing, and has faith.

But there is a surprise. Lieutenant Joe Goodrich raises his hand.

Perry looks at Joe in disgust. "We don't pay lieutenants to run bulldozers." Perry says to Joe.

Roscoe comes to Joe's defense. "Lieutenant Goodrich is the best operator I have."

"I don't care," Perry says. "Put an assigned operator on there."

Joe and I walk back away from the hedgerow with Perry. Close behind we hear the starting of engines and the falling of trees. That pleases me. The common man is competent and reliable. But Joe Goodrich is not the common man. Neither is Perry.

Goodrich and Perry are a couple of weirdos. They are ideological opposites, both of whom insist upon having things their way. I get the impression neither of them understands or cares about anything I say.

"Guys," I say, "we have a few problems here."

Joe doesn't even let me finish my sentence before he interrupts. "You're the first problem."

"First of all," I continue, pointing at Perry, "I'm not going to take orders from somebody who wears no rank."

"Neither am I," Joe adds.

We wait for Perry's reply. Finally, after a long period of silence, Perry speaks. "I'm an officer with Special Forces. I don't wear rank because I don't want the enemy to recognize me. There is a price on my head. I'm marked for assassination."

"Yeah, right," Joe Goodrich replies sarcastically. "And you're also with the CIA."

Joe has made another mistake. He has again talked down to Perry. Perry reaches out and grabs Joe by the arm with a tight, crushing grip. "Are you ready to die?"

"No," Joe says.

"I am," Perry replies, tightening his grip on Joe's arm, "and I'm ready to take you with me."

I believe Perry. He has made his decision. He is willing to die. That puts him in a strong position.

"Yes sir," Joe says apologetically. "That won't happen again, now that I know who you are." Joe realizes he has irritated Perry and tries to rectify the situation. "What I meant to say, sir, with all due respect, is that we have a problem."

Perry releases his grip on Goodrich and we all three laugh. We may not agree on much, but we certainly agree that we have a problem. We have several problems, not the least of which is defining the perimeter of the base camp. None of us really knows where Perimeter Road should go. The centerline of the road needs to be staked out for the bulldozers to follow. We wait for Division Engineers to stake out where they want to.

Another problem is security. Darkness will soon set in. I tell Perry we cannot work in the dark. Perry tells me we can. Perry tells us to turn the headlights on and keep working all night long.

Another problem we have is chain of command. Perry is not in the chain of command. He is in an advisory role only. John Slaughter is our commanding officer, but John Slaughter is not here. I am in command here, and Joe Goodrich will not accept that. He will not accept it because, as Joe puts it, I am incompetent.

"Joe," I remind him, "I outrank you."

"By one lousy day."

"Those are the rules of the game."

"Well," Joe rolls his eyes, "I cheat."

I look to Perry for support, but support is not coming. Perry doesn't care about our personal problems. He tells us to work it out. Perry doesn't want to be bothered with disagreements between lieutenants. Perry has only one thing in mind: the mission.

And the mission is An Khe Base. We are to help build a base camp for the 1st Air Cavalry Division, and to build it with the utmost speed. Twenty thousand men will pour into this camp in the next few days. They will bring with them the newest machine of war: the helicopter. We are told that helicopters will make this division the most mobile fighting force in history; one which can strike with the suddenness of lightning at the heart of the enemy.

CHAPTER 3

Initial contingents of combat troops begin to arrive, not by helicopter but by cattle cars—large stake-bodied tractor-trailers with wooden staked sides. Each trailer holds about two hundred men. The cattle cars are loaded in Qui Nhon and driven up Route 19 to An Khe, with the men standing all the way. It is all most undignified. I am disappointed to see young men being shipped to war this way. Practical wisdom should tell them they deserve better, but it doesn't, and that is to be expected. *Young men are not possessed of practical wisdom. Practical wisdom comes with experience.*

With troops soon to arrive by the thousands, our first priority is to cut a rough access road part way around the perimeter for the arriving forces to maneuver to bivouac areas. Perimeter Road will completely encircle the heliport. Troop camps are to be located along the Perimeter Road, with the inside being devoted to helicopters, artillery and support units. Division Combat Engineers arrive early to take over supervision of construction. They drive construction stakes and direct our dozer operators where to go and what to do. Although the camp is a simple circle, it is easy to lose direction and get lost because it is so large and much of the perimeter is located in forested areas. There are many trails. I maintain my bearings by thinking of the camp as a big compass with due north pointing straight up at twelve o'clock, toward China. The main entrance to the base is at the opposite pole, at six o'clock, away from China toward Saigon.

We have been assigned to a gentle, sloping piece of terrain near the entrance at 0530, facing toward the town of An Khe. We set our tents up on the inside of

Perimeter Road. Across the road is a slightly suppressed open field where we park our equipment, and beyond that a small stream, another open field, and then woods. I stand and stare across the open fields to the woods, which separate us from the town of An Khe, searching, looking deeply within for people. I know people are watching us. They are watching us from the concealment of the woods. For us, however, the woods acts as a blindfold that separates us from, and prevents us from seeing the people. Clockwise to our right is Division Artillery. They position their 105 howitzers and commence firing barrages to the southwest. The noises are deafening. The impact zone is visible a few miles away. Counter-clockwise to our left is the 7th Cavalry. That makes me feel very secure. We are immediately adjacent to the Artillery. The 7th Cav is a few hundred feet away, the area between us and them being yet unassigned. That leaves me a little uneasy. We dig defensive manholes along the road immediately in front of our bivouac area. The manholes are located about twenty feet apart along the inside shoulder of Perimeter Road, which permits us a field of fire across the road into the open fields between us and the concealed town of An Khe.

Our party consists of about forty men, quartered within three general-purpose tents. Lieutenant Goodrich and I share one tent with Sergeant Roscoe. We have installed a room divider between our quarters consisting of a piece of communications wire hung with ponchos. Officers and NCOs are separated from sight, but not sound. In the officers' side there are two cots, a field desk, and a field phone. Roscoe's end is almost empty. Joe and I have dug two foxholes along Perimeter Road immediately outside the entrance to our tent. Each foxhole is about four feet deep. The rest of the men have dug their own foxholes nearby and are quartered within the remaining two GP tents, except for three equipment operators. These three have chosen to build their own private hooch out of two-man pup tents neatly tied between trees. I have decided that the private hooch is unacceptable and have directed Roscoe to order the men to tear it down. Instead, more hooches get built. So much for my authority!

We have a good latrine, three holes. It consists of the bottom halves of three fifty-five gallon drums under a wooden board. Three holes are cut in the board with swinging wooden covers over each hole. We positioned the latrine across

the Perimeter Road in the construction equipment parking area next to
Division Artillery. There, the latrine is partially concealed by a hedgerow,
which offers some privacy. When sitting on the latrine our backs are to the
hedgerow, but we face the perimeter, looking into open fields. I suppose we can
be seen from the woods, but we don't mind because it is too far for snipers. It
is just a nice view, but it is occasionally noisy. On each side of the latrine there
is a P-Tube—a pipe stuck in the ground. The soil below the pipe has been provided with a bed of stones for drainage. The P-Tubes offer permanent disposal.
The latrine barrels, on the other hand, must be pulled into the open, fueled
with kerosene and burned on a daily basis.

Division Engineers are located immediately adjacent to us, to the rear, along
a center-access road, which will run north and south, conveniently intersecting
the circle at 0600. That is where we receive orders. It is just a short walk away
from our bivouac area. A command tent has been set up there and a meeting
has been scheduled for 1200 hours.

At 1130 hours Joe Goodrich and I walk to the command tent, fold back the
canvas flap door and enter. The tent is filled with several rows of empty folding
metal chairs. At the front hangs a large map, showing a detailed design layout proposed for An Khe Base. Joe and I sit down in the first row of chairs and stare at the
map. Looking at the map, for the first time we begin to understand and appreciate the magnitude of the effort at An Khe. The sheer size of the base camp is
mind-boggling. It is a town of twenty thousand people, a small city large enough
to get lost in. It is a community which must provide for the needs and welfare of
its residents, but one which is totally non-self-sufficient. It must be constantly
supplied and re-supplied, for it has no farms or factories, no utilities, no source of
anything. Everything needed here—from food and ammunition, to medical supplies and fuel—must be constantly re-supplied by land or air. There is a small airport about three miles to the east, large enough for C-130 cargo planes. The next
closest supply point is the seaport at Qui Nhon. There will have to be a lot of sup-

ply runs between Qui Nhon and An Khe.

Another striking thing about the camp is its apparent vulnerability to conventional weapons. Joe points to the map, with five fingers extended, and then rolls them into a tight fist. "One bombing run could wipe out this whole facility," he comments.

I agree with Joe. It is obvious this base camp could easily be totally destroyed by a major power like the Chinese or the Russians. But we're not fighting a major power, yet. We're fighting a peasant army, supported by a bunch of local insurgents.

"I'm sick," Joe says. "This is insane. This defensive position separates us from the very people we are trying to win over."

"No, Joe," I respond. "This must be good. This has been well thought out by experts."

At 1200 hours the briefing party enters the tent. Perry is there, as I was sure he would be, but I am surprised to see Major Powers and Captain Slaughter. They have flown in from Qui Nhon. Powers talks a lot. Slaughter says very little. It doesn't take Joe and me long to figure out what Powers and Slaughter want. Powers wants to finish at An Khe and move back to Qui Nhon as soon as possible. Slaughter wants to move the whole company to An Khe and provide combat support to the 1st Cav. But Perry runs the meeting.

Perry asks us to be seated. "Well," he says, "here we are." He appears to be relaxed as he begins his briefing. He exudes great confidence in what he says, assuring us that the plan for An Khe Base has been well conceived for the utmost security and efficiency.

The principal feature will be the defensive perimeter—a three-hundred-foot wide bare perimeter strip, measuring five miles in outside circumference. The perimeter strip is to be cleared of all vegetation, allowing open fields of fire. The open fields will be wrapped with barbed wire. Defensive foxholes will be dug along the inside of the strip to provide crisscrossed interlocking fields of fire. There is no way anyone will ever be able to cross the defensive strip and enter the camp. It is absolutely impenetrable.

Inside that is Perimeter Road, or what is to be Perimeter Road. Right now, most of it is uncleared woods and muddy trails. Perry stresses that we are to work twenty-four hours a day to gain access around the entire perimeter. Our work includes site clearing, rough grading and finished grading. We have several motorized scrapers, but for the most part we must depend on fill from the gravel quarry to bring the road to final grade. Division Combat Engineers will construct necessary drainage culverts and several timber bridges.

Troop bivouac areas will be located along both sides of Perimeter Road. Large general-purpose tents will be utilized to house the troops. Each soldier is provided with a folding cot. Each tent has two rows of cots—one row on each side of a center aisle with up to ten cots in each row. Everybody will have individual mosquito netting. Most troop units will have their own mess facilities. When in base camp, soldiers eat K rations prepared in field kitchen facilities. The food in not great, but it is hot and usually pretty good. You can even expect steak on occasion. But never milk. There is no milk at An Khe. Each troop unit will have access to a water supply and shower facility. Chlorine tablets are plentiful. Ion-exchange water-purification units will be initially set up near streams. Supplementary wells will then be driven to provide a reliable source of good ground water. Interspaced with the troop bivouac areas are artillery emplacements, hardstands, and supply storage areas. Artillery pieces are located on open terrain to allow for unobstructed trajectories. That also allows easy access for helicopters to lift and transport artillery pieces to remote fire-bases. The artillery unit next to us often fires directly over our heads. The noise is deafening, and at night it is difficult to sleep.

Of course there will be a hospital. Perry explains that the initial hospital will be housed in MASH-type tents and that Quonset huts will soon be built. Generators will be provided for twenty-four hour electrical service. The hospital will be located adjacent to an area designed to accommodate med-evac helicopters. The new hospital will be well-equipped and well-staffed, although small—just large enough to treat casualties on a temporary basis until they can be transported to troop medical ships or other area hospitals. The initial temporary MASH hospital is near enough to our location for us to witness some activity there. We see that there are several dozen nurses. The nurses stay pretty much to themselves except at mealtime. At mealtime they eat in the hospital mess tent. Since we are only a detachment, we have no mess facilities or personnel. Joe Goodrich tells Perry we want to eat at the hospital mess tent. Perry says so would he, but we can't. He has made arrangements for mess to be delivered directly to our bivouac area.

Several other specialty units will be located nearby. Graves Registration is immediately adjacent to the hospital. Next to that is a small POW compound where we occasionally see hooded prisoners stooped down in a squatting position. Scattered among the troop areas are supply depots stacked with conex containers and equipment hardstands for parking vehicles. Without exception, these areas are mud holes. We are directed to build stabilized hardstands as soon as possible. We want to build them of crushed stone, but there is none, so we will use gravel.

Our work is of considerable urgency. Perry is explicit. He directs us to work twenty-four hours a day and operate the borrow pit outside the perimeter, with no security. The remote location of the borrow pit worries us because the borrow pit is located on the far side of Hong Cong Hill. No security is provided at the borrow pit or along the entire length of the haul road. At the gravel pit, level plateaus are cut by bulldozers, with gravel being plowed into loading areas where front-end loaders scoop it up and drop it into dump trucks for the haul to fill areas. The borrow pit is located about one mile from the base camp perimeter. The entire area between the perimeter and the quarry is heavily forested. We can see only a few dozen feet into the woods. The fear of ambush is constantly with the truck drivers. They drive as fast as possible along the bumpy dirt road from the perimeter to the quarry and back. At the quarry, a sense of fear is constantly with the equipment operators because they ride totally exposed to potential snipers. Surprisingly, we haven't been attacked—yet. Quarry operations run pretty smoothly in daylight hours. One truck is loaded and departs about every three minutes. It is a rather comfortable operation, except at night. Nighttime is bad. At night the trucks invite disaster as moving targets with headlights on. They drive dangerously fast along the narrow, winding dirt road and dangerously close to the large trees. At night the equipment operators are sitting targets with large, blinding headlights shining into the night air. Nighttime at the borrow pit is terrifying. The nights are long.

Against my better judgment I broach the subject of nighttime security. I raise my hand and interrupt Perry. "Sir," I say. "Sir" seems fitting, even though I don't know his rank. "Nighttime operations outside the perimeter invite disaster. We need additional security or we should suspend operations." I knew immediately that it was a mistake for me to say that.

"Lieutenant, would you rather be in the bush with the infantry?" Perry asks. Then Perry looks at Major Powers and confidently says, "I'm sure we could arrange that."

Powers doesn't reply. I think he is afraid of Perry. But John Slaughter is not afraid of Perry. "The Big Deuce can take anything you throw at us," John says.

Joe Goodrich isn't afraid of Perry either. "Are you guys crazy?" Joe yells. "We're engineers, not infantry."

"We're soldiers first," Slaughter yells at Goodrich, "and don't you forget it."

That shuts Joe up. Joe is out of line, and he knows it.

"We must make better progress," Perry says. "The monsoon season will soon be here, and when it hits, these dirt roads will turn to mud."

Slaughter wants to move the whole company to An Khe. "Gravel roads will turn to slippery slide boards in heavy rains," Slaughter warns. "We need crushed rock, and we have a rock crusher to produce it."

Major Powers stands and stares with concern at the map. He knows the pending monsoon season has the potential to seriously disrupt motorized traffic on the gravel roads, especially critical fuel trucks. If An Khe were a temporary facility we could somehow live with the disruption, but An Khe is obviously being built for permanency. Permanency demands a justifiable degree of stabilization. For road stabilization we can build gravel or rock. At present, we have only gravel.

Powers looks at Slaughter and says, "Rock crushers need rock. There is no rock at An Khe."

"There's rock at the Pass," Slaughter says. "There's plenty of rock at the Pass. And we have a rock crusher."

Powers replies, "We would first of all have to find a suitable location for it." There is no way Powers will ever let Slaughter move the whole company to An Khe.

But Slaughter is insistent. "We could haul rock from the Pass and locate the rock crusher at the heliport."

Perry interrupts. "Forget the heliport. No construction equipment is permitted on the heliport." A large area at the center of the base camp is reserved for helicopters and helicopter maintenance units. Right now it is covered with knee-high elephant grass and scrub hedgerows. Construction equipment would strip the helicopter landing areas of vegetation. That would create muddy conditions in wet weather and dusty conditions in dry weather, both of which are unacceptable. Perry continues. "The heliport area will be hand prepared by a civilian labor force."

The prospect of a civilian labor force is a surprise to all of us.

Slaughter and Powers are disgusted with the prospect of a civilian work force at An Khe. It is counterproductive to their objectives. But Joe Goodrich is elated.

"Several hundred civilian laborers will be needed," Perry says. "They will be paid forty *piasters* per day to remove brush and to cut knee-high grass to golf course length sod."

With that said, the meeting quickly breaks up. Powers returns to Qui Nhon. Slaughter returns to Canh Van Valley. Joe Goodrich and I continue to argue over who is the boss.

Each morning, for the next few days, a civilian labor force of several hundred peasants arrives at the main entrance to An Khe Base. Most are men and boys; a few are middle-aged women. At dawn they are escorted by armed infantry to the helicopter landing pad areas where they spend the day cutting knee-high grass and brush to ankle height. They work hard, bent over like bows, in back-straining positions. It is hard work with little pay, but they don't seem to mind. They are used to that type of work in the rice paddies, and the work they do is work that cannot be done by machine. Many of them travel miles to work—walking, riding in buses or Lambrettas, or on bicycles. Most are from the surrounding highlands area, but many come from as far away as Qui Nhon and Pleiku. The large number of civilian workers who have shown up in the last few days to work on the helicopter landing pads is revealing of the great need for jobs. Their willingness to work hard for meager wages is a tribute to humanity.

We do our part, too. While the civilians clear the helicopter pads, we continue to haul gravel onto Perimeter Road and the main north/south artery, widening the roads to two lanes with shoulders. Unfortunately, we are completing only a few hundred feet a day, which means we will not be finished for several weeks. Wet weather will delay us even more. With the monsoon season approaching, we are all aware the road network would be of a much more permanent nature with a good supply of crushed stone. I am hoping Group Headquarters will assign the rock crusher to An Khe, rather than to Qui Nhon. A rock processing operation could also provide additional jobs for local civilians.

It seems like a lot of progress is made in a short time, but all good things come to an end. Perry gives us the bad news. The entire civilian labor force will be laid off. Only military personnel will be permitted inside the base camp. This is upsetting for all of us, especially Joe Goodrich.

Joe and I sit alone in the officers' end of our general purpose tent. We sit on two folding chairs at the field desk. Due to the heat of the day, the tent flaps are rolled up. Being dry, the dust rolls through the tent around us. It is quite warm, but a slight breeze keeps the sweat from forming on us. We sit together for a long time without saying anything. What is there to say? The civilian labor force is gone. That doesn't make much difference to me. The plan, to my way of thinking, is simple: keep our mouths shut and do what we are directed to do. We don't need any civilians.

But Joe disagrees, violently. He pounds his fits on the field table. "What's more important—people or roads? Without civilian involvement there is little use of us being here. Leave this place to the infantry," he says.

"So what can we do?" I ask. "When Perry tells us what to do we have bend over and say, 'Why, thank you.'"

"Not me," says Joe. "I'm my own man. If people don't want to do things my way, then people can do without me."

I can't do without Joe. I need Joe. But I can't let him walk over me. "Well, that's a noble approach," I say respectfully, "but it won't work." Joe must already know that. Joe is smart. I remind him that we all have to do what we are ordered to do, regardless of whether we like it or not. That's how the system works.

"Not me," says Joe. "I live by higher standards."

"Yeah, right," I say. "Don't you wish?"

Joe sees an opportunity—an opportunity to offer the hand of friendship and provide needed jobs. We could build a model city here where local people can interact with us and feel secure. But we are not going to build that. What we are going to help build here is a gigantic, impenetrable fort. And neither Joe nor I have the authority or wherewithall to do anything other than what we are directed to do. Most people don't. Most people just have to do what they are told. But wouldn't it be wonderful if instead of building an impenetrable fort we could build a caring environment? Good jobs could be created—good, simple jobs that can easily be performed by good, simple people. No high tech! High-tech jobs here will make a few people rich and a lot of people poor. Fair wages could be paid. Just print more money. And make the money plentiful and easily accessible to the common man through jobs. People would participate. It would be easy to transport people to work. A transportation network could be established to transport as many people as warranted. That is what Joe wants.

But that is not going to happen, not at An Khe, at least. At An Khe, security rules. Inside the perimeter will be secure. Those inside the perimeter will enjoy the peace of mind security brings. There will be a roof overhead and a place to sleep. Basic needs will be met. Friendships will develop. Inside the perimeter will be security, peace and trust. Thank God for that. But the outside is a different world, where nothing or no one feels secure. Outside the perimeter there may be both friends and foes, but when the shooting starts there is no distinction on our part. Under those conditions, everybody must be assumed to be a potential foe. That is what Joe does not want to see. But that is the way it is. Joe Goodrich must know that. Why won't he yield to reason?

"So what are you going to do?" I ask Joe. "Are you going to see this through or are you going back to Canh Van Valley?"

"I'm not going to get killed in a pile of dirt for anybody." Joe is direct, but also tactful, in order to avoid court-martial for insubordination. "Besides, you don't need me here."

Joe insists that he is more needed back in Canh Van Valley to help with equipment repairs. He has a good point there. The twenty-four hour work schedule is taking a heavy toll. Equipment breakdowns become more common. Two dozers and a grader are already deadlined for major repairs which we are incapable of performing in An Khe. Joe tells me in no uncertain terms that we are remiss in not insisting on shutting down night operations at the quarry and not performing scheduled maintenance.

"You are in charge here," Joe says quietly. "I hereby inform you that everything here should be deadlined for maintenance right now."

"We can't do that." I remind Joe that Perry will never let us shut down anything that runs. He must know that. But Joe won't cooperate. Joe is his own man. Joe stands his ground.

"So relieve me," Joe finally says. "Get me out of here."

Joe is really smart—and courageous. I greatly admire Joe for his strong beliefs and the courage to stand behind those strong beliefs. But in this case, I am deeply disappointed with Joe because of his lack of commitment to his own set of values. He is so willing to pursue his own personal set of values in the relative safety of Canh Van Valley, yet unwilling to continue to pursue them here at An Khe. Joe may have strong beliefs, but he is unwilling to pursue them under adverse conditions.

The 1st Cav in not here to make peace. The 1st Cav is here to make war. The 1st Cav is here to kill North Vietnamese Regulars and Viet Cong. That is what the 1st Cav is equipped and trained to do. The 1st Cav is not here to win the hearts and minds of the people. Joe Goodrich knows that. Joe Goodrich knows that the strategy for An Khe has been set by others—others who paid the price and earned the right to make such major decisions—and that those decisions affect the rest of us. *The benefits received and the prices paid affect the fortunes and misfortunes constantly circling others and ourselves.*

Prices have been paid. A lot of people have already been killed here. As a result, people of power have made decisions. Some have taken steps to unite North Vietnam and South Vietnam. Others have taken steps to secure independent freedom for South Vietnam. Those decisions have been made by others, not by us. We must live with those decisions, right or wrong.

Joe Goodrich may think he is right, but he is not the only person in this world. Joe Goodrich can't always have things his way. In these matters Joe Goodrich is a nobody, just like the rest of us. At An Khe, Joe Goodrich merely causes problems.

As much as I want to accommodate Joe at An Khe, I can't. And that is all right. Joe may do just fine back at Qui Nhon. I make a phone call to John Slaughter, explain the situation, and ask him to take Joe back. Slaughter agrees with one provision: I have to continue efforts to get the whole company moved to An Khe, including the rock crusher. He will send Fallon up to replace Goodrich. Fallon is a rock quarry man who Slaughter expects will find a good location for the rock crusher.

With that finally decided, Joe Goodrich loads the two deadlined bulldozers and the grader on lowboy trailers and returns to Canh Van Valley. I advise Perry of the change in staff. He is delighted and tells me to expect a nice surprise.

The next day I return from the daily meeting at Battalion Engineers to find Perry's surprise: a large conex container. The new container sits right in front of my tent. It is eight feet deep, eight feet wide, eight feet high. And it is filled with American beer.

Roscoe has already opened the doors and counted the cases. "Sir, heaven has arrived." He reaches out and offers me a beer. "The army runs on beer."

It is a tempting offer, but it is only early afternoon. The day shift is still working and the night shift sleeps. We decide to wait until supper time to pass out beer. We also decide on a three-beer limit. That should be just enough to keep everybody happy.

A three-beer limit should be perfect. Three beers will help the day crew to relax, while still not having too much of an adverse effect on the night crew. The crews normally operate with three bulldozers, two front loaders, and usually about eight dump trucks. The borrow pit is located at the end of a long, narrow haul road cut through the jungle. Working conditions are rather pleasant in daylight hours, but at night the dozer and front-end loader operators are sitting ducks for snipers. The nighttime operators deserve at least three beers.

To see to it that everybody has a good time but nobody gets soused, I intend to personally pass out the beers and then put a padlock on the beer conex container. I intend to make that part of my responsibility for the welfare of my detachment. Moderation is important; however, I also feel some obligation to provide some well-deserved entertainment. So far it has been all work and no play. We all need to have some fun. Besides, there is reason for celebration; Joe Goodrich is out of here.

On the other hand, with Joe gone I need to take a more active role in the borrow-pit operation. I have spent most of my time on the construction sites and let Joe worry about the gravel pit. Joe had never given any indication of anything wrong out there, except for the dire lack of security.

Joe didn't want me to give his men orders, so I didn't either. Joe always gave his own orders and I assumed he had a good working relationship with his men. I had never heard anything different, so I just assumed relationships with Joe's men were acceptable, but I wasn't sure. I just assume everything is fine with Joe's men because I never heard anything to the contrary. They seem to be a boring lot. And that is good. Good government is boring.

Even so, there are several men I want to get to know better. Spec 4 Sam Bennett is the first. Sam is typical of several other operators who appear competent. He works hard, does what he is told and keeps his mouth shut. Then there are the apparently less competent, like Hayman. Hayman screws off, does what he wants, and runs off at the mouth. I have Roscoe assign Hayman to Bennett. Maybe he will learn something.

It is about 2230 hours on the first night with Joe Goodrich gone. Roscoe and I have settled down for the night, me reading by Coleman lantern in my end of the tent and Roscoe asleep on his cot in the other end. That has been our normal routine because we let Joe Goodrich take care of nighttime operations at the quarry. Joe was always good about that, never complained or asked to be spelled.

PFC Hayman sticks his coal-black head through the tent curtains at my end of the tent and rolls his ivory-white eyes in a circle. His voice quivers. "Sir, they told me to come on in." Hayman smirks, his white teeth glowing. "There's all kind of shootin' out there," he says. "We had to quit."

Roscoe rises and looks over the cloth partition. "Get your ass back here where you belong," Roscoe yells. We had all become accustomed by this time to the nightly artillery fire screaming overhead and the small weapons fires along the perimeter. "Don't bother the lieutenant. You come see me."

"But Sergeant, there's all kinds of shootin' out there. The VC's on Hong Cong Hill."

I politely interrupt. "They are?"

"Yes sir. We were working up there. You know what I mean? We were up there all by ourselves. You know what I mean? Just me and the guys. You know what I mean?"

Roscoe is not so polite. "Yes, damnit, we know what you mean."

Hayman pulls his arms up into a runner's stance and begins to jitterbug. "Somebody shot at us." Then he starts laughing uncontrollably.

"Well it must have been hysterical," Roscoe growls with disapproval. "Get the hell out of here and go back to work."

Hayman stops dancing long enough and tries to give me a serious explanation. "I guess there was only one man shooting at us. Couldn't really tell. I heard this here *ting ting*." A grin comes across Hayman's lips. "Then Bennett came over and said somebody was shootin' at us. I turned the engine off and jumped to the ground, but forgot to turn off the lights. Bennett and I were squatted down behind the dozer with the headlights on. Bennett said we didn't have to work no more."

Roscoe, visibly irritated, begins to pace the tent. "Why, I'll kick the hell out of that little junior buck-sergeant."

"I left my gun up on top the machine," Hayman snaps his fingers. "Bennett told me to go up and get it. I told Bennett to go get it." Hayman stops dancing, comes to attention and addresses me. "You can go out there and see the bullet marks on the engine, Lieutenant, if you don't believe me."

Our conversation is interrupted by a jingle on the field phone. I lift the receiver to hear Perry on the other end, complaining that the quarry had been shut down. He directs us to open operations back up immediately.

I place the receiver back down onto its olive drab receptacle. The tent is quiet. Roscoe has been listening. "What's wrong now?"

"That was Perry. The quarry is shut down and he wants us to start operations back up right away."

Roscoe and I walk outside with Hayman, where we stand huddled together in the cool air of a black night, watching tracer bullets zoom into the camp from atop Hong Cong Hill. The usual aura of glowing lights is absent this night. Black it is; black on black except for blue white tracers grazing into the camp—first one, and then another—round after round, random shots countered by machine guns hailing a rain of tracers back into the night.

Hayman speaks. "We ought not to be workin' tonight. There's somethin' goin' on out there."

"It sure looks like it," I say, wishing Joe Goodrich was here to handle this.

"I'm not going back out there," Hayman declares.

"Oh yes you are," Roscoe replies.

"But Sergeant, I can't go. I'm sick."

"You're going to be a lot sicker if you stay here," Roscoe says.

To me, Hayman looks sick enough already. Even though he smiles and laughs, his hands shake uncontrollably, and he obviously is not thinking straight. I rarely overrule Roscoe, but this time I do. Hayman is not going back to the quarry. Hayman is going to bed.

Roscoe and I will go alone. If only Joe Goodrich were here. But Joe is gone.

We walk to my jeep. Roscoe climbs into the driver's seat. I throw a couple of sandbags onto the floor directly under my seat, hang four hand grenades on the dashboard and chamber a round into my M14. I point to the back seat. "I wish that radio worked," I tell Roscoe.

Roscoe flicks the ignition switch to the right, just far enough to trigger the electronic fuel pump, leans back over the driver's seat and turns on the radio. "Can't get nothin' on this radio but Chinese music." The radio blasts forth with Chinese Rock and Roll. Roscoe rams the ignition switch all the way to the right and yells over the roar of the engine. "What did you say, sir?"

"I wish I was in bed," I reply.

"Wanta' leave the radio on?"

"Might as well. Maybe it will confuse the enemy."

Our jeep pulls out with the radio blasting and headlights on high beam. We drive a short way along Perimeter Road and then turn off onto the haul road and head toward the quarry. It is an eerie ride. I feel a little bit like waiting for the headless horseman to appear from the woods around every turn. The VC must be out here. We are lit up with blinding lights. We expect to be ambushed, but we are not.

For some strange reason, nobody bothers us. To me, that doesn't make sense. By the time we reach the quarry, it is back in operation. That doesn't make sense either. It doesn't make sense for the VC not to kill us all because we have no security and no protection from ambush and attack. When fired upon, we cannot even shoot back. We are too few and on the wrong side of Hong Cong Hill for the infantry to support us.

Instead of bothering us, the VC opt to climb up to the top of Hong Cong Hill and fire tracers into the base camp at the infantry. That doesn't make sense either. The tracers give away their exact position and draw immediate return-ing fire. That doesn't make sense.

Roscoe and I sit in the jeep at the quarry, talking about the inconsistency of it all. We sit in an area lit up brightly by headlights. There are two levels of work—one high, one low. At the high level the bulldozers scrape gravel from the face of Hong Cong Hill and push it to the lower level where front-end load-ers load the gravel onto dump trucks. The bulldozers hang high in the night sky with their headlights blaring over the jungle below. The front-loaders work against the exposed vertical ledge of the quarry, lighting the exposed face first, then turning to light up the jungle as they load the dump trucks. The dump trucks wait patiently in line, their bright lights lighting up the work areas, inviting snipers.

The VC leave us alone. It bothers me that it doesn't make sense. I'm an engi-neer. Things are supposed to make sense. But then this is real; this is non-fic-tion. And after all, like Roscoe says, non-fiction doesn't have to make sense. Only fiction has to make sense.

CHAPTER 4

I awake at dawn to eat a bowl of cereal made of dry oatmeal, sugar and hot water. It tastes good and leaves me content.

Fallon will arrive today to recon sites for the rock crusher. I don't know where the rock crusher belongs, but Fallon will. Fallon is experienced and I feel sure his expertise will insure success. We must have an accurate and truthful appraisal from him to make sound decisions. It is a matter of principle. *Principle is the basic starting point.*

At mid-morning I sit at my desk. Roscoe enters the tent. "Sir, Sergeant Fallon's here," he says in a low tone.

"Good," I enthusiastically reply.

"But he's sick."

"What do you mean, he's sick?"

"He needs to sleep for a while."

"You mean he's drunk?"

"Yes sir, he's pretty drunk, too."

I step outside the tent into the sunlight and look across Perimeter Road at the motor pool to see Sergeant Fallon sitting slouched over in the driver's seat of a three-quarter ton truck. He looks like he is asleep, but I know he is not. I yell across the motor pool for him to wake up.

Fallon sits up alertly, renders a hand salute, blinks his eyes and says, "Sir, that Pass is a sonofabitch."

Fallon is drunk. I can see it in his eyes and smell it on his breath. Although I don't yet know how drunk he really is, I give him the benefit of the doubt, assuming he is thinking clearly. "You didn't have any trouble, did you?" I ask.

"No sir. Sir. Sir." Fallon staggers out of his truck, swerving from side to side. Nearly falling, he catches himself on the open door where he stands, trying to remain upright. He holds his M14 tightly in his right hand, with the muzzle pointed directly at my stomach. "I don't like the looks of that Pass."

Slowly, I reach out and gently push the weapon aside. "I'm glad to see you, Sergeant Fallon. We need you."

The muzzle of Fallon's rifle pointed at my stomach was unnerving. I know he doesn't intend to pull the trigger, but I know also that he is drunk enough to pull it by mistake. And I am sure the gun is loaded.

"I brought my own tent. Won't bother Roscoe," Fallon mumbles.

It is obvious Fallon is incapable of erecting his own tent. I have no intention of permitting it, in any event. I intend to have him bunk with Sergeant Roscoe in the NCO Quarters. "You won't need your own tent," I tell him. "We'll put your things in with Sergeant Roscoe."

"No sir," Fallon insists. "I want my own tent."

This is an embarrassing situation for me. I have just denied three men a private hooch and now here comes Sergeant Fallon, insisting he have one. I absolutely do not want to permit it. It is not fair to the other men that he would have private accommodations. I tell Fallon that, but not too forcefully. I am a little afraid of Fallon because of his experience. Fallon is a Korean War veteran, with medals. He claims he even killed a few people. That is what he claims. But I am beginning to have less and less confidence in what Sergeant Fallon claims. Now is not the time for Fallon to be drinking. Too much is happening here at An Khe for me to tolerate a drunken platoon sergeant, no matter how much experience he has or what kind of expert he claims to be.

I am disappointed with Fallon. He may be an expert on rock and rock crushers, but to me he is nothing more that a common drunk and an opportunist who serves no real cause other than his own self-centered interest. But then after all, the world is full of eccentric experts. This is the way things are. This is the hand

I've been dealt. This is the hand I have to play. So under the circumstances I yield, permitting Fallon to have his own private tent, at least for the time being, and even help him erect it. We pitch his tent—a small command tent—next to our GP. Fallon unfolds his cot inside, lies down and goes to sleep.

Early the next morning Hayman pulls the jeep up in front of my tent for me to climb in. I am determined to start a recon and ask Roscoe to find Fallon and tell him I am ready. We cannot wait any longer. Decisions must be made.

"Sir," Roscoe explains, "Sergeant Fallon is sort of incapacitated."

"What is he, sick again?"

"Yes sir. He's pretty sick."

"You mean he's drunk."

"Yes sir, he's pretty drunk, too."

I don't care how sick or how drunk Fallon is, or whether he pukes all over himself. There will be a recon this day and Fallon will be on it. I tell Roscoe to get Fallon into the jeep. Roscoe says he already tried, but Fallon is out cold. I don't accept that and accompany Roscoe to Fallon's tent where we find him wrapped in a blanket on his cot.

I nudge him, gently at first, and then shake his shoulder. "Sergeant Fallon."

"Uh?" Fallon moans.

"Come on, Sergeant Fallon. It's time."

"It's time?" Fallon asks. "It's time, America." Fallon throws back the blanket and points to a half-empty bottle of bourbon. "Sirr—I bought you a little present." He speaks slowly, slurring his words, but I clearly understand what he says. "This is all yours, Lieutenant. I'm done with it."

I motion for Roscoe to get Fallon up and prepare him for a recon. We grab Fallon by the shoulders, lift him to his feet and drag him to the jeep. After placing Fallon in the back seat, Roscoe sits down alongside of him. I climb into the front passenger seat. Hayman drives.

Hayman moves the jeep up from the equipment hardstand and pulls onto Perimeter Road. We head south along the main entrance road and turn east onto Route 19. As the jeep speeds along Route 19 toward An Khe Pass, Sergeant Fallon sways silently back and forth, eyes closed, mumbling to himself, but he is alert and aware of his surroundings. "I knew Slaughter was going to do this to me," he says. "I knew he was going to do it. I knew he was going to do it."

I turn around and put my arm over my seat and speak to Fallon. "You know more about rock than anybody in this company."

"I know more about rock than anybody in the United States Army. That sorry Slaughter, I knew he was gonna' do this to me." Fallon sways from side to side, peering off into the distant jungle hills, first to one side, then the other. "I'll bet these hills are just crawlin' with Cong. And we've got to come out here and set a rock crusher right in the middle of 'em."

After reaching the Pass, we pull off onto a narrow, winding road to survey a potential site. The site is heavily wooded with steep cliffs rising on one side about one hundred feet straight up into the air. Roscoe and I hop from the jeep and walk closer to inspect the site.

Fallon stays seated, yelling from the jeep. "There's not enough rock around here to keep a rock crusher going for a week." He points to the heavy vegetation growing out of the side of the cliff. "Look at that overburden. There's no use staying here any longer. I'm telling you, there is no rock in that hill."

I don't know if Fallon is right or not. It looks to me like there is plenty of rock there, but Roscoe seems to agree with Fallon, so we leave that site to drive further down the Pass.

The further we go, the louder Fallon gets. "Sirr, sirr, where's my weapon?"

"I think you left it back in your tent."

Fallon's face wrinkles with horror. "I gotta get my weapon."

"It's OK, Sergeant Fallon. The rest of us have ours."

"No sir. We gotta' go back and get my weapon. We gotta' go get it."

I pick my rifle up out of the vertical mount, reach back and hand it to Fallon. "Here. Take mine."

Fallon grasps the weapon and pulls it to his chest. "You might know we'd have to set this damn machine up right here in the middle of VC territory. These hills are just crawlin' with 'em. Sirr. Sirr. You know what we gotta' do? We gotta' bring the platoon out here and sweep this whole area. Kill every VC within five miles. And sir, we can do it. Yes sir. I'll bring 'em all up here. We'll clear this jungle out, and when we get done we'll put the crusher right here and there won't any VC come anywhere near this place. But we gotta' clean it up first. We gotta' clean it up."

I am about to give up the hunt when there appears just ahead another vertical rock face. This one is right alongside of the road and only about fifty feet high. As we pull off to the side of the road to examine it we notice three ropes dangling from the top of the cliff, snapping against the rock near the base, where an infantry sergeant stands, shouting orders to three infantrymen from the 1st Cav halfway up the rock face. The climbers slide down the nylon rope about four feet at a time, stopping, crossing their legs tightly, then releasing and dropping another four feet.

Hayman pulls the jeep off to the side of the road, slowly applying the brakes. When it comes to a full stop, Fallon gets out. "If you want rock," he yells, "I can give you all the rock you need. I know where the rock is. It's right here in the Pass. This is where we got to set the crusher up because this is where the rock is, right here in the Pass." Fallon closes his eyes and continues rambling. "I don't know how we're going to secure it, but if you want rock, if you really want rock, you got to come down here to the Pass to get it."

Fallon sits down on the ground near the cliff and leans against the rock face, watching the infantrymen propelling down the vertical rock face. None of us knows why they are doing it. For the fun of it, I suppose. Rock propelling must be their thing, I guess. Fallon seems to like it.

Roscoe and I sit in the jeep, staring at him, discussing the alternatives. There aren't many alternatives because the area is undefendable without infantry, especially at night, and we know the infantry will not help. For them this is only a playground. We would have to defend it ourselves, which we can't.

The trip home is quiet. I spend most of the time wondering what to tell Perry. He probably already knows the site at An Khe Pass is not feasible because it cannot be secured, but I have to report to him anyway. I turn back to confirm the decision.

"Roscoe," I say, "I don't see how we can possibly provide adequate security at the Pass without the infantry."

"No sir," he answers back. "You're right. We can't do it."

We can't do it. We can't provide our own security. We're engineers, not infantry. We have neither the manpower, nor the skills, nor the interest, nor the ability to provide security for a rock quarry at the Pass, or anyplace else for that matter, outside the limits of Perimeter Road. It would be nice if we did, but we don't. And why should we? Why should we have to? What are we providing security against—the NVA, the VC, or the Vietnamese civilians down the street or around the corner? Why not let the local Vietnamese provide security? Why not let the local Vietnamese run the rock quarry? Why not let the local Vietnamese run the whole show?

"Unless," I tell Roscoe, "we could hire civilians to guard it."

"Oh hell no," Roscoe says. "We would need the infantry out there." Roscoe looks at Fallon for approval.

Fallon, sitting close to Roscoe, sways from side to side. "It's time, America," he moans. "It's time."

I think it might work. Of course to be effective, a civilian operation would have to be run our way. It would have to be efficient. In addition, the civilians would have to guarantee safety and security. Somewhere in this country, someplace, there must be people who could do that. Somewhere there must be civilians who, if paid enough, could guarantee safe operation at the Pass. They may not be immediately available to us, but they must exist. All we need to do is find them and strike a deal.

With great confidence, I direct Hayman to drive to the town of An Khe. People must have returned to the town by this time. If so, we will study them. We will study the type of people they are and we will study their needs. We will find those who are willing to make commitments for success at the Pass.

The town of An Khe is only about a mile from the entrance to An Khe Base. It is offset to the north of Route 19, along a dirt road. There is an eastern entrance and a western entrance, both of which branch off from Route 19 through wooded areas surrounding the town. We enter from the east along the narrow, two-lane dirt road, which runs through the center of town. For the most part, each side of the main street is lined with bamboo huts and rusty tin shacks, with very few civilians present. Initially, it looks like a peaceful little country town. At the far end of town, however, something out of the ordinary is apparent.

Several new buildings are going up there, wooden frame with shiny tin roofs and shiny tin exterior walls. Most of the new buildings are still under construction, but a few are recently completed. The recently completed buildings have brightly colored signs mounted over the front entrance. Initially, they look like bars.

We notice too many off-duty GIs in town carrying weapons. Some of them walk right down the middle of the street like they own the town. One man has even rented a cart drawn by a water buffalo. The cart is a small farm wagon with large wheels and a high center of gravity. The man in the cart is heavyset. He sits high, holding the reins loosely in his left hand, slapping the water buffalo gently with the long whip in his right hand. He carries an M16 in his lap. Everybody carries a weapon. They must feel it is not safe to be here without a weapon.

Near the end of the street there are two new buildings with lines of armed soldiers standing in front, waiting to enter. They look like bars, but they are not. They are houses of ill repute.

Against Roscoe's advice, I get out of the jeep and walk inside one of the yet-to-be-completed buildings. Inside there is an entrance foyer and a waiting room with comfortable-looking wooden chairs much like a doctor's office. Down the middle of the building is a dark center aisle. On each side of the aisle there are cubicles, each about eight feet by eight feet, three on each side of the center aisle. Full-height metal partitions separate the cubicles. It is quite noisy inside, with workmen pounding and banging. This shop is nearly finished and there are several more going up. Signs to be mounted over the entrances are already being painted in bright decorative colors—the Neverforget, the California. Nearby, I see some girls who have already arrived—Chinese, Korean, and Malaysian—black, brown and oriental. Although I may be over-reacting, I see danger here. There are no MPs. I mention to Roscoe that I want to talk to the men when we get back.

It doesn't take us long to get back. An Khe Base Camp is right around the corner from the town of An Khe. We are neighbors, separated by an impene-trable armed perimeter. From our bivouac area I look across the open fields to the dense woods which separate our two worlds. It seems incredibly ironic that I live this close to moral corruption.

Now, in addition to a drunken platoon sergeant, I have to worry about loose women. Oh well, one thing at a time. Fallon comes first. Roscoe and I help Fallon from the jeep to his one-man command tent and load him into bed. He seems to have sobered up a little bit. At least he lies down peacefully and keeps his mouth shut. That gives me time to concentrate on the other problem. After leaving Fallon's tent, I tell Roscoe how upset I am about loose women we saw in town, and that I want to talk to the men.

"You mean them whores, Lieutenant? You don't need to talk to them about that."

"I want to talk to the men about this, Sergeant. I want to explain to them about the different types of venereal disease. I want to tell them the only sure way to prevent disease is by total abstinence."

"Pardon me, sir, but that's not necessary. I already told them to wash up good with soap and water."

"I once saw a man die of syphilis," I say. "In his last days he sat in a rocking chair with big sores all over his face and head. He had sores on his arms and hands, and his legs were bandaged up and once a week the doctor would stick a needle into his scrotum."

Sergeant Roscoe brushes off his fatigues, straightens his cap, and marches directly to the troop tents. He stands at attention and yells at the top of his lungs, "All right, all you rinky dink little mutherfuckers get out here in formation. The Lieutenant wants to talk to you."

Only about a dozen men fall into formation. They form up directly in front of me in two ranks. At this time of the day they appear to be a motley bunch. Some have shirts on, some have only tee shirts, and some wear no shirts at all. Some have their trousers tucked neatly into their boots, some do not. Some wear hats, some do not. Nobody has combed their hair and everybody wears dirty clothes and muddy boots. Of forty men, this is all Roscoe can muster together. The rest are either working, or sleeping, or are downtown.

I stand erect before the men and lecture. They listen, and I think they understand. They smile. It is good to see them smile. Maybe I should not be so hard on them. After all, they deserve to experience life to the fullest, for tomorrow they may die. Even so, it is my duty to try and instill in them some sense of lasting morality in which they can take pride. I do that, knowing well it is their decision what they choose to do. I remind them that some decisions are easily made—those which they attribute to affect only themselves. Other decisions are not so easily made—those that they attribute to affect not only themselves, but to others. I hope they stay away from the Neverforget and the California. Some will, some won't. I tell myself that it is OK, and then I forget about it. I have bigger problems. Perry has scheduled a meeting at 0800 hours tomorrow morning in the Battalion command tent to discuss the rock crusher.

It is now 2400 hours to be exact, or as near exact as I can tell. I'm not much good after midnight. We have turned off the generator, so there is no electricity. I am sitting in my end of the tent, reading by candlelight; Sergeant Roscoe is in the other end, talking with a short, skinny little buck sergeant from Battalion. Roscoe calls him HD. HD has spent the last several nights drinking beer with Roscoe, but I haven't paid much attention to them before tonight.

They speak rather softly so as not to bother me, but tonight HD has brought his guitar. Even though late, it is good to hear the sergeants joking around. Roscoe kids HD, insulting him in a fun way, kidding him about only being a buck sergeant. HD reminds Roscoe of his overwhelming experience.

The noise is rather loud through our makeshift room partition. I can hear their discussions quite well. Roscoe first makes insulting remarks about HD. HD in turn ignores Roscoe's remarks by strumming on a guitar, surprisingly well.

HD had once been a staff sergeant. Now he is only a buck sergeant. I can see why. He is a drunk, but he is a harmless drunk. HD confidently strums his guitar. "Lieutenant Jefferies," he says in a loud voice, "I'll bet you think we're all crazy back here."

I am surprised that he plays the guitar so well and remark, "You are pretty good on that guitar."

"Well, I'm from the Blue Hills of Kentucky and I've been playin' this guitar since I was a little boy. Learned it from my daddy."

"What else did they teach you?" Roscoe asks. "What else did they teach you, you little junior buck sergeant?"

HD laughs loudly. "Bluegrass." He grins from ear to ear. "My daddy taught me how to play bluegrass."

"And to drink whiskey," Roscoe says.

"Yes, that's what I learned to do." HD continues strumming his guitar. Then he turns to me and asks, "Lieutenant Jeffries, are you related to any Jeffries from Hohenwald, Tennessee?"

I reply that I am not, but that I know where he is coming from because I spent one summer working on a surveying crew in Mississippi.

"Now that was good country down there. Did you ever have any bootleg?"

"One day I was out on a surveying party and some old codger came out with a bottle of something that had charcoal floating in it."

"That was it. Did you try it?"

"No, I was afraid it would poison me."

HD stretches his neck, scratches his whiskers and yawns. "Those chunks of charcoal in it might have. But when you get a hold of a bottle of the real thing, nothing's any better."

Roscoe, grinning broadly, lifts his right foot and slaps his knee, forcing it back to the ground. "You ought to know, you old corn runner you."

HD stammers. "Almost got caught one time. I was on this run from Hohenwald to Natchez. The night after I left, the feds got there. Well, you see my old lady, she didn't know anything about this because I had my still out in the woods. Had all of these pipes strung up, you know? You got to distillate, run it through a distillation unit. I jammed some good stuff, best stuff in Tennessee. I just…well, after I left, the feds had a four-state alert out on my car. I was lucky because I stopped at a gas station and called my old lady. She told me the feds had been there, so I took the stuff and threw it out. They never did stop my car. I was sweatin' that one out, because if they'd caught up with me I'd have been busted clear out of the army."

Roscoe buries his face, distorted with laughter, in both hands. Then he lifts his head and stares at HD's three stripes. "They damn near busted you out anyway."

HD offers to sing one more song before we all go to bed. He says, "This is my favorite good-night song. It's a song about my old dog Blue." HD sings loudly, while Roscoe roars with laugher. It is fun listening to HD. HD may be a drunk, but he is a harmless drunk. Not like Fallon. Fallon is a dangerous drunk.

The next morning I rise early for the meeting with Perry. I take Roscoe with me to the meeting, but I leave Fallon behind. I can trust Roscoe not to say the wrong thing, but not Fallon.

We arrive at the Battalion command tent precisely at 0800. Perry is there, waiting for us. He has rolled the sides of the tent up so we have a clear, unobstructed view of the main north-south road from the troop areas to the heliport. There are two others there with Perry: a bird colonel and a brigadier general. Impressed, I immediately snap to attention.

Perry puts us at ease while the three of them study the situation map. The general does all of the talking. The colonel nods his head up and down in agreement. Perry remains silent. Then the general and the colonel take off, leaving Perry to do all the talking.

Perry begins by approaching the situation map and pointing to the Pass. "What do you think of that?"

"I don't understand the question," I say.

"You were out there looking for rock. Did you find any?"

"Yes sir, we did."

"Can you mine it there?"

"Yes sir, we can mine it if you can secure it for us."

It is at that precise moment that we see several companies of men marching down the road, past our tent, toward the heliport. They are heavily armed and prepared for battle. They march down the middle of the road in military formation, eight abreast, company-by-company at the route step, young men in jungle boots pounding little puffs of dust into knee-high fog. *Kids!* I think. *Just hollow-faced kids in warriors' garb, one step from the cradle, one step from the grave.* Their eyes follow the ground beneath their feet as they trod along like cattle to slaughter in unpretentious obedience.

"Sure, we can secure it," Perry says, "but why don't you secure it yourselves? Why does Group want to keep you guys back in Peaceful Valley?"

"You mean Canh Van Valley?"

"If that's what you want to call it. There are lots of valleys over here." Perry points outside. "Those men you see out there are going to a valley— Ira Drang Valley"

"Is that a peaceful valley too?" I ask sarcastically. I sort of resent Perry's comment. I should not, but I do.

Perry quickly interrupts me. "Not hardly. There are NVA Regulars in Ira Drang Valley. There aren't any NVA in Qui Nhon. Why does Powers insist on staying in Qui Nhon?"

"I think it has something to do with winning the hearts and minds of the people," I reply honestly, or as honestly as I can. I don't really understand his point. I don't know where Ira Drang Valley is, and I really don't care, as long as I don't have to be a part of it. Ira Drang Valley is not a part of my world.

Perry points to the columns of combat uniformed men marching in formation toward the heliport. They are loaded down with machine guns and ammunition. "That's the 2nd of the 7th," Perry proudly says. "They are going to Ira Drang Valley to relieve the 1st of the 7th. They bivouac right next to you. You should be going with them."

Now that the general and the colonel have left, I feel free to speak. "We're construction engineers, not infantry. We don't belong in Ira Drang Valley, unless you want us to build something there."

"We'll let you know. It sort of depends on how things work out with the NVA. In the meantime, we have decided you should leave your rock crusher at Qui Nhon, but we want you to stay here with us for a while."

Even though I don't know much about Perry, I am beginning to trust him. "Sir," I say. Sir seems appropriate. "We want to do whatever you want us to do, as long as we are capable of doing it."

"Maybe instead of supporting us you world rather directly serve in support of the South Vietnamese Army. That might be more to your liking, and to Powers."

It is obvious that Perry doesn't like Major Powers. Maybe it's a power thing. Perry is not in the chain of command, and we are not even assigned to the 1st Cav. We are here merely to support the Division Combat Engineers with construction of the 1st Cav Base camp. That rubs Perry the wrong way. Perry wants absolute control.

"I don't think so," I say. "I wouldn't want to trust my life to the South Vietnamese Army."

"Then what do you want, Lieutenant? What does Powers want? You want to go back to Peaceful Valley? You want to go back to Peaceful Valley and leave the Cav to do the dirty work? If that is what you want I'm not going to let it happen, and you can tell Powers I said so. In the meantime, just do what you are told."

Sergeant Roscoe and I leave the briefing tent in complete bewilderment. We don't know what we are supposed to do. The only thing we do know is that the rock crusher is not coming to An Khe. That means we don't need Fallon. Roscoe and I agree to send him back to Slaughter.

It is not a minute too soon to send him away. On the way back to our tent we hear Fallon's screaming voice. It is only 1000 hours in the morning and Fallon is already in what appears to be a drunken stupor. We enter one of the troop tents to find Fallon dragging PFC Hayman around by the shirt.

"I'll teach you how not to be scared." Fallon shakes Hayman by the collar, forcing him to the ground. "I'm gonna' make a man out of you."

I can't believe this is happening. I just can't believe Fallon could do this to us. "Get back to your tent," I tell Fallon.

"Sir, this ain't none of your business. I'm the platoon sergeant and I'll handle this." Fallon's enraged eyes glow with fury as he yanks Hayman from the ground, then he pushes him back down again and stomps back to his tent.

Hayman looks terrible. His eyes are red and full of tears and his arms and hands shake. I walk over and kneel down beside him.

"I'm not going to make it," Hayman sobs. "I'm not going to get out of here alive."

"You're tired," I say to him.

"I'm a coward." He buries his head in his hands. "If my father ever saw me like this, he would kill me."

Fallon yells at me from the seclusion of his tent. "Sir, I want to talk to you."

Hayman is still shaking. "Sergeant Fallon is going to beat me up."

I reach down and turn Hayman's face toward me. "You're all right," I say. "You're not a coward. You're only scared." Roscoe and I help Hayman to his feet. After we clean him up and put him to bed, Roscoe asks if I'm going to have it out with Fallon. I tell him "yes," and to have Fallon report to my quarters. Being most disgusted, I go to my tent and sit down behind my field desk to await him.

Fallon is prompt. He reports to me immediately. He acts drunk, but he doesn't smell of alcohol. I can't tell if he is drunk or sober. I can only tell that he is out of control.

Fallon staggers into my tent, where he stands at attention and cocks his hand in a military salute. "Sergeant Fallon reporting as ordered, sir." Fallon's physical size and loud voice are imposing, but he no longer frightens me. He stands at attention, showing respect, but he is still belligerent. "Lieutenant Jeffries, I'm the platoon sergeant up here and I know what has to be done. That man is a coward. There is no place in this army for a coward, and if you hadn't come along I would have straightened him out."

"Sergeant Fallon, sit down."

"Sir, I would prefer to stand." Fallon has been around long enough to know he better not refuse an order.

"You can stand there all day if you want to," I tell him, "when you're sober. But you're drunk. And there is no place here for a drunken platoon sergeant."

"Sir," Fallon says looking down at me. "You're not very proud of me are you?"

"No, I'm not."

"Are you afraid of me?"

"No, I'm not afraid of you."

"No sir, I mean are you afraid I will cause embarrassment?"

"Yes, I am, and I'm afraid you will hurt someone."

"Sir, I wouldn't do it. You can trust me. I'll stick by you." Fallon wears a drunken grin. "I'm a bluffer, sir. You can trust me."

I dismiss Fallon. I suddenly feel sick. I haven't had much sleep, so I lay down on my cot. The pain is a piercing one. I lay there, tossing around in pain, wishing the bathroom was a carpeted walk from my bedroom. The bathroom is a convenience I miss a great deal.

In an attempt to feel better I get up and walk across Perimeter Road to the latrine. To get there I have to walk around two foxholes, navigate a ditch, and climb a bank. I then mount the throne and adjust my rear end into the circular hole formed through a scratchy one-inch plank. I sit there with my elbows on my knees and my chin in my hands, staring off into the distance. It is peaceful here. The beauty here cannot be matched by a simple bathroom, not even in the most luxurious surroundings. As I sit on the latrine, watching the helicopters taking off for Ira Drang Valley, I think to myself that it may be pretty there, too. Maybe if things work out we can move there. But right now things are not working out. Fallon must go.

Between Fallon and Goodrich, there is one thing I now know. *Incompatible objectives cannot coexist side by side.*

It is a perfect opportunity to dump Fallon. He has been of little use since his arrival here. Much of the time he has been drunk. Even when he was sober he stayed to himself and let Sergeant Roscoe run things. He would come out of his tent only at mealtime, and then never saying much. Even if he stays off of the booze, I fear that sooner or later he will cause trouble. I like the man, but I don't trust him. I admire his experience but abhor his unwillingness to take a risk for others. He is a totally self-centered individual who seeks to escape responsibility. He thinks constantly of himself—of his needs only. He is an arrogant person who rarely gets out of the first person singular.

Fallon packs up and leaves. I plan to drive down to see Slaughter later in the week to explain why Fallon has to remain in Peaceful Valley with Joe Goodrich. In the meantime, I wait to see if Perry plans to send us to another valley.

CHAPTER 5

Each week An Khe takes an increasing and accelerated toll on our construction equipment. I had no idea how fast machinery deteriorates under continuous use. Operating twenty-four hours a day, there simply hasn't been time available for scheduled maintenance other than for oil, lube and filters. We have ignored engine noises, so now we have several major problems which are adversely effecting production.

We have had to weigh rapid initial production against slowdowns for maintenance. I have felt that the construction had to be accomplished as fast as possible, even if that meant delaying maintenance. I knew that *choices must be made,* and I made them.

In retrospect, perhaps we should have worked to keep the equipment running rather than operate twenty-four hours a day. However, there is limited maintenance talent and capability available at An Khe. The talent for maintenance is in more secure areas near the coast. I have two bulldozers with transmission problems loaded onto lowboys for transport to Canh Van Valley.

Our little convoy leaves An Khe Base early in the morning. Hayman and I lead in the jeep. We are followed by two lowboys with deadlined dozers on top. Bennett brings up the rear in a three-quarter ton truck.

Route 19 is desolate. We ride with our rifles loaded and peer with anxiety at every turn. We should have grown accustomed to insecurity by this time, but it is not easy waiting for somebody to try and blow your head off. We ride along near the jungle, where ambush would be so easy. I am anxious because there has been a lot of trouble recently with the 1st Cav in Ira Drang Valley.

I probably should not dwell on Ira Drang Valley. Ira Drang Valley is west of An Khe. We are headed east. But I worry. The Cav lost several entire platoons to ambush in Ira Drang Valley. I have heard many tales and now try and imagine what it must have been like there. It must have been terrible. Men were trapped at night, unable to escape. Many had been knifed to death. Some had even been barbed wired to trees.

The short journey from An Khe to the top of the Pass seems to take forever. We pass a few civilians, which is comforting, and an occasional water buffalo. But for the most part, riding this road leaves us with an uneasy feeling. It may be safe. But we do not feel safe. We feel like moving reference points on a big rifle range. We feel helpless to defend ourselves. And ahead lies the Pass. Our stomachs wrench with anxiety as we approach the top of the Pass.

From the top of the Pass on this clear day we can see nearly forty miles longitudinally down the Dak Krong River Valley to the South China Sea. Rich green rice paddies line the valley as far as the eye can see. Pausing near the top, slowing momentarily, we gaze downward and to the left across shoulder high elephant grass bordering the ridge toward a winding snakelike Route 19 crudely notched into a sloping mountainside.

We descend the Pass in low gear, using the tractor engines to slow the heavy loads. To avoid any danger of collision, our jeep stays well ahead of the lowboys. Otherwise, the three-mile descent is uneventful.

Once through the Pass and into the lowlands we travel swiftly—fifty miles an hour—bouncing, turning to glance back occasionally to see that all is well with the trucks which follow a good distance behind. I nestle down comfortably into my seat and watch the countryside whiz by, green rice paddy after green rice paddy, sporadically dotted with peasants. Some, driving mud-laden water buffalo, slush barefooted behind handmade wooden plows. Some walk narrow dikes, separating rice paddy from rice paddy, walking the narrow paths of poverty from the village beyond to work at the family livelihood. They are dressed in cheap black dress and the customary thatched cone-shaped hat. Peaceful it is—poor perhaps, but peaceful—the way it has been for hundreds of years along these narrow paths which separate rice paddy from rice paddy.

There is a more comfortable feeling for us here in the fertile lowlands than in the desolation of the highlands central plain. Here in the lowlands we feel secure seeing workers in the fields. We can see for miles. There is no danger. In the joy of this peace I pause to wonder who originally built this road through the fertile valley along which trucks of war now roll. I wonder who originally cut this narrow path along which we now travel, separating rice paddy from rice paddy.

Ahead of us, along the right shoulder, there is a lone civilian riding a bicycle. I first see the civilian in the far distance and watch the rhythmic pedaling as we approach him from the rear. I can't tell if it is a man or a woman. The rear brim of the white thatched cone-shaped hat resting on the shoulders is restrained by a chin strap worn not militarily at the chin, but loosely around the throat. The cyclist is of medium build, and dressed in white.

The cyclist is about a quarter of a mile away. We are traveling at sixty miles an hour, so it will take us about fifteen seconds to reach him. We don't give much thought to this civilian cyclist. It is a natural thing to see civilians here in the valley, for this is a peaceful valley and one that is relatively secure. This is a fertile valley, where God is in control. It is God who decides the upcoming course of events in this peaceful valley. It is God who decides. It is God's doing.

Hayman sees the cyclist, I am sure of that, but for some reason he speeds up as we approach from the rear. There is no particular reason to speed up to pass this civilian. The lowboys are a quarter of a mile behind us. But Hayman speeds up. I don't know why he speeds up, and really don't give much thought to it. Hayman is driving. Hayman is in control of the jeep and is the person responsible and in charge.

We are about five car lengths behind the bicycle when suddenly and without warning the cyclist swings to the left and pulls directly in front of us. I can see now the cyclist is an old man. He is a very old man and we are going to run right over him.

There is little time to react. Hayman slams down on the breaks and turns the steering wheel to the left, as far to the left as possible without flipping the jeep. The locked tires squeal as the jeep slides forward. I stabilize myself against the windshield to absorb the impact. We feel the initial impact against the front bumper. There is little resistance. The tires easily override the bicycle and the old man.

The jeep skids for about thirty yards beyond the scene of the accident. As the jeep comes to a halt, I reach back to grab my seat and, nearly falling out, turn to see the old man lying on the asphalt pavement next to the mangled bicycle. The two lowboys with dozers atop slow down and swing to the left lane to avoid the accident and park alongside the road. Behind them is Bennett in a three-quarter ton truck. He passes the lowboys and then stops his truck directly behind the old man.

The accident has occurred near a cluster of four huts which sit back about one hundred feet from Route 19. As I watch the old man lying in the road, several young men come out of the huts. One is yelling at me in Vietnamese and pointing toward the old man lying facedown in the road. I reach out and pick up my rifle. The young man stops where he is in the front yard of what I presume to be his home. But I fear it may not be his home. There are too many combat troops in this area for a man of this young age to be living here. I lift my rifle and chamber a round.

The old man lying in the roadway starts to move. Slowly, he moves one hand to the pavement and pushes himself up onto his hip. Blood flows from his mouth, down one side of his chin and onto his shirt. He raises his head and looks forward to me, then raises one arm over his head and waves.

I am not prepared for this. I have not been trained to care for civilians or render aid to civilian casualties. The matter of accidentally injuring civilians was never addressed in officers' basic. We do not carry a first aid kit on the jeep. We do not speak one word of Vietnamese. We have been trained by infantry officers, not by missionaries. We are trained only to take care of our own and kill the enemy.

The young men who have come out of the nearby huts stand in quiet observation. They first look at the injured old man, and then at me and my loaded rifle. My God, I am not prepared for this! I am prepared only to suspect they are VC carrying concealed weapons. I am trained to trust no one and always suspect a trap. The old man may be a lunatic who intentionally pulled in front of our jeep to draw us into an ambush and the young men dressed as civilians may really be Viet Cong about to carve us into little pieces. My God, I am not prepared for this.

I am trained to react promptly and make decisions. That was drilled into us with tactical field exercises at our summer camp in officer basic training. It was also drilled into us by our classroom instructors in college ROTC. I am not prepared for this, but I am trained to make decisions.

Surprisingly, my decisions are made by impulse, not logic. There may be time to think, but I do not take time to think. I do not take time to reason right from wrong, to weigh the dangers, to envision the alternatives. There is time only for reflex and conditioned action. I lift my arm forward and wave Bennett and the two lowboys forward, then I climb into the jeep and order Hayman to move out, leaving the broken old man lying in the road.

The accident occurred about halfway between the Pass and Canh Van Valley. This is a relatively desolate area of rice paddies, except for the group of four huts near the accident site and the young men who emerged from those huts. I am sure the witnesses are limited to three or four natives. I assume that some of those people will care for the man, but worry that there is no nearby means of transportation.

I look at Hayman. He is staring straight ahead down the road and far off into the distance. "Jesus," Hayman says. "Jesus forgive us. Maybe we should go back."

"Oh no," I say. "A decision had to be made and I made it."

I desperately try to convince myself I made the right decision. We are in a combat zone. Danger is present. The young men coming out of the huts might have been Viet Cong. It was not worth risking any American lives for an old man who is going to die anyway. I struggle to dispel the doubt. I must clear from my mind any thought that they may have been the man's relatives or friends. Whoever they are, the old man is their problem now. The old man lies broken in front of their homes. We have left. Now someone else must care for him, or bury him.

I try to forget the accident, to put it out of my mind, but I cannot. The problem we created now becomes someone else's problem. But whose? Ahead on the road we can see coming toward us several military vehicles. They are going to pass us and they are going to pass the old man. Two of the vehicles are jeeps with officers. Soon, those officers, too, will have a decision to make. Soon they too must decide whether or not to stop and render aid to a helpless old man. Soon they too must decide whether to risk potential dangers to stop and help. They too will soon have to make those decisions.

They may decide to stop. If they do, they may discover a hit and run—a criminal act. I doubt, however, that they will remember our vehicle markings, but they may remember the lowboys hauling dozers. We may be criminals. Even somebody in our own unit could incriminate us. I decide to see if anybody wants to go back.

I pull off to the side of the road and wave to the others to pull off behind me. The lowboys with dozers pull off onto the shoulder and park behind the jeep. Bennett pulls the three-quarter ton truck up and parks in front of the jeep.

Bennett steps from his truck and walks toward me, staring at me straight in the eyes. "Sir, you made a mistake back there," Bennett says to me. Then he looks at Hayman. "And you made a big mistake."

I can see now that Hayman is visibly upset, even more so than I am. Hayman's hands shake. He won't look at me. He looks off into the distance. "I probably killed him," he says.

"You probably did," Bennett replies to Hayman. And then he turns to me. "And if he didn't, you did."

I respond to Bennett immediately. "Would you have stopped?"

"No," he says, "but you should have."

"Would you have stopped with me?"

"Probably not," he says. "I would have kept going. But you should have stopped. You're the officer. Even if those people had turned out to be Viet Cong, you should have stopped." Bennett stares me in the eye. "I'm not saying that I expected you to stop. I just said you made a mistake, sir."

"Well, there is still time to correct it," I say. "If you want to go back, you can all turn around right here and go back."

No one speaks. No one even looks at me except Bennett. Bennett stares at me. I stare back, upset by his insinuation that it was my duty to stop. He is the last person in the world who I thought would accuse me of neglecting my duty. I might have expected it from one of the truck drivers, but not Bennett. Bennett is too competent to question my decision. I turn to see if the others concur. The two truck drivers stand along the shoulder of the road, kicking stones with their feet. Neither speaks. Rather, they look to Hayman, who is standing near them.

Finally, Hayman breaks the silence. "If we go back there those people might kill us," Hayman says softly.

Bennett and the others understand. We all agree to keep the incident quiet and to tell no one, except Slaughter. I do feel obligated to tell Slaughter. I wish I didn't have to bother him with this matter, but I feel that I must. After all, Slaughter is the commanding officer. He may tell me to forget it, or he may decide to court-martial me. I haven't seen Slaughter for a while, so I plan to break this news to him slowly. After all, I haven't even explained to him my reason for sending Sergeant Fallon back yet. He must still be furious about that.

Returning to Canh Van Valley under these circumstances is somewhat traumatic. To make things worse, the environment there has changed radically. The camp, once tucked neatly into the native countryside, now lays stripped bare. The surrounding vegetation has been removed and replaced with concertina wire. The camp sticks out boldly, being easily seen from a half mile away. Instead of the neighborhood-friendly site I remember, Slaughter's campsite now appears as an armed fortress. The compound is in the form of a circle, surrounded with trenches and barbed wire with open fields of fire in all directions. Inside are a few GP troop tents and several equipment maintenance tents. Construction equipment is parked neatly between the tents. Along the perimeter just inside the concertina is a system of trenches, not entirely unlike those of World War I. The company has an entrenching machine for laying pipe. It looks like Slaughter decided to use the trenching machine for purposes other than laying pipe.

At the rear of the camp, fields of fire have been cleared for about three hundred feet, all the way along the foot of the westerly hills, which are still huge, wooded and unchanged. Those hills are steep, heavily wooded and a still unsecured barrier separating us from the mysterious unknown valley on the other side. That area invites danger.

To the north and south are small rice paddies. Those areas are relatively innocuous. Nobody would ever make a ground attack across a rice paddy. That would be suicide.

To the front of the camp, along Route 1, the fields of fire have been cleared less than a hundred feet to the east, just far enough to see all of the civilian huts along Route 1. Most of the huts I remember are still there, even the hut of the old man who complained about us moving into a graveyard. The graveyard issue now appears moot. The graves the old man had marked are no longer visible, as the entire site has been graded into a barren, sandy parking lot.

John Slaughter watches from his command tent as we drive into camp. I thought Slaughter would come outside to greet me, but he doesn't. I fear he is upset over Fallon's return and I decide it is best to get that issue resolved before I tell him about the accident.

I go directly to Slaughter's CP and enter the office. Slaughter is seated at his desk. He is huge. He is physically impressive. I had almost forgotten how impressive Slaughter is. The muscular six-foot-two airborne ranger demands respect. I come to attention and render a salute. Slaughter returns my salute and nods for me to sit down.

"How are you, David?" he asks in an unusually quiet subdued voice.

"Just fine, sir," I reply.

"Why did you send Fallon back to me? I wanted him at An Khe to find a site for the rock crusher."

"I'm sorry about that, sir. We looked, but we didn't have much luck. Fallon says the only place to find rock is at the Pass."

"He did, huh?"

"Yes sir."

John turns and looks out through the open side of the tent. "I hope we can straighten him out." Then he turns and bows his head toward his desk, picks up a pencil and starts doodling. "He back-talked me, the fool. He wouldn't support my decisions."

Slaughter is quiet, reserved, and thinking clearly. Now is the time to tell him about the accident. "Sir, I have had some other trouble."

"I was afraid of that." John stops doodling and puts his pencil down. "If he gave you trouble at An Khe, I'll see that he looses a stripe."

"No sir. I mean other trouble."

"I don't like to hear problems, Lieutenant. Didn't anybody ever tell you not to let your problems become your boss's problems?"

"No sir. I don't believe they ever did."

"So what's your problem?"

"We killed a man."

John Slaughter slams his fist down onto his desk and sits back in his chair. "Congratulations," he says. "Tell me about it."

"It was an automobile accident. We ran over an old man on a bicycle with the jeep and left him lying in the middle of Route 19. He was hurt badly. I'm sure he is dead by this time."

"It was an accident?"

"Yes sir."

"Did anyone else see it?"

"No sir. I mean just a few local civilians. I probably should have stopped and taken him to the hospital, but I didn't know where the local hospital was." I wait for John to say something, but he lets me do the talking. "I don't even know where the nearest military hospital is. And if we had attempted to move him he would probably have died in our jeep, and then we would have had to deal with that. I mean, I wouldn't have been able to find his next of kin and we would have probably had to keep the body here at camp over night."

John Slaughter motions negatively with his hand. "Forget it."

I breathe a sigh of relief. With those two words Slaughter has relieved me of accountability for this tragedy. For me it is over, thank God. I rationalize my actions that when faced with a crisis I did what I was trained to do: save American lives.

"What other problems do you have, Lieutenant?"

"I brought two dozers back deadlined."

"How bad are they?"

"I think one needs a clutch, and there is something wrong with the transmission of the other."

"You want two more to tear up?"

"If you want to give them to me."

"You've got them. What you are doing at An Khe is more important than what we are doing here." John glances out of the side of the tent, "Whatever this is."

John stares intently out of the side of the tent toward a nearby village. The entire area has been cleared of brush; the tents and the equipment are lined up in neat military fashion so we have a good view of the village through two rows of concertina wire.

John Slaughter doesn't look well. "I'm tired," he says. "I'm really tired. I think I'll come up and spend some time with you, maybe a day or two. I need to get out of here for a while. I have to do something besides sit here in reserve while the rest of the army fights the war."

I assure John he is welcome to come up any time, although the accommodations may not be very comfortable, and that when he gets there we would probably put him to work fixing broken-down equipment.

"Fix equipment?" he says. "With what? We already need more repair parts than we have on hand. I sent several people to Saigon to look for repair parts. They keep coming back empty-handed. I finally sent a man down there and told him to stay until he found some, which may take forever."

We don't have forever. I don't know how long we do have, but we don't have forever. John Slaughter is upset. That is not like John. "You should have sent Joe Goodrich," I say. "Joe would love it in Saigon."

"He wouldn't go. He wants to stay here to win the hearts and minds of the local people, and play missionary."

John excuses me. I leave the CP and walk to the officers' tent and go inside where I find Joe Goodrich seated in a shallow, low, handwoven chair, reading a book.

Joe looks up when I enter. "What are you doing here?" Joe asks.

"I've come to the rear for a little rest and recuperation," I say to Joe, hoping he will welcome me.

"Well, you have come to the wrong place, because there is none of either around here." Joe pretends to ignore me and keeps reading his book. "This place down here is driving me crazy," he says in a quiet voice. "Slaughter is crazy."

"Oh yeah?"

"He calls alerts—two, three, sometimes even four times a night."

"Alerts?"

"Yeah, in phases. Phase one means everybody gets up and puts their clothes on."

"Phase one?"

"Then when he calls phase two, everybody gets in the trenches. Since we have an entrenching machine, Slaughter has found it necessary to dig trenches all around the perimeter. Some are too deep to even see out of. At night the trenches are full of vermin, and when it rains they fill with rainwater to become a muddy mess."

"Nobody has even fired a shot down here yet. What is he so excited about?"

"I don't know, but I'll tell you one thing. The rest of us around here are about sick of it. We're not getting enough sleep. We don't have enough people to work all day and then pull guard duty at night."

"Well, I tried to help you out."

"Oh?"

"I sent you another guard: Fallon."

"Thanks. Remind me to return the favor sometime."

"How about now?" I had heard that Joe had been appointed communication officer and I have been waiting to lay somebody out.

Joe nods his head.

"Are you the communications officer?"

"Yes."

"You know we are on the AM net?"

"Yes."

"Well, did you know there is nobody else on the AM net in this country except us?"

Joe answers without looking up from his book. "The Army issued you an AM radio and that's what you have to use."

"Thank you, Lieutenant."

"So what do you want me to do, go steal you one?"

"Yes, if you have to. I need a radio. I have to be able to communicate. The only thing I can get on my radio is Hanoi Hannah and Chinese Rock and Roll."

Joe drops the book onto his lap, looks up at me and says, "I hear you have beer in An Khe."

"We have about five hundred cases."

Joe gives me a disgusted look. "We don't have one ounce. Listen, the next time you come down here you bring me fifty cases of beer and I'll see if I can get you an FM radio."

"Look, Joe, I really need an FM radio now."

Joe smiles. "You look tired," he says. "Why don't you spend the night here and we'll talk about it in the morning?"

The morning sounds just fine to me. It has been a long day, and I am really not up to returning to the scene of the accident so soon, so I tell Joe I really don't want to return to An Khe and that I will spend the night here if they can find me a cot to sleep on.

"Great," Joe says. "Maybe Slaughter will call an alert."

Joe calms me down somewhat and puts me at ease by assuring me that I am welcome to spend the night. I even get the impression he wants me to stay. Even though he and I have opposite points of view philosophically, we do respect each other. We need to talk.

"Great," Joe says. "You stay here tonight, and tomorrow I'll take you on a tour of Slaughter's special project for peaceful coexistence."

Peaceful coexistence. That should be interesting. So far I haven't seen much evidence of it. I haven't seen any civilians around, except for those presumed to be living in the nearby huts along Route 1. I ask Joe about training civilians to work in the camp. He merely replies that there is a security problem. That means Slaughter doesn't want any civilians working inside the camp. Slaughter refuses even to let them in to shine shoes. Slaughter insists that his men shine their own shoes. Slaughter insists that there simply isn't enough work for civilians. So much for peaceful coexistence.

Slaughter is concerned with security. He cannot understand why he hasn't yet been attacked, particularly from the south. All the VC have to do is walk up Route 1. The marines pulled out weeks ago. Slaughter's camp is the southern-most camp in the valley. He has requested an infantry unit to protect his southern flank and armed outposts atop the adjacent hills to protect the western flank. He insists that we should be building an infantry base.

Instead, Slaughter has been ordered to improve an unmapped road eastward through the mountains that separate us from the coast, and westward for a short distance. He hasn't yet been told what this road leads to, only to widen it and somewhere along this road build a dump. He has also been ordered to pick a suitable site for the rock crusher and rock quarry along this road.

I spend the evening chatting with Goodrich and Slaughter. We sit in the officers' tent, John complaining about the lack of security and Joe complaining about unnecessary alerts. As they argue, I think about today's accident. Slaughter doesn't mention the accident. I appreciate that. Maybe he has already forgotten. He spends most of the evening discussing this matter and how disappointed he is to be assigned for peaceful coexistence in a combat zone. I decide not to tell Joe Goodrich about the accident. Joe is too idealistic and too ready to do right. I'm afraid Joe would not cover for us.

In the morning, Joe, John and I prepare for a recon. There are three jeeps—mine and two machine gun jeeps. We all ride in John's jeep, Slaughter in the front and Joe and me in the back. The other two jeeps have been rigged up with thirty-caliber machine guns. One machine gun is mounted shoulder high in the center of each jeep. The gunner stands behind the machine gun.

We ride out of the main entrance, past thatched huts of straw, turn right onto Route 1 and head south. It is a very secure feeling to ride between two machine gun jeeps. The Canh Van River is to our left, and beyond that a ridgeline of mountains which separate us from the coast. To the right lies a higher ridge of mountains that separate us from the unknown valley to the west. Straight ahead, only about a half a mile from camp, there is a fork in the road. The straight leg continues south along the valley as Route 1, a narrow paved road. The right leg is a dirt road that branches west over the mountains. The small dirt road nestled neatly through a narrow pass has been widened for a distance of about four football fields to reach the top.

We drive as far as the fork in the road and then stop. "There it is," Slaughter says.

"It looks peaceful enough," I reply. "I wonder why the VC don't hit from this direction."

"Beats me," Slaughter answers. "It would be so easy. They could walk right up this road and tear us to pieces."

Joe Goodrich now speaks up. "But they can't attack from this direction," Joe says, "because they can't get here."

"We don't know that," Slaughter insists. "No one has given us that assurance. We have to assume the worst, that being that we can be attacked at any time."

"Impossible," Joe says. "You are creating dangers that don't exist. The NVA will not attack from the south because they cannot supply their troops from there."

John Slaughter is furious. He says he is not worried about the NVA, but the entire country is infested with Viet Cong. He reminds us that they have weapons and ammunition, and that they are merely waiting for the opportune moment to attack us. Slaughter believes the VC will soon attack us from the south.

From what I can see, I think Slaughter is wrong and Joe Goodrich is right. There is no danger of assault on Canh Van Valley from the south, or from anyplace else, for that matter. I agree with Joe that Slaughter's fears are ill-founded and that those fears are jeopardizing his mission here. But I dare not voice my opinion.

"Now over here," Slaughter explains as he points to a relatively open area where water buffalo graze between scattered trees, "is where Group wants me to build a dump." John lifts his helmet and wipes the sweat from his forehead. He looks disappointed.

Joe Goodrich stands up and points ahead, beyond the section that has been widened. "This is a stupid place for a dump," Joe says. "People live here."

Ahead, along the road, two ill-clad Vietnamese men shuffle toward us. They each come carrying a load of sticks on their backs—firewood. As they approach, we can see that the sticks have been burned to charcoal, a smokeless product they will sell in the Town of Qui Nhon.

"I agree," I say. "This is a stupid location for a dump."

"People live down this road," Joe says. "Just plain people live down this road," he says. "They don't bother anybody and nobody bothers them." Joe raises his arm in gesture. "They don't support any armies, and no armies support them. That's why we won't be attacked from this direction."

John Slaughter becomes excited. He stands up and points toward the pass. "Yes," he says. "And if we build a dump here it will draw rats and rodents—and other vermin."

"That it will," says Joe Goodrich, "but a rock crusher won't." Joe then turns and points one hundred and eighty degrees and points in the opposite direction. "Now there, across there on the other side," he yells, "is the perfect place for the rock crusher."

Slaughter and I turn and look. The area to which Joe refers is on the easterly side of Route 1, at the side of a stone-faced hill which separates Canh Van Valley from the coast, only about a quarter of a mile from camp, at the unsecured end of the Valley. The area is heavily wooded, but there is also rock. A large outcropping of rock is visible with a large high, dry flat area that could be used for the rock crusher.

Joe is probably right again. There is plenty of rock there. And it is so close to camp that at night we could simply leave it unguarded, or as a last resort try and guard it ourselves.

Slaughter is visibly upset. "The VC will blow it up in a few days," Slaughter says as he looks out over the terrain. He wants the rock crusher and the entire company moved to An Khe, but I doubt that will happen.

I doubt that John Slaughter will get his way. Canh Van Valley is an acceptable site for the rock crusher. It is close to camp, and from what I see, is in a reasonably safe area. I can't imagine anybody attacking us in such a beautifully peaceful setting. Obviously, this is where Engineer Group will want the rock crusher. John Slaughter may not like it, but that is the way it will be. That is what Engineer Group Headquarters will insist he do because it is in their best interest to have it located near Qui Nhon. It may belong in An Khe, but it will remain in Canh Van Valley. *Men wish what is honorable but choose what is profitable.* Now, it must work.

CHAPTER 6

Early in the morning Hayman and I prepare to leave for An Khe. Immediately before leaving I speak with John Slaughter and thank him for ignoring the accident. I have great respect and admiration for John Slaughter. He has supported me. He has forgiven me. Instead of a court-martial, there is a cover-up.

I am anxious to leave Canh Van Valley, but I am reluctant to return to An Khe because of having to pass the scene of the accident. Still painfully vivid in my memory, I imagine the old man lying in the road, propped up on one hand, bleeding at the mouth and waving his other arm at me. I ask myself repeatedly why I did not stop to help him.

Are we soldiers, or are we murderers? I wonder that—not seeking forgiveness, for Slaughter has forgiven us—but rather in an effort to determine the significance of what we did. Why did we run over a helpless old man and leave him in the road to die? How could we have done such a thing? To justify my actions I must *look for the higher value*. For me, the initial justification is easy. I simply did what I was trained do. It is easy to decide that. It is not so easy to *believe* that.

The trip back to An Khe is quiet, lonely, and emotional. I continually imagine seeing the old man in the road, bleeding at the mouth, with his hand in the air waving at me. I repeatedly keep asking myself, "Are we murderers?" I feel like a criminal returning to the scene of a crime, wondering who is there, wondering if blood stains are still on the road, and wondering if there is any evidence of the accident, wondering if the old man is dead or alive.

Driving past the scene of the accident, passing the point of impact, there is no evidence that an accident ever occurred. There is no visible evidence whatsoever of any violent act. That act now lives only in the minds of those who were there to observe it. No one else will ever know what happened, except of course, the old man's relatives and friends, if he had any, and if they cared enough to tell about it. I think that perhaps they did care. Perhaps the memory of that tragedy has instilled in them a thirst for revenge. Perhaps, one way or another, they will seek revenge.

I cannot live with thoughts like that. Instead, I must rationalize that we had no control over any of the circumstances presented to us—or our reactions. We did what we were trained and conditioned to do. Somebody got killed. Here it happens every day. Every day there is another killing, and when the killing is over all is forgotten. We tell ourselves to forget it. Forget it. It is over.

Perhaps what happened really was significant. Perhaps it was not. To help forget the accident, Hayman and I decide to drive home through the town of An Khe. On the way we chat about what possible changes may have taken place there. We had seen several brothels under construction the last time we were in town and we are now curious to see how many have been completed.

We enter the town from the east, along Main Street, a dirt road, to see that there are, by now, several new brothels. Each is a pole frame with tin siding, tin roof and a large, brightly-colored sign hanging over the entrance. The new tin shacks sparkle brightly against the rusty older buildings and dusty street. Long lines of men stretch into the street from each brothel. Many other men roam the street sites, shopping for trinkets from the shops and street peddlers who have arrived there. As Hayman drives the jeep slowly down Main Street, I am in the passenger's seat, holding my weapon by the stock, butt on the floor. The town seems somewhat safer than the last time we were here. There are more soldiers in town. Most still carry loaded weapons. Some, but not many, are obviously drunk, which is a bit unnerving.

This once peaceful town is peaceful no more. It is now noisy and rambunctious, somewhat like a Wild West town during the gold rush, I imagine, with one major difference: common people live here, people whose families have lived here for several generations. Children play in the street. Seeing those children playing here leaves me with a sickening feeling because, I think, they deserve better upbringing than this den of iniquity. Here they cannot be screened from corruption. There are no alternatives here for these children. This village is too small for screening. The highland villages are much smaller than the coastal towns such as Qui Nhon.

There is a great difference between the opportunities children have here in the highland villages like An Khe compared to the opportunities children have in coastal towns like Qui Nhon. In Qui Nhon there are schools, several run by missionaries, but not here. In Qui Nhon there are Buddhist temples with high towering pinnacles, but not here. Many areas of Qui Nhon are clean and relatively safe, but not here. In Qui Nhon, children have a choice of where to play, but not here. Here children play in the streets between flashy bars and brothels and rusty tin shacks they call home.

Hayman pulls the jeep over and parks alongside a rusty tin shack that stands next to a shiny new brothel. He turns the ignition off and points toward a clothesline in the back yard. There, hanging on the clothesline, is a pair of women's panties—white panties with black polka dots. "Those must belong to one of the whores," Hayman says, then he jumps from the jeep, runs to the clothesline, steals the panties, returns to the jeep and ties them with a knot around the top of our radio antenna. "We need a flag," Hayman says with a smile on his face. "A Peace flag," he says. "Do you mind, sir?"

"Why should I care? We can't get anybody on the radio anyway." And we need to talk to somebody. If we can't talk on the radio to our own people, maybe we can try and talk to the local people here on the street. There are several people here who might want to communicate, even though we don't speak the same language.

Nearby, there are several street merchants. One is selling bamboo matting. Everybody needs bamboo matting. We need bamboo matting. We could use it as rugs for the troop tents. We could use some to wrap around the latrine for privacy. The matting is cheap, so I give Hayman twenty dollars and tell him to buy as much as he can.

Many other items are for sale, things I could use for my hooch. I buy a coffee-pot and a small Dutch oven. The merchants wage in bitter competition, so I barter with two merchants side by side for a lower price. They want greenbacks, of course, but I have none left by this time and give them a combination of Military Pay Certificates and *piasters*. There are many things for sale here, mostly junk, but some good stuff too, such as silk fabric and Japanese radios. I am particularly drawn to one merchant selling hand-crafted goods, including a collection of china dolls. I plan to buy one until Hayman reminds me the Stars and Stripes Newspaper recently carried an article about a bomb scare where terrorists planted bombs inside dolls.

Hayman convinces me to pass on the little dolls, although I wish I had bought one because they appeared to be handmade by artisans. God knows, we should be supporting those selling handmade goods instead of the bars and brothels. But Hayman convinces me otherwise by pointing out a nice safe-looking establishment with MP's standing in front. It looks like a bar.

"Sir, you look like you could use a beer," Hayman says.

"I don't think officers belong in a place like this," I say. On the other hand, I can easily justify stopping for a beer. That would be perfectly innocent. Besides, Hayman has convinced me that it is my duty to go inside one of these places to see what is going on. We have our pick of several interesting establishments, including the Never Forget and the Last Chance. With two MP's in front, we pick the Last Chance. Hayman opens the swinging front door and motions for me to enter. But it's not a bar.

Inside there is a small lobby with several chairs and a sofa. On the sofa there are two rather unattractive Oriental girls, lounging in skimpy pajamas. I get the impression more girls are in the back rooms.

"I wonder what and who is back there," I say.

"I imagine it is rather dirty," Hayman replies. "Too dirty for officers."

"I'm sure it is," I answer. "I probably shouldn't let the men come down here. I already told them that, you know. I told them how dangerous this can be to their health, and even to their psyche."

"It's OK, sir. They're soldiers."

"Yeah, maybe so, but I haven't heard anybody say it is worth it yet. Maybe it's just something they feel they have to do before they die." And we know men do die here. And we know they have money to spend here. And we know that is why the girls come. And we know somebody, somewhere, is making a lot of money.

"It's OK, sir. They're soldiers."

"In a once peaceful town? That's not right. War and peace-keeping activities just don't mix."

"That's the way it is, sir. That's the way it's always been."

We return to An Khe Base, pass out some of the bamboo matting as rugs for the troop tents and use the rest for screening the latrine. We also use some to build a roof over the latrine to keep it dry in rainy weather. The rain clouds have been accumulating now for several days. The monsoon season is nearly upon us. That will bring construction operations to a halt.

The monsoon season begins with gentle rains. The first rains are light and bring relief from the heat. We welcome the first rain. The sun soon appears through the mist. The sun lasts a couple of days and then it rains again, this time longer and harder. The second rain does not go away so fast.

Eventually the monsoon rains have a devastating effect on the gravel roads. The gravel here is laterite clay. When it rains, the surfaces of the roads turn to mud and become so slick that rubber-tired vehicles lose traction and slide off the pavements into the ditches. It is nearly impossible for us to move dump trucks to the quarry, so we cease operations. This would not have happened with crushed stone pavements. But we don't have crushed stone because the rock crusher cannot be secured in the highlands. The rock crusher remains in the peaceful valley near Qui Nhon. Maintenance of gravel roads in monsoon weather is no easy task, so I decide to use our most experienced operator first and let him train the others.

Spec 4 Bennett enters the dispatch office dressed in GI rain gear with rubber pants, a rubber hooded jacked and rubber boots. He chews on a water-soaked cigar. "Sir, this is the damnedest mess I ever seen in my life. You can't do any work in this kind of weather."

"Look, Bennett, I'm just following orders." That sounds all right to me. That's what the Germans used to say.

"It's no wonder all the equipment is falling apart. This army needs some old civilian construction foreman to explain what a waste of time it is to try and work in weather like this."

"Would you rather be in the infantry?" I ask.

"No sir. I'll tear it up as fast as the army issues it. No sir, I don't want anything to do with the infantry."

"We need a little road maintenance."

"Well sir, let me tell you, when we get done out there we'll need a lot of road maintenance to fix up the mess we're gettin' ready to make. I'll be glad when I get back to Brown Construction Company. There's an outfit that knows how to do things right." Bennett shakes his head as he leans down to sign in the operators' log-book. "Lieutenant, let me ask you something. Has anybody got any plans of what this place is supposed to look like? I mean these people…we go out there and the instructions we get is that the road's supposed to go off in a general straight line between two trees. There aren't any grade stakes, elevations or nothing. Haul in some dirt, dump it in a rice paddy, push it around a little bit, get stuck, pull yourself out, bring in some more dirt, push it around, and get stuck. It's about time somebody sat down and figured out the alignments so when we did something we wouldn't have to do it over again."

"Bennett, you must have heard there are three ways to do things, the right way, the wrong way and the Army way."

"Yes sir, I believe I heard that somewhere before. But just between you and me, he Army way here in this place is screwed up. We have all this old equipment—dump trucks, rubber-tired equipment, rollers, front-end loaders. We haul dirt in bad weather from a borrow pit two miles away. We need some big pans. Take 'em up there on Hong Cong Hill and haul some fill. Don't do any work when it rains. Work when the rain stops. Take them pans, take 'em up there on Hong Cong Hill and build us a camp here that looks likes something. If somebody around here would take the time to plan and get the right equipment to do the job, why then you could haul some dirt. Can't haul no dirt with five-ton dump trucks. No, sir. I mean, you need some eighteen-yard pans. Sir, you give me some dry weather and big pans and I'll build you some roads."

"The Army, unfortunately, is not set up for civilian operations."

"Yes sir."

"You're a little Spec 4 who used to work for a civilian contractor and you probably know more that ninety percent of the people you are working for."

"Yes sir, that's right. I know a lot more."

"But you're only a Spec 4."

"Yes sir."

"Well, let me explain to you how the system here works. The system works on progress reports. Progress reports go forward: man hours expended, equipment hours, tons of fill hauled and miles of road constructed. What the wheels want to see is the maximum number of hours in the given time period, regardless of whether we're moving in the right direction or not."

"Yes sir."

"Now my advice to you is to forget Brown Construction Company and just do what the wheels want done. If they want you to push mud from one side of the road to the other side of the road, that's what you do—you push it. If they tell you to build a road between two trees, that's where you build it. If they want you to waste equipment hours in bad weather, that's what you do. And when your tour of duty over here is finished, you go home and forget it ever happened."

"That's what you're doin', ain't it, Lieutenant?"

"That's exactly what I'm doing. Just doing what I'm told. And I'd advise you to do the same. That, Mister Bennett, is the higher good."

Totally disgusted, Bennett bites down on his cigar, pulls the rubber rain hood over his head and trudges back out into the storm.

The monsoon season seems to last forever. It goes on for weeks in the Orient. We spend the days moving mud from one side of the road to the other. The evenings we spend drinking beer and playing cards. At night we try and sleep, but we never sleep well with the nightly artillery barrages whistling overhead.

Some nights the artillery is quieter than others, but it is always present. So are the helicopters. The helicopter landing area for the 7th Cav is just to the east, and north to our back is a landing area near the hospital for med-evac helicopters. Many helicopters land hourly during the day, even in bad weather. When the sky clears, dozens land and take off. The killing goes on. There is little letup in the fighting. Even now, a battle rages nearby. Between the monsoon rains, the artillery, and the helicopters, the noise is deafening.

I lie on my cloth army cot, trying to sleep, but I never sleep well. I toss and turn and curse nightly, counting the artillery rounds, watching the helicopter landing lights approaching the hospital.

I am still awake late this night when someone enters the tent and wakes Sergeant Roscoe. There is some sort of commotion in Roscoe's end of the tent. I hear Roscoe putting his boots on. He yells for someone to get his truck started, then he yells at me to call the hospital and get the doctor. It takes me a few minutes to comprehend what is happening. A bulldozer has overturned in the quarry and one of our men is pinned under it.

I arise and dress quickly, grab my rifle and jump into the passenger seat of Roscoe's truck. Roscoe drives directly to the hospital to pick up a doctor, and then the three of us ride to the quarry. Roscoe is driving. I am in the passenger's seat. The doctor is seated in the rear behind us. The doctor advises us that he has a med-evac helicopter on call. We don't bother with the normal blackout lights but ride with headlights on high beams, traveling the muddy road as fast as conditions permit. The tires grind their way through puddles of rainwater, splashing mud against the towering trees that surround the road like a tunnel.

As we pull into the quarry site our headlights beam onto the laterite face of the mountain where a bulldozer lies upside down like a giant beetle helplessly upended on its shell. Next to the overturned dozer is another dozer. Bennett is driving this machine. After seeing us arrive, Bennett places the blade of his dozer under the upended dozer and lifts gently. There, beneath the dozer, lies a crushed body.

Somebody says, "Give him some air," so we move back into a semi-circle. The doctor climbs down beneath the machine and feels the man's pulse. "This man is dead." The doctor says. "Cancel the helicopter."

"It's Fitzgerald," Roscoe says softly.

God help me! I didn't even know we had a Fitzgerald.

Some of the men reach down and help the doctor pull the broken body from beneath the dozer, lifting it like pallbearers and placing it into the back of a dump truck.

Bennett is crying. His eyes are red and the tears have dampened the dirt beneath his eyes to mud. "He must have fallen asleep." Bennett and Fitzgerald were good friends. They had grown up in the same town and had known each other's families.

Roscoe is also crying. He is crying too hard to drive, so I help him into the passenger's seat, then I drive back to camp. The doctor rides in the back, sitting on the floor.

"Fitzgerald was a tall fellow with blond hair, wasn't he?" I ask Roscoe.

"Yeah, that's him."

"Tall and slender?"

Roscoe reaches up and brushes the tears from his eyes. "Yeah, that was him. Three o'clock in the morning. I told those guys that if they got tired to get off of those machines and rest. He has sat up there on that machine night after night like a sittin' duck waiting to get shot at. Every hour of the night he has lived in fear of a sniper's bullet. Now he is dead because he fell asleep."

We drop the doctor off at the hospital and then deliver the body to Graves Registration. At Graves Registration, Fitzgerald's body is stuffed into a green plastic body bag. I then call John Slaughter and report what has happened. John decides to drive up immediately with Fitzgerald's personnel records.

Three hours later, John Slaughter arrives. He steps from his jeep and grabs my hand firmly and shakes it. John says he is sorry to hear about Fitzgerald but gives the impression he is somewhat pleased we have finally taken our first casualty.

We take the personnel records to Graves Registration, where John signs the necessary papers, then John and I walk alone. We talk about Fitzgerald and what a shame it is that he had to die in an accident. Slaughter jokes that I must be accident prone because this is my second fatal accident.

"John," I say, "we are moving too fast."

"I know," he replies, "and we are not all moving in the same direction. Sometimes I wonder if we are even in the same army."

"What do you mean?"

"Fallon's been arrested."

"For what?"

"He got drunk and stole a jeep. He drove it through Qui Nhon and ran it into a Lambretta. Someone signed a statement that after the accident Fallon took the antenna from the jeep and whipped civilians with it."

That sounds incredulous. Nobody in their right mind would do that, not even Fallon. But apparently he did. "I'm sorry to hear that, sir."

"So am I," Slaughter replies as he bows his head. "So am I."

John's apparent meekness is surprising. John Slaughter is not one to be sorry about anything. John Slaughter is a tough, hardened man who calls the shots his way. John Slaughter doesn't need anybody's approval, or opinions, or direction. John Slaughter is what I consider to be a true soldier, an airborne ranger, an army engineer, a career officer. John Slaughter doesn't have to be sorry about anything.

We spend the rest of the day touring the job sites. John likes that. He likes being near the infantry, watching the helicopters land and depart, listening to the artillery firing overhead. For John Slaughter, this is where the action is—An Khe, not Qui Nhon. For John Slaughter, this war is at An Khe, not Qui Nhon.

At An Khe, men die. A lot of men die. This is war. War is what John Slaughter lives for. War is what John Slaughter has trained for. War is what John Slaughter needs and wants. The war is in An Khe, not Qui Nhon. An Khe is where John Slaughter belongs, not Qui Nhon. There is no war at Qui Nhon. At Qui Nhon people work to obtain the necessities of life. A lot of people there seek the necessities of life. That is peace. Peace does not interest John Slaughter.

John raises his head and looks me directly in the eye. "There is something else," John says, "something I don't intend to put up with."

"Oh?"

"The new executive officer."

"I thought I was the executive officer."

"No more you are not. Powers has sent us a lieutenant who outranks you. His name is Swartz." Slaughter rolls his eyes in disgust. "He is rather bossy and wants to run things. I'm not going to let him."

That sounds more like John Slaughter. That sounds more like John Slaughter the warrior, the airborne killer ranger for whom I have the greatest respect. The man who knows what should be done and who insists things be done his way—the army way.

We spend the rest of the afternoon chatting together, surmising that Lieutenant Swartz is Powers' spy, and about the best way to handle him. After much discussion it is obvious that John Slaughter lacks the tact and political finesse to successfully deal with Swartz, let alone Powers. Diplomacy is not of John Slaughter's nature. It would be nice if it was, but it is not. It would be nice if we could all be diplomats at the appropriate time, to be capable of convincing others to do what we want without creating discord and resentment. How many times must we be told that it takes but one cruel word to make an enemy for life? How is it that some of us have diplomacy and others do not? Is it in our training and upbringing, or is it related to natural intellect and talent? Why do some of us have it and others do not? It seems some people are born diplomats; they know how to talk politely to others. Does that make good diplomats better than the rest of us? It probably does. Diplomacy certainly makes life more pleasant for everybody. But John Slaughter is not a diplomat. That is just the way it is.

John, insisting I meet the new executive officer as soon as possible, suggests I come to Canh Van Valley within the next few days. I really do not want to go, but I feel that I must, to support John's command. As competent as John Slaughter is, he seems pretty much alone. There seems to be little support from Major Powers. There also seems to be little support from Slaughter's own officers and NCOs. That is sad, when your own people fail to support you. John needs me as a friend. I enjoy being with John. John supports me. I decide to be John's friend. That is appropriate. *Friendship is for pleasure or profit.*

Three days later I travel to Canh Van Valley to see Slaughter. I thought a three-day break would be appropriate. As it turns out, I shouldn't have waited so long.

Returning to Canh Van Valley, I find a lot of unexpected activity there. There are several jeeps from Group Headquarters parked near John Slaughter's command tent, which makes me suspect a personnel problem. I look around for strangers, but I see none. I see only John Slaughter sitting in his command tent, slumped over his field desk. It is not like John Slaughter to sit slouched over like that. Something is obviously wrong. Maybe it has something to do with Fallon, or maybe Joe Goodrich, or maybe the accident I had on Route 19. I don't bother to ask anybody else what is wrong. I go directly to Slaughter's command tent, walk to the front of his desk, snap to attention and salute him.

John Slaughter fails to return my salute. He slowly raises his head and says quietly, "I've been relieved of command."

Oh no. Not this. It can't be. John Slaughter is an Airborne Ranger. He is my hero, my mentor.

"I've been relieved of command of the Big Deuce." He is visibly upset, and obviously disappointed. "Powers is taking over."

"Taking over what?" I ask. "Powers is a major, not a captain."

"Powers is taking over my job as commanding officer of this company. The TOE slots a major for CO of this company, not a captain. Powers has taken my command away."

For Slaughter, there may be nothing quite as humiliating and humbling as being relieved of command before his time, especially when he has tried his best to do what he thought was right. But he tries to maintain a good attitude. "At least I'm not being kicked into a staff job. I've been given command of the 524th Dump Truck Company." That is quite a fall for John Slaughter. "A damn dump truck company. The good news is that I will be moving that damn little dump truck company to An Khe."

John smiles, just a little. John Slaughter is finally coming to An Khe. Good. That is an answer to prayer. Not exactly the answer he wanted, but good enough for government work. It will do him good to get away from garrison and up where the action is, even if it is only in command of a little dump truck company. I congratulate him, the best way I know how, even though it is hard for me to find the right words. What do you say to a man who gives up his farm to become a cowboy? You can't be too hard on a man who sticks by his principles when he knows he must lose power to maintain those principles. How many of us are willing to do that? How many of us will sacrifice power for principle? How many of us will risk losing everything we have to do what we really want to do?

I'm not. There is no way I will jeopardize what I already have for what might be. For me, progress is building upon what I have, not tearing it down to start over. Tearing it down and starting over is for people like John Slaughter and Joe Goodrich. Me, I just set my sails to the wind and watch what happens. When the wind is right, I sail. When the wind is not right, I jib, or come about. When the weather is bad, I pull into port. For me, life is a trip—a trip that begins only after you know which way the wind is blowing, and how to use it. Tearing down is for people like John Slaughter and Joe Goodrich.

John Slaughter and Joe Goodrich are aggressive people. Politically, they are complete opposites. Yet emotionally, they are a lot alike. They are both headstrong, bullheaded and uncompromising. And they hate each other. Even now they hate each other so much they cannot stand to be in each other's presence. That is painfully obvious to me as I watch Slaughter leave the command tent as Joe Goodrich enters.

Joe Goodrich walks in like he owns the place and sits down in John Slaughter's chair. "Did you congratulate the major yet?" he asks. Apparently Major Powers must be on site, although I have not seen him yet.

"No. And I don't plan to either," I tell Joe.

"Did you meet the new XO?" Joe asks as he rises up out of John Slaughter's chair. I think he is doing that as a courtesy to John, but I am wrong. He gets up to make room for somebody else. Without me noticing, the new XO has entered the tent. Joe tells me to turn and greet him.

It would have been nice if he could have knocked, or at least announced himself before entering so I could leave. Instead, he sneaks in on me like a predator quietly approaching for the kill. I feel an uncomfortable presence, like standing next to the aggressive kid who stole my high school sweetheart after telling her to get rid of me. This is a man who I really don't care to be near, ever. Although not justified yet, I feel he has come here to take from me. He has come to take my command, to take my reputation, and to take my independence. His mere presence leaves me offended. It shouldn't be that way, but it is. I wish there were some way I could better deal with my emotions, but there isn't. Maybe a course in psychology would help, or a course in how to take defeat and criticism without becoming emotionally upset.

When I turn around, there he is. Just like that, I am outranked. "I'm Lieutenant Swartz," he says smartly. The fat little officer steps forward with a smile and stares me directly in the eye. I resent his presence and expect him to realize that, but somehow get the impression he does not. He reminds me of a fast-talking trinket salesman on Times Square who once swindled me out of three dollars for a worthless set of pearls. His uniform is sloppy, perhaps unavoidably so to fit over his pear-shaped body, broad at the stomach and broader still at the hips. I watch his face as he addresses me, but I notice more his broad rear end swelling obtrusively from beneath his bulging round stomach.

"Pleased to meet you," I say politely.

"I've heard a lot about An Khe. When are you coming back here?"

"Not until it is time to go home, I hope."

"Isn't there enough equipment up there without yours?" he asks sarcastically.

"No. We need all the equipment we can get."

"I've been talking to Major Powers about you guys. He is very interested in having you return. He wants to get the whole company back together again so we can function properly. We are awfully shorthanded here. We need more men to pull guard duty."

"That's a worthy aim."

"And build a garbage dump. Group wants us to build and operate a garbage dump." Rodney senses I could care less. "The major is here and wants to meet with you now."

Rodney Swartz leads the way to the officers' tent where we find Major Powers already moving into Slaughter's old quarters. Powers doesn't even have the courtesy to wait for Slaughter to leave. Instead, he has begun unpacking and placing his clothes into a handmade bureau he had purchased in Qui Nhon.

In contrast to John Slaughter's ruggedness, Major Powers looks like a former high school whiz kid that skipped two grades. He has a narrow mustache which, although well-trimmed, fails to cover his boyish features. His uniform is pressed and his boots are waxed to a bright, but slightly dusty shine. "It's good to see you in the civilized world, Lieutenant," Powers says to me over the partial-height cloth partition that separates his quarters from the rest of the officers—the junior officers.

"This isn't going to be much of a meeting." Powers keeps talking while he unpacks his clothes. "I just want to explain to you that my philosophy here is much different than what you have been used to at An Khe. I want you to know that I plan to be very easygoing and I want you to be the same. I want things to run smoothly. I want to function primarily as an administrator here, and I want you and the other officers to act as supervisors. Of course you are still at An Khe for the time being, but even there I want you to act primarily as a supervisor. I'm going to let the first sergeant run the company and I want you to let your platoon sergeant run your platoon. Tell him what you want done, leave him alone, and let him do it. Keep checking to see that he follows your orders."

I find the whole situation to be quite extraordinary, to say the least. Powers is now the boss. Yes, he is. But, as John Slaughter has on many applicable occasions asked, "Are we all moving in the same direction?" No, we are not. We are still moving in opposite directions: war at An Khe, peace in Qui Nhon. In my opinion, for what it is worth, these are opposite and interfering objectives. Can we live with this? I suppose we can for a while, if we must.

But after a while, sooner or later, we must win. Powers is now the boss. Yes, he is. To me, that means it is Powers' responsibility to pull it off, to see that we are all moving in the same direction, to see that we win. I wish him well. Then I say good-bye to John Slaughter and return to An Khe.

CHAPTER 7

It is dawn at An Khe. I lie awake on my cot. I haven't slept well. I am upset because Slaughter was relieved of command. Slaughter tried to do what he thought was best, but in the end, he couldn't. I guess *there are some things we just can't do.*

The night shift gets off duty at 0600 hours. Many skip breakfast and go straight to bed while the cool night air still lingers. Most of them sleep only three or four hours before their sleeping bags become soaked with sweat. For relief from the heat they roll the tent flaps and tie them back, then the dust floats in from Perimeter Road and settles about collecting on the mosquito nets. By midmorning it is time to get up. It is ungodly hot here. By late morning it is time to shower.

Just before noon we hop a truck for the shower point. We wear our shower shoes and sit in the back of the deuce-and-a-half truck, clutching tightly to the canvas cover that funnels dust up into our faces. We cough. We bounce with every pothole in the road. We curse the potholes and we curse the wooden seat on which we sit. We try to think about other things, like getting a new car as soon as we get home, maybe an Impala with bucket seats, sleeping in an air-conditioned motel and swimming in a heated pool. Never going to take another dusty ride.

At the shower tents we off-load onto a muddy trail where our shower shoes stick in the mud and the mud oozes up between our toes. Inside the shower tents our shoes click-clack against the concrete floor as we carry our little bars of soap to the portable showerheads, there to wait in line and duck under the warm water, then to back off, soaping ourselves, and duck back under once again. The showers are as crowded as they were in high school, but now we feel alone. Here we are naked with strangers. Here we feel alone and insignificant. Here there is no rank, no bankers or laborers or millionaires.

After showering we have lunch. Lunch is more palatable now that we are clean. Even so, lunch is no gourmet meal. Lunch consists of Spam, beans, and bug juice. There is no milk. We used to have milk on occasion delivered from Pleiku. But no more milk. The milkman got shot.

Milk is the one thing we miss most, besides peace of mind that we will not be shot at. After that come the women. This really is a lonely place here without women. There are a few female nurses at the hospital, but they stay pretty much to themselves. We rarely see the nurses.

In the early evening Roscoe rises from his bunk and tosses an empty beer can onto a cardboard wastebox. "What we need around here is a little recreation," Roscoe says. "There's a nice little old empty field right here alongside of us. If it's all right with you, sir, I'll have the operators grade us a ball field."

After thinking about his request for a brief moment I nod my head in the affirmative.

Roscoe is delighted. "We'll push all that elephant grass off to one side, smooth us up a diamond and play us some ball. Yes sir."

The heavy monsoon rains have subsided. I think a ball field may not be a bad idea. Maybe some recreation will help us take our minds off the heat. And it is certainly hot enough. Roscoe is right. We do need some recreation. The location he has chosen for the ball field—between us and the 7th Cav—is a perfect location. Roscoe builds his ball field. The rains come again and the ball field turns to mud.

Within a few days, Captain Slaughter arrives with his dump truck company. I stand near the main entrance to the base as John Slaughter enters, leading the convoy of twelve dump trucks. This must be embarrassing for him, but I am glad to see him anyway. I salute him. He returns my salute, smiling, pointing to a new addition riding in the back of his jeep—a dog, a German Shepherd.

"Only on command," John yells from the moving jeep. "He attacks only on command."

It is good to see John smiling, but he doesn't smile for long. John Slaughter's Dump Truck Company has been assigned to the small tract of land between us and the 7th Cav: the ball field. The location makes John happy, but not the terrain. I follow John to the site to see if I can be of any assistance.

Approaching the site, John stops his convoy and directs them to park along the shoulder of Perimeter Road, just in front of our bivouac area. John then parks his jeep in front of the ball field. I park alongside of him. John steps from his jeep and walks onto the ball field, leaving his German Shepherd behind in the jeep, watching his every step. I follow John, expecting the worst—expecting him to explode with anger.

He folds his hands over his stomach, looks over the site and speaks to me in a disgusted tone of voice. "Do you see that mud hole we've got?"

"Sir, that's a good area."

"Like hell! Somebody has built a motor pool in the middle of it."

"No sir, that's a ball field."

"That's a mud hole."

"Well, sir, you see I had no idea your company was being assigned to this site."

"This was to be somebody's site." John Slaughter is really very irritated. I am surprised, in fact, by how irritated he really is over such a seemingly insignificant matter. John Slaughter wants to always be the boss. "Lieutenant," John says, "we are not all moving in the same direction."

"I feel terrible about this, sir."

"So do I, Lieutenant." John motions for his German Shepherd to come forward. The dog leaps from the jeep, jumps through several mud puddles and charges at me. I wince, but do not budge. The dog stops at my feet and growls. "Only on command, Lieutenant," John says. "Only on command."

As soon as I leave, John Slaughter moves his dump truck company onto the ball field. He places his CP tent right were we had located the pitcher's mound. I don't know why he did that. He just did.

I stay away from John for the next few days. Instead of baseball, Roscoe settles for a volleyball net strung between our tent and one of the troop tents. He sets up two floodlights, one on each side. We play volleyball nearly every night. Sometimes guys come from the Dump Truck Company to join us.

For us, work here is now becoming rather routine. We grade roads and haul dirt. The weather is such that there is enough sun each day to permit good progress. The road system here is nearly finished. Our mission at An Khe is nearing an end. As we relax and take stock of the work at An Khe it becomes evident that we must soon either return to Canh Van Valley or be prepared to support the infantry in its efforts elsewhere in the highlands. Each time I make a trip to Canh Van Valley I see more and more reason why we should return there. Major Powers has opened up a rock quarry in the valley near his encampment and is in the process of moving the rock crusher to that site. For him, security is becoming an increasingly pressing problem. He simply doesn't have enough men there for proper security.

The days pass slowly, as every hour we expect orders returning us to Canh Van Valley, but we hear nothing official. I imagine Major Powers is running things there pretty much the way he wants to. I imagine things there move slowly because there really isn't much to do other than operate the rock quarry. We do know it is relatively safe there. There is no shooting. There is no artillery fire, no helicopters. At Canh Van things are much different than at An Khe. At Canh Van things are quieter and more peaceful, and things there are apparently becoming even more laid back. Major Powers has reduced the number of nighttime guards he provides. He has abandoned the system of trenches which

John Slaughter had constructed and is instead constructing berm fortifications with guard towers. Fewer men are now required to guard Canh Van, which gives Major Powers more time to work on his projects for peaceful coexistence.

Powers has also made some staff changes. Rodney Swartz, of course, is the new executive officer. That was my old job. But Powers has given Swartz an additional duty that I did not have: paymaster. Rodney Swartz has been appointed Paymaster. John Slaughter always did that himself.

Each time I travel to Canh Van Valley, I kid the guys down there about how easy life is in Peaceful Valley and how rough things are at An Khe. They really aren't. I just like razzing Rodney Swartz. I don't like Rodney Swartz. He out-ranks me. I tell Rodney that as Paymaster it is his duty to pay the men at An Khe personally. He promises to do that.

At the end of the month, Rodney Swartz travels to An Khe to pay the troops.

Roscoe and I chuckle as Swartz pulls up in his windshieldless jeep. The floor is sandbagged. The back seat is sandbagged. The fenders are even sandbagged. Swartz sits, glassy-eyed in web gear and steel pot. He holds the butt of his M14 in his hand and rests the muzzle on the hood.

Roscoe grins broadly as he greets the lieutenant. "Sir, you look like a travelin' sand pile."

Lieutenant Swartz strains to remove his two-hundred-pound gut from the confines of the fortified vehicle. "Sergeant Roscoe, I always come prepared." At that very moment, a battery of 105's fire a volley overhead. Swartz jumps straight up in the air. His helmet bounces down over his eyes. He drops his rifle, lifts his helmet from his head and turns to me. "Jesus Christ, what was that?"

Roscoe calmly leans against the side of the jeep. "Sir, you're on the front lines now. You better pick up your rifle and put your helmet on."

"Do they fire like that all the time?"

"Every hour or so," Roscoe says.

"I bet you guys will be glad to get out of here," Swartz says in a waning voice.

Roscoe shakes his head in the negative. "No sir. We're getting along just fine right here. You tell the major that we are fine right where we are."

Rodney composes himself. After he picks up his rifle and puts his helmet back on, he is again ready for confrontation. Rodney looks briefly around the platoon area. "This is the sloppiest place I've ever seen. How can you people live like this?"

I look around to see what he is talking about. Although I hadn't really thought about it before, I now realize Rodney is right. The place is a mess, a real mess. The parking lot is a mud hole of ruts and puddles. Our equipment is dirty—filthy dirty, in fact.

Rodney leads us across Perimeter Road to the motor pool, talking all the way. Still talking, he steps from the laterite road surface onto the water-logged motor pool. There, the mud oozes up around the rim of his spit-shined boots. "This is mud," he says. "Nothing but mud."

"Yes sir, you're right," Roscoe sarcastically agrees. "That is mud." I admit that things look rather poor, but I let Roscoe do the explaining. Roscoe opens the doors of two conex containers. "This here's the tool shanty." It is embarrassing. Tools are slung around over the bottom of the two conex containers into wads of grease and rags. Some of the hand tools are rusty.

"Lieutenant Jeffries, this is a disgrace. Just look at this filth. What are you people doing here anyway?"

"As much as we can with the personnel available," I say. "We need more people." That is the best excuse I can think of, even though it is a weak one. I want to get away from the motor pool as soon as possible, so I turn and walk back toward the troop tents.

The inspection tour continues into one of the troop tents. I really hadn't been inside the troop tents for some time. I had left that to Roscoe. I have been more concerned that the men have been working long hours. I wanted them to have some place where they could relax without having to worry about inspections.

We enter the first troop tent, where a dozen men lie, racked out on their cots.

"What are these men doing in bed?" Rodney asks. "They should be cleaning tools."

"They have been working all night," I reply.

"Yes sir." Roscoe reinforces my defense. "They been workin' all night."

Rodney points to two men in the corner, drinking beer and playing cards. "They don't look like they need sleep."

"Well, sir, it's like this," Roscoe explains. "They don't need as much sleep as the rest of the men, but they get just as much time off."

I am amazed myself at the mess. Things have gotten pretty bad—beer cans on the floor, trash paper under the cots, dirty clothing hanging from the tent ropes.

As we leave the troop tent, Rodney keeps looking down, staring in disgust at the mud on his boots. It had showered the previous night and there are small puddles of water remaining all round the bivouac site. Rodney hits each one like a game of hopscotch, trying to wash the mud from his boots. All the time he rambles. Roscoe and I pretend to listen as he talks and sloshes his boots in the puddles.

I recognize a lurking foxhole, disguised as an innocent puddle. So does Roscoe. I see the grin on Roscoe's face as Rodney approaches the puddle. I smile and Roscoe smiles back. Rodney talks and mouths and with a splendid splash stumbles into three feet of muddy water like falling through a trap door.

Rodney looks up at us with a surprised, disgusted and embarrassed look on his face. "What the hell is this hole doing here in the middle of the platoon area?" he screams.

"Sir, that's a foxhole," Roscoe replies.

"Full of water?"

"Yes sir. I've been meanin' to cover that up." Roscoe reaches down with his hand to help Rodney up.

"Sergeant, I should think you should," Rodney says as he climbs from the quagmire with both pant legs bulging with water.

Roscoe tries to reassure him everything will be all right.

"I know it will, Sergeant. I know it will. But how am I going to get my pants dry in time to pay the troops?"

Rodney and I walk alone toward my tent. "I hope you know what you are doing," he says. "This place is a disgrace. I'd be ashamed to let the major see it."

"Well, he was here a few days ago and he is certainly aware of the conditions we are under. I'm sure he approves."

"He has changed his mind," Rodney says. "This is a waste of manpower as far as he is concerned. He wants you back at Canh Van Valley."

"Doesn't he think what we are doing is important anymore?"

"I doubt it." Rodney looks down in disgust at his mud-soaked fatigues. "Say, do you have a pair of trousers I could borrow?"

"Yeah, but they won't fit."

"Forget it. I'll pay like I am."

Rodney Swartz is quite irritated. I suggest that he might hide his muddy pants behind a desk. He agrees that sounds like a good idea, so we set him up behind a desk in the dispatch office, in my end of the command tent. To his relief, that works out well.

Rodney pays the troops. No one seems to notice his muddy trousers. That pleases his ego, and Rodney has quite an ego. I sense his ego grows further as each payee has to render him a salute. I invite him to spend the night, but he respectfully declines.

I am glad to see Rodney Swartz leave for Canh Van Valley. His critical comments about the conditions of things under my watch are upsetting. We have been here at An Khe for several months now, from the very beginning. I expected the new executive officer to offer me a few kind words of congratulations for what we had accomplished to date. Unfortunately, he did not. I don't think he ever gives a thought to what happened before he arrived. To him, it is like the world begins when he enters it. History must include him; otherwise it is unimportant and not germane to his decisions or actions.

There is nothing more dejecting than having someone tell you that you are doing a lousy job. Coming from a superior, it is extremely hard to take. For some people, criticism comes naturally. Rodney Swartz is one of those kind of people. People like that are no fun to be around. I don't like being near them, ever. I will do almost anything to avoid being in the presence of a critical superior. I dislike confrontation, especially with a superior. Critical people tend to drive me away, to force me into another camp. How many times must we be reminded that it takes but one harsh word from a critic to make an enemy for life?

Swartz has left me depressed about the future. I don't want to have to put up with Rodney Swartz. I don't want to put up with his criticisms and his stupid insinuations of my incompetence and misdirection. I don't want to put up with any of them—Swartz, Goodrich or Powers. I don't even want to return to Canh Van Valley. Maybe it is time for a transfer. Maybe I should request a transfer to John Slaughter's little dump truck company. I decide to request a transfer and to ask John Slaughter what he thinks about me doing that.

I spend that evening with a double ration of beer, thinking a lot about what I should say to John Slaughter. It is dark. It is pitch dark as I leave for John Slaughter's tent. I can hardly see where I am going, but I am determined to get there anyway. I trudge along the narrow footpath, through a thicket where I rip my trousers below the knee. To heck with it! What's a little rip? I'm going to see Slaughter.

After stumbling though the thicket for a while, I finally come to John Slaughter's encampment and find his tent. He has a CP tent with an office seating area in the front room and his sleeping quarters on the back. The front flap is open and a Coleman lantern hangs in the center above where John Slaughter sits, staring outside into the dark night. His German Shepherd is at his feet.

I haven't talked socially to John Slaughter in several weeks. We have met on occasion during working hours, but never just to chat. John seems glad to see me and I am certainly glad to see him. We exchange greetings and John invites me in for a visit. There are two chairs in the front end of the tent. John sits in one and I sit in the other.

John is in a friendly and talkative mood. "David, I have a good company here. It's not the Big Deuce, but it's a good company," John says as he pets the German Shepherd.

I look down lovingly at the handsome animal and ask, "Where did you get him?"

"From my new first sergeant. Top said he didn't want me to be lonely." John grabs the dog by the back of the neck and gently rubs his back. "You cute little rascal. I have a dog at home." John reaches around and pulls his wallet from his back pocket. "Say, did I ever show you my family?"

"No, John, you haven't." Actually, I know nothing of John Slaughter's family, or of his personal life. I know only that he is a serious-minded career officer.

"I have two children." John reaches into his wallet and pulls out a family portrait. He points first to one child, "The little one is only ten months old," and then to the other. "This is Nancy. She's three and a half."

I have to admit John's children are cute. John's wife is pictured with them. She is very attractive. "You sure have a nice looking wife," I say, hoping to flatter him.

"Yeah, Betty's OK. I married her when I was only a Spec 4. We didn't have much money then. She had to work."

"I'll bet you weren't even considering the Army as a career then, were you?"

"No, but I'll tell you something. I passed the OCS test about the time I was due to make Sergeant E5. I talked it over with Betty because I had just about decided to make a career of the Army. I liked it and so did she. Both of our families are poor. My father is an unemployed coal miner. Bets—well she doesn't have a father. Anyway, I told her I passed the OCS test and that I was going to turn it down. I told her I wanted to be a first sergeant. She said, 'No, John. I will not have you used as a stepping-stone for some officer.' We both knew that being an officer is a lot different that being an NCO. Officers aren't supposed to pitch in and do things like sergeants. Some people think officers are not supposed to do anything except stand around and look important and be responsible."

"John," I say, "that's what I want to talk to you about."

"Betty?"

"No, no. Not Betty. I want to talk to you about being responsible. I want to talk to you about Qui Nhon and Canh Van." It takes time to bring myself to say this, but I finally do. "I don't want to go back there."

"Well, that's two of us," John says. "I don't want to go back there either. What's that have to do with being responsible?"

"I don't really know. I guess it is like—well, like they say—it's not the job, it's the turkeys you have to work with."

"I know what you mean. Change of command is tough on the palace guard. I know what you mean."

"It's more than that. It is more than about personalities. It has to do, I think, with a more basic principle of where do I belong: here at An Khe with you, or in Canh Van with Joe Goodrich."

"Listen." John bends forward in his chair. "Powers will have no more luck at peaceful coexistence in Canh Van Valley than I did. It is impossible to work civilians into our operations over here because there is no security. People can't work effectively until they can work safely. That is why we have to win this war militarily first, then live in peaceful coexistence."

John and I talk late into the night, discussing eternal truths and the world's problems. I wish we could just go on talking. I wish we could just philosophize rather than make decisions. But we can't. Decisions must be made.

With great reluctance, I explain to Slaughter that I am considering requesting a transfer to his dump truck company. I tell him I want to stay here with him.

John says he would welcome having me stay if I were able to adapt. He reminds me that his dump trucks may sometimes be in direct support of combat operations. He reminds me that if I stay with him I will be expected to play the role of a combat engineer as well as a construction engineer. He reminds me that my chances of living through this war will be considerably less at An Khe than in Qui Nhon and Peaceful Valley. I listen intently to what John says, and then I assure him that I understand.

I know John is right about wanting me to be sure of what I want and am willing to do. I know that to transfer I must be willing to take the necessary risk.

"I'll give you a chance," John says. "There is an operation coming up in a couple of days. Some place called My Canh. I am to take a helicopter ride over there and check it out for truck deliveries. You can come along for the ride, if you want to."

That sounds to me like a good idea—maybe. "Will we be safe?"

"Absolutely. This is a huge operation. We are only a small part of it—the ground-supply part. My trucks will deliver supplies. But first we need to reconnoiter and check things out. Perry and I have scheduled a reconnaissance helicopter to locate and confirm decent ground access to a proposed supply point. I wouldn't go if it wasn't safe."

Yeah, right. I think I've heard that before, from Perry. Anyway, it is decision time. I have seen Perry in action. I trust him. And I trust John Slaughter. I decide to go with them.

At dawn, John Slaughter and I stand in full combat gear at the heliport, along with John's German Shepherd. We excitedly watch as several dozen choppers amass at the heliport, engines whirling and props turning. The choppers are lined up parallel to Perimeter Road so as to be easily accessible to the combat troops who arrive by deuce-and-a-half trucks. Boarding looks simple and easy to implement; just get on board one of the choppers, like everybody else. The choppers are loaded one after another. As each troop truck arrives, those men mount the next available airship. Everyone seems anxious to climb aboard and get a seat. The boarding is very efficient. These men must be used to this now. They move efficiently, like nobody wants to be left behind. Nevertheless, each is a bundle of nerves. Make no mistake about it; these men are anxious, concerned about their immediate future.

Slaughter and I are no exception. We're both nervous and a bit confused, particularly about which chopper to get on. We haven't seen Perry yet. That bothers me. That bothers me enough to ask John if he knows what to do. I don't want to go without Perry, and I suggest that we might want to cancel out.

John says that is impossible, that he is committed, and that if I want in I have to go with him now.

Now looks like the time for me to go, after finding Perry already sitting inside the next chopper alongside of several heavily armed infantrymen. Relieved to see Perry, Slaughter and I approach to mount the chopper, but we find it is full. Perry motions for us to catch the next chopper. Slaughter and I pull back and look into the next chopper where there are four infantrymen with M16's. We quickly climb in, me with my M14, John Slaughter with his 45, and his German Shepherd. The dog has a seat all to himself alongside of John.

The noise is deafening, with choppers lifting off all around us. We can hardly hear one another above the roar of the engines. "Are you sure this is the right chopper?" I yell to Slaughter.

John nods his head in the affirmative. He nods his head, all right, but I don't think he heard one word I said. I grab hold of a bulkhead strap, I stand up and lean over the infantryman sitting between us and yell the same question to John.

"What?" John yells back. "I can't hear a word you are saying."

The pilot motions for me to sit down. Refusing to sit down, I yell back at the pilot. "We're engineers. We're here for a reconnaissance."

The pilot again motions for me to sit down, but there is no way I am going to sit down until I get a straight answer. "Wait a minute," I scream, but it is hopeless. I cannot be heard above the roar of the engines.

Helicopters are taking off all around us. Suddenly ours lifts off, forcing me back into my seat. The infantryman alongside of me turns and yells in my ear. "You better fasten your seat belt," he advises.

I reach down and pull the seat belt from the floor and wrap it around my waist. I then turn to the infantryman and ask, "Do you know where we are going?"

"Puc Yu, sir. That's what they told me. We are going to Puc Yu."

"Well, damn it!" I reply. "The Captain and I are supposed to go to My Canh. We must be on the wrong ship."

"So am I, sir," the PFC replies. "So am I."

This man must have wisdom far beyond his years, far beyond me. I might as well stop complaining. Slaughter is not complaining. Slaughter is staring off into the distance, his arm around his dog, admiring the countryside. I might as well relax, too. I lean back, rest my helmet against the bulkhead and look out the open door. The countryside is beautiful. Here, high in the air, the war seems to disappear. The clear blue morning sky carries freshness to the moist green jungles below. It is beautiful up here, but not for long.

There are ten choppers flying in our formation—that means about two platoons of men. A lot more helicopters originally took off. I wonder where they went. I wonder where we are going. We are supposed to be going to John Slaughter's proposed resupply point, but by this time I begin to doubt that.

For most of the trip we fly over thick heavy jungle. There are a few roads, but not many, and certainly none that I want to ride over in a dump truck. Then, like a well-choreographed ballet, the choppers begin to lose altitude. Straight ahead, in the middle of thick jungle there appears a large open field— a landing area. Our group of choppers circles twice, then lands.

We hear small arms fire. I yell over to Slaughter that it looks to me like we have landed in the wrong place. He doesn't answer me or even notice that I said anything. He stands up and motions for me to jump out, which I do— after him.

I land hard on the ground, my feet firmly dug in. Surprisingly, I feel comfortable, like I belong here, like this was intended to be. Then I suddenly feel pain.

Within seconds of landing I am hit.

A sharp, piercing pain drives through the calf of my right leg.

It's the million-dollar wound. What a break! I glance down, looking for blood, but there is no blood. There is only pain.

Slaughter's German Shepherd has bitten me in the leg. I punch the dog with the butt of my rifle, but the dog won't let go. The choppers lift off, leaving us in an open field with eighty men, two platoons, me yelling and screaming at the dog—the damn dog.

After the choppers lift off, Slaughter pulls the dog away. "Are you all right?" he yells over the roar of the engines.

"Hell, no," I yell back. "I'm wounded."

You would think that would get somebody's attention, but it doesn't. Nobody cares. John Slaughter doesn't care. Neither does Perry. Nobody cares. They are all crouched down, trying to avoid incoming small arms fire. Somebody is shooting at us.

Now that the choppers have lifted off, we can more clearly hear the bullets whistling close by. Slaughter and I both hit the ground. Not knowing what else to do, that is where we stay.

"Maybe we got on the wrong chopper," Slaughter whispers to me.

"Listen, John, we have a problem here," I whisper back.

"Yes, we do," he says. "We're not all moving in the same direction."

"You have to get us out of here."

The shooting has started. Neither of us knows what to do. Neither of us is prepared for this. We need Perry. Perry was on the chopper just ahead of us. It landed. We saw it land. So where is Perry? We need him. We're engineers, not infantry.

The infantry knows what to do. Thank God for the infantry. When the shooting starts, the infantry knows what to do. And they do it, most effectively. The fighting lasts for no longer than a few minutes. Our casualties are light. The NVA casualties are heavy. The infantry knows what to do.

After the bloody encounter is over, John Slaughter and I walk the site. We stare at the bodies. We smell the blood. We study the faces of those who died. We walk around the site to each body. We don't miss a single one. We hit them all, friend or foe, every mother's son of them, each of God's creation, each put on this earth by God to be taken away at God's will. How is that? Why must some of us go so young while others stay so long? Is it really God who decides, or is it man? How can God keep track of all of us individually? How can he know us all? How can he hear each prayer? How can he know enough to judge each of us upon death? God must have a very big computer to keep track of so much information.

Walking from body to body, it drills into my head the realization that for each of these men, nothing matters anymore. For each of these men, life is over, final.

No more battles. No more troubles. Only, I pray, eternal peace, happiness and joy. Most of them must deserve that. Those who do not, we leave to God's judgment.

Painful as it is, I study each face with great diligence. My attention lingers a while with each before moving on to the next. That is, until near the end. Near the end I notice off to the side what appears to be a dead American soldier, lying face down. I motion for Slaughter to roll him over. John appears reluctant, like he already knows something about him that I don't. John motions for me to turn the dead body over. I roll the dead body over to see that he has been shot once in the forehead just between the eyes. I look at him in utter disbelief. It can't be. God wouldn't let this happen, not to this man, not to Perry.

Christmas at An Khe is a most lonely time. The Cav has erected a twelve-foot high cross atop Hong Cong Hill. The cross is decorated with small white light bulbs that glow brightly in the night as beacons on the sea. The cross shines high above the camp, and at night it appears suspended in the free air, visible for miles. It is never turned off. In the early evening hours we take our chairs out into the cool darkness and watch the cross while listening to Christmas music on Armed Forces Radio.

For our troop tents, the USO has provided small Christmas trees with little red balls. The men decorate them with pieces of hard candy, neatly scotch taped to the branches.

A two-day cease-fire is declared over Christmas. We cease work at 1800 hours Christmas Eve. After cleaning up, we open the bar. I want to stay with the men, but Roscoe says no, I have to go to the officers' club. The officers' club is located in a large timber frame building with a tin roof, mounted on a concrete slab. There are four cinder block walls on the sides and bare ceiling rafters overhead. The officers drink themselves drunk and sing silly songs. It is dumb. I want to leave, but after three martinis I decide to stay.

At 0200 hours in the morning I stumble back to the troop tents, where much to my surprise everyone is asleep. I then go to my tent and pull two large duffle bags full of gifts provided by the USO from beneath my cot and drunkenly stumble back into one of the troop tents.

Bennett is still awake. "Sir, are you feeling well?" he thoughtfully asks.

"Merry Christmas."

"What do you have there?"

"There aren't any names on these, but there is one for every man."

"Thank you, sir," Bennett says. "Thank you from every man here."

Christmas morning is quiet. Around noon I have Christmas dinner with John Slaughter, full course turkey. The food is good and we gorge ourselves. John is in a very good mood, so I take the opportunity to tell him I have decided not to request a transfer to his Dump Truck Company. John understands, and wishes me well.

In the afternoon we are to be treated to a USO show: Bob Hope. Bob Hope is coming for Christmas, with Carol Baker, Jack Jones and Anita Bryant.

The division theater is set up on a sloping field where the troops sit close together in a diamond-shaped formation. Two giant Chinook helicopters float down from the sky with a machine gunner at one side and long flowing blond hair at the other. Excitement flows from one side of that sea of troops to the other, back and forth; the current tosses us, sweeping us up, then back down again. The waves rise, front rows first and then back. Heads bob up and down, back and forth, and then from side to side. Men are smiling.

Then there he is. The back end of the helicopter lowers and Bob Hope struts forth, swinging a golf club. We all cheer. We all feel great. We all feel important. For us this is a great honor, an honor that we deserve. *Honor is the motive from which the brave man withstands fear and performs acts of courage.*

CHAPTER 8

We return to Peaceful Valley—all of us.

An Khe is history. Our tour of duty with the 1st Cav is over. We have been through hell. We have been through hell, and we now expect to be greeted as returning heroes.

Our convoy arrives at Canh Van in midmorning. The site is immaculate. All equipment is clean and lined up in neat rows. Everyone has their shirts on. Our entrance is disruptive. Our equipment is muddy. Our uniforms are dirty. To avoid ridicule, I will *try something that looks right and might work*. I will try to keep my mouth shut.

I can do that, I think. It should be easy to keep my mouth shut. It will be easy, provided others do also, or if they don't, they at least speak to me with honor and respect. But they won't. I know they won't. Instead, I can expect to be ridiculed and told what to do. Why? Because these guys down here are out to get me. And they probably will, because they are thoughtless, ruthless, and experts at intimidation.

Even so, I know I must prepare. I must prepare to defend myself against the pending assault—the pending assault to usurp my power. That assault begins, innocently enough, with the motor pool.

Powers has arranged the site so we cannot park all of the equipment we are bringing back in any one area. Instead, we are forced to decentralize by squeezing equipment into individual spaces between existing vehicles only where Powers has left room. To me, that means it is no longer my equipment. It now all belongs to Powers, and there is not much I can do about that. I can't do much about my men, either. Roscoe is assigned to the NCO tent, where officers are not allowed. The rest of my men are split up and sent to several different troop tents where individual cots have been inserted between those troops already there. To me, that means I no longer have any men. They all belong to Powers, and there is not much I can do about that, either. What I can do is to insist upon decent accommodations for myself.

My accommodations should be good, much better than the muddy conditions I have been used to. Here, instead of muddy dirt floors there are clean concrete slabs under each troop tent, as well as the CP, the mess tent, and the officers' quarters. I forgo reporting to Powers and instead go directly to the officers' quarters.

The officers' tent is neat and clean. Five cots are lined up along open tent flaps and there is a footlocker at the foot of each cot. There is a broom at one end of the tent and butt cans on the floor. At the far end of the tent, behind a bamboo partition, is the major's quarters. The officers' quarter are immaculate, peaceful, and quiet until Joe Goodrich walks in.

Initially, it is good to see Joe. He gives me a warm greeting, shakes my hand and then helps me carry my bags inside. But then, as expected, Joe takes over.

"Your bunk is made up," Joe says, pointing to a neatly-made cot with mattress, sheets and a small pillow. "I put you next to Lieutenant Swartz."

"Thanks a lot," I say sarcastically.

"Rodney's not a bad guy," Joe says with a smile. "He's at one end of the tent and I'm at the other end, as far away from each other as possible."

Joe is also at the far end of the tent from Major Powers' Quarters. He has put me across from Swartz and next to Powers. The major has his quarters set up in the far end of the tent, private quarters with private entrance separated from the rest of us by bamboo matting.

"That must be the major's penthouse," I comment.

"Yeah. Swartz built it for him."

"Nice job," I remark as I unfold a chair in the middle of the floor. I slowly straddle the chair backward and sit down. "Good idea to keep him separated from the rest of us."

Joe stands with his hands on his hips and stares down at me. "Get comfort-able, David. You will spend the rest of your tour here right there in that chair. Powers won't let you touch a thing."

"That suits me. I'll sit here for the rest of the war and be perfectly content."

"You'll never do it. You will go out of your mind in this place."

"Not me. What more could I ask for? I have clean accommodations, no responsibilities, peace and security. What more could anyone possibly want?" I am sincere about that. Joe Goodrich may not think so, but I am very sincere. Joe knows something I don't know—that Rodney Swartz has snuck quietly into the tent and is standing behind me, waiting to ruin my day. Joe Goodrich walks out.

"Get up and get to work," Rodney yells, nearly scaring me out of my wits.

After regaining my composure, I politely reply, "Sir, I'm resting up from a long tour at the front." I am tempted to say something more confrontational, but I decide not to.

Swartz coolly strolls over to his bunk and lies down. "You are going to go nuts in this place," he says. "I'm going nuts here myself. I'm the perimeter defense officer."

"What are you guarding against?" I laugh. "Spider monkeys?"

"Listen, there are a lot of monkeys out there." We may joke about defense, but defense is foremost in everybody's mind. "We have guards on duty all night long," Rodney says. "The major even has us pulling officer of the guard."

"Oh yeah? What does the officer of the guard do?"

"He gets up twice a night and walks the perimeter and makes sure all guards are awake."

"What time does he do that?"

"Anytime between the hours of midnight and five."

"Does the officer of the guard get any time off the next day?"

"Are you kidding? We get every day off. Some people," Rodney laughs, "some people even have part-time jobs off post."

"Oh? Like who?"

"Like Goodrich. I'll explain that to you some day. In the meantime," Rodney reaches into the duffle bag under his cot and pulls out a pair of combat boots into which he has sown zippers into the sides, "you need a pair of these." Rodney proudly zips and unzips the polished boots. "These are my 'get up in a hurry' boots. All I have to do is slip them on and pull the zipper."

I am about to comment on what a good idea Rodney has when our discussion is interrupted by a rough voice from beyond. "What zipper?" Major Powers has entered his side of the tent.

Rodney and I rise so we can see him over the bamboo partition. "The zippers here in my boots, sir."

"That is an unauthorized modification," he tells Rodney. It is good to hear the major put Rodney down, even though I know he doesn't mean it. It is good to see the major again. We kid and joke around. He praises me for all the glorious work in the highlands and then tells me how proud he is to put his trust in me as officer of the guard.

I respectfully tell the major that I expected something better. He tells me he intends to find an appropriate assignment for me and expects to make the announcement at tomorrow's staff meeting. He tells me he hopes I find that acceptable, and in the meantime I will serve Lieutenant Swartz as officer of the guard. That seals my fortune for tonight. I'm officer of the guard. I can do that, for one night, at least. Maybe it will do me some good. Maybe I can learn something.

That night, while the other officers prepare for bed, I prepare to inspect the guard. Before leaving the officers' tent I ask Joe Goodrich if I should take a weapon. He says no, but that a flashlight may be of help, and to be sure and make a lot of noise.

There are several guard post locations spaced somewhere around the perimeter: one at the main gate near Route 1, two along the north and east berms and the rest scattered somewhere around the south and west sides where the berm is yet unfinished. As I am totally unfamiliar with the guard post locations and as it is a very dark heavy overcast night, I expect to have trouble finding my way round. I start with the only one I can see. I start at the main gate.

A lone guard stands in the road at the main gate. I can make him out from light spilling from of a nearby tent. His silhouette stands out as a tall, thin man with arms extended downward, holding his rifle in both hands. There is some-one with him, a much shorter person, a girl. The girl stands close with one arm around the guard's waist. Nearby, barely visible, two small children stand qui-etly. When they see me approach, the girl and the children turn and walk away.

The guard challenges me as I approach. "Halt," he says. "Evening."

"Good evening," I reply.

"Halt. Evening."

"I said good evening."

"Halt. Who goes there?"

"This is Lieutenant Jeffries."

"Sir, don't you know the password?"

"What password? I don't know anything about a password."

"Sir, you better go back to the orderly room and get the password. You're liable to get shot."

The girl and the two children have stopped only a short distance away. It is obvious they plan to return as soon as I leave. I can see a little farther down the road now, and clearer; my eyes have become more accustomed to the dark night. I see not far away what I assume to be a group of teenagers. I'm sure the guard has been talking with them, too. "What are these people doing here?" I ask.

"Sir, they're just talking. They come up here every night."

"It's midnight. You should have run them off at dark."

"Yes sir," the guard says to me. He turns and yells "*didi*" to the kids, chasing them away, and then whispers to me, "The password is Evening-Dancer."

"I'm sorry, I didn't know the password."

"That's all right, sir," the guard replies. "But you should always know it before you come out here to inspect. I nearly killed one of our own men one night who was trying to climb through the barbed wire. I yelled three halts and three *dung lyes* before he responded."

The girl and the two children run back down the road toward the group of what I perceived as teenagers. My night vision is improving and I can see more clearly now that about half of those whom I thought were teenagers are actually our own men. The rest are young girls. My first reaction is one of disbelief. This violates all principles of security. Fraternization of this type must be against regulations.

"Those men have no business sneaking off in the middle of the night," I tell the guard. "Some night they may not come back."

"It's safe," he says. "The kids here are safe. They wouldn't hurt anybody. It's all harmless fun, sir."

I stand and look down the road for a few minutes, watching the kids laugh and giggle. Somehow, this is a welcome sight. After seeing the killing in the highlands, it is good to see affection and hear laughter. This probably violates some sort of army regulations, but I approve, in spite of the potential risk.

I ask the guard, "How do you know they aren't Viet Cong?"

"We have gotten to know them. They're OK. They are just hanging out. They don't have anything to do here at night except hang out. We wouldn't allow any troublemakers here, Lieutenant."

"I hope not."

"And not everybody knows about it, just a few of us. Just the ones we can trust. You won't tell anybody, will you, sir?"

Why would I want to tell anybody? The kids are having fun, and God knows there is not a whole lot of fun to be had around here. Accepting the guard's explanation, I ask him how to get to the next guard post. He points in a clockwise direction, southwest along a dark path, and tells me to be careful not to fall into a trench. With that bit of information, I move in what I hope is the right direction. The berm in that area has not yet been completed. The area is level and very dark. I can hardly see where I am going and wonder to myself what poor fool could have been assigned to guard duty here.

"Halt. Who goes there?" The next guard yells at the top of his lungs.

I whisper back, "A friend."

"Advance and be recognized," he says, more quietly this time. To that I advance to within a few feet of the guard before coming to halt when he shouts, "Evening."

"Dancer," I reply softly. Then I proceed to chew him out for yelling loudly enough to be heard at a considerable distance. "When you give the password," I tell him, "you're supposed to say the challenge softly so that the enemy can't hear. If he knows the challenge, he might sneak up here and give you evening and you give him dancer and then the enemy will know the entire password."

"Yes sir. I'll do better next time."

It is terribly dark. I ask the guard if he sees anybody out there, knowing he cannot. He tells me he can't see much of anything except what he thinks might be a water buffalo nearby on the other side of the perimeter's barbed wire. Well, after what I just saw at the main gate, the water buffalo is welcome. I assure the guard he is doing a good job and that I am proud of him.

I have a terrible time finding the next guard post, the one on the west side. It is pitch dark and I am not at all sure where the perimeter is. After stumbling around for about fifteen minutes, I wander across a hole in the ground and onto a Spec 4 staring glassy-eyed up at me.

"Good evening, sir," the guard says.

"Good evening." The kid really scared me. "Didn't you see me walking around out here?"

"Yes sir, "I saw you."

"Why didn't you challenge me?"

"I didn't need to. I knew who you were."

"Didn't you know I was out here looking for you?"

"No sir. I figured if you were looking for me you would have given a yell."

"Listen, man, when I'm out here inspecting the guard and I come upon you like this, you are supposed to give me the challenge. Don't you know what the password is?"

"I forgot."

"Everybody else out here knows it. The last guard yelled it at the top of his lungs." I give him what I think is enough time to become thoroughly embarrassed, and then tell him the password. "When I come around here the next time I want you to say 'evening' and I will return with 'dancer.'"

"What about if you don't say 'dancer'?"

"Well, you will know it's me. Just don't shoot anybody unless he's a foreigner."

Finally, to my relief, at the northeast tower I come across a guard I recognize: Bennett. I desperately need somebody to talk to in whom I can confide. Bennett is the only one on guard duty I really know. Bennett has been in An Khe. Bennett knows what is going on over here.

As I approach the tower I can see Bennett, lit up by distant flares sitting high in the air between four wooden uprights under the roofed guard post. He is smoking a cigar and his weapon is lying on his lap. He turns as he hears me approach.

"Lieutenant Jeffries, is that you?"

"Yeah." I climb up into the tower and sit down beside him.

Bennett looks out into the night sky across the valley. In the far distance we see flares. The flares light up the northern sky, occasionally penetrating the low clouds, permitting us a partial view of valley.

"So what do you think?" I ask him, believing he will understand the question. When he fails to answer me I ask, "Do you want me to be more specific?"

"No sir. I understand. You want to know what I think about Fitzgerald and Perry getting killed. You want to know if I think we belong here in Peaceful Valley or back where the war is in An Khe."

"Well, yes. You got it. What do you think?"

Bennett doesn't answer right away. He thinks first, then answers. "I think this livin' down here is a whole lot better than up at An Khe. Yes sir. I'll take guard duty here every night." It is generally very peaceful here at night, looking out across the night sky. It is very much of a relief for us to be here. "The guys down here really got it made," Bennett says as we watch flares flicker in the cloudy sky.

Bennett appears to be relieved, greatly relieved, to be away from An Khe, away from the tiring night shifts of operation at the gravel quarry and of the fears associated with operating at night outside the security of a defended perimeter. He must be exhausted mentally and in dire need of rest. Having heard of several allotments for rest and recuperation available in either Bangkok or Hong Kong, I ask Bennett if he plans to take some R&R.

"No sir. No R&R. Gonna' save my money to get married."

"And go back to work for Brown Construction Company?"

"I may not go back with them. My father wrote me and told me he has a job lined up for me sellin' fertilizer."

"Fertilizer? You don't want to spend the rest of your life selling fertilizer. I thought you wanted to be a builder."

Bennett pulls the cigar from his mouth and looks me in the eye. "I don't reckon this to be my kind of life anymore. I want to sit in a fancy air-conditioned office with pretty secretaries, sit on my fanny from eight to five, and play golf on the weekend."

We continue to sit quietly for a short time. Bennett and I understand each other. We both feel the pain of Fitzgerald's death, he more than me, of course, because he grew up with Fitzgerald. Bennett tells me he has written to Fitzgerald's parents and plans to visit them when he returns home.

"What does the major have planned for you?" Bennett asks.

"Not much, apparently."

Bennett shifts his eyes and smiles across his cigar. "You ain't complainin', are you?"

"No. I guess not. There are a lot of men over here with something to complain about, but not me. I have no gripes with this lousy assignment."

"You just keepin' your mouth shut and doin' what you're told," Bennett chuckles. "Don't cause no problems, and when it's over, go home and forget about it." Bennett looks me squarely in the eye and reminds me there's a lot of fertilizer to sell back home.

The next morning I sleep late, have a late breakfast of cold cereal and then walk around the bivouac area, looking over what I couldn't see the night before. Powers soon joins me, talking my ear off with his profound wisdom. Powers is convinced that too much time in the Valley is devoted to security and not enough time to hiring and organizing civilian work crews. Powers wants work on the berms speeded up. That will not only generate more work for the civilians, but will also release more of our men from guard duty since we will then have to provide guards for only four guard towers. Besides that, he is mostly concerned about the mountain to the west and the valley beyond. That concerns the rest of us, too, for it is most uncomfortable having our backs to the unknown. We rationalize that it is pointless for us to worry, because if we were to be attacked from the west it wouldn't make any difference how many people we had on security. There would never be enough and we would all be picked off like sitting ducks by snipers atop the mountain. I really would like to know what is on the other side of the mountain, and so would Powers. Powers tells me he wants to make a recon into the area and asks if I want to go along. I emphatically tell him no. He understands my reluctance to go there, but does insist that I accompany him on an inspection tour of his current work sites to see if I would be interested in getting involved with any of them.

The major insists that I ride in his jeep. He drives himself, which is rare for the major. He normally uses a jeep driver. As I walk toward the passenger's seat, I ask him if I need to take a weapon. He says "no," he has his forty-five. I am a bit hesitant to get into the major's jeep without a rifle. Slaughter would have us all armed to the teeth and escorted by a minimum of two machine gun jeeps. But I figure the major knows what he is doing, so I hop into the passenger's seat and we take off.

The major pulls out onto Route 1 and heads south. We travel only a few hundred feet when he points off to the left. "That's the rock quarry," he says. "You can work over there if you want to. But if you do, you have to work with Fallon. It's his show."

"I could probably do that, as long as he stays sober."

"A civilian work coordinator," the major replies, "that's what he needs most. I have hired several civilians and sent them over there, but he doesn't seem to give them any work. He spends so much time blasting rock and setting up the rock crusher that he hasn't had time to allocate jobs for the civilians. He needs a coordinator."

The major swings the jeep off to the left onto a dirt road that leads to the rock quarry. As we enter, it is obvious to me that from a technical standpoint the quarry meets all of the requirements for a good quarry site. There is plenty of rock in locations easily accessible so that each day the drilling crew can safely blast enough rock to keep the crusher going for the next day.

The crusher has been set up at one end of a large flat piece of open terrain, well away from the exposed rock face. The crusher consists of three basic pieces: a receiving hopper, a crusher unit, and a screening unit. Shot rock from the blasting operation is picked up with front-end loaders and loaded into the receiving hopper. It is next transferred to and crushed in the crushing unit and then lifted by conveyor to the screening units where the crushed rock is separated into various sizes, ranging from less than a half an inch to about four inches. There are several conveyors at the screening unit which convey the different size stones into separate piles, where they are eventually picked up by front-end loaders and loaded onto trucks for delivery to various construction sites such as the airfield in Qui Nhon.

I can tell how proud Powers is by his enthusiastic explanation of the whole operation. Still, he is disappointed to see the civilian laborers just sitting down under a tree. He pulls the jeep up next to the noisy crusher and motions to Fallon his disapproval. Fallon nods his head and motions to indicate that he will take care of things. I wave to Fallon and he waves back, smiling. It is good to see him again, working, and sober.

We leave the rock quarry and head across to the west side of Route 1 and to the road which Slaughter had widened before he left for An Khe. The major stops the jeep at a fork in the road and points off to the left. "This is where they want me to build a dump," he says. "You can have this project if you want, but I don't advise it. If we build a dump here, people will come from miles around to scavenge everything we dump there. Group wants us to build a dump here for everybody in Qui Nhon. If there is not enough room for a dump in Qui Nhon, then there are too many people in Qui Nhon. "That's poor planning, Lieutenant," the major says. "Those people in Qui Nhon should have planned for a dump when they moved in there. We don't want their dump," he says, and then reminds me, "you can have this project if you want it."

The major then pulls back onto the widened road and heads westward, straight up to where the road again narrows to a single lane and curves over the mountains to the other side. I nervously ride down the other side through the jungle until we reach the valley below, where the jungle thins enough for us to see a few hundred feet through the trees. We see no people—only trees. I am very uncomfortable without a rifle, and I tell the major that I would appreciate it if he would please turn around and go get it. But he says not to worry. He has his forty-five.

We continue to ride along the winding, bumpy dirt road for a couple of miles through the thick jungle. The area looks desolate. I ask the major if he knows where we are going. He says no, but he is sure we will be safe. That is, of course, until we come to a narrow stream which the major tries to ford.

The bottom of the stream looks sandy, and stable, but it is not. Halfway across, the tires sink in about six inches deep. We are stuck.

"I'll try and back up," the major says, putting the jeep into rear drive and trying to back up.

"Try and get a rocking motion going," I suggest. "Back and forth."

He rocks the jeep back and forth, but it only sinks in deeper. "We're stuck," he says. "You'll have to get out and push."

I step out into the stream, and as I do I notice a group of Vietnamese watching from a short distance away. It is a mixed age group of civilians, mostly barefooted, some little children, a couple of boys and three men. One of the men is very old.

"We have company," I say to the major as I move into position behind the jeep to push. "I hope those people are friendly."

The major glances at the civilians. "Oh, I don't think they are anything to worry about," he says casually. "Push harder. Try and get a rocking motion going."

I bend over and grab the jeep by the rear bumper. I place my knee under the bumper and push back and forth, following the movement of the jeep. It seems useless. "We would probably do better if we had some help, sir."

"Keep rocking," he says.

But the jeep won't budge and the civilians are approaching. "The heck with this," I say, as I get directly behind the rear wheel and prepare to push as hard as I can. "You let her rip."

The major floors the accelerator and mud flies everywhere, covering me from the waist down. The effort is useless. Wiping the mud from my hands, I tell the major he will have to call for help on the radio.

"We can't use the radio," he says.

"Sir, I don't understand. We are only five miles from camp and we all have the same AM radio."

"I mean the radio works, but there is an AM blackout. Nobody's on the other end." The major watches intently as the group of civilians continues to approach us. "I heard a patrol got ambushed not far from here," Powers blurts out. "There's not a soul out here except us, those people over there, and the VC."

The civilians can now easily hear us, even if they do not understand, when one little boy, hearing the word VC, runs to us saying, "No VC. No VC." He points toward the distant hills, westerly, across the wooded valley. "VC over there. No VC here. We help."

Soon there are about ten Vietnamese in the water, standing near the jeep where I am by now becoming quite nervous because I don't have a weapon, not even a pistol, and the civilians are edging closer. "Well, what the hell…" I say. "If these people aren't friendly, we're dead anyway." Maybe they can help. I motion for the civilians to move closer and to grab each side of the jeep. They do, and lift with great strength. Even though none of them can weigh more than a hundred pounds, they possess surprising strength. Even the very young struggle hard. It soon becomes evident, however, that their efforts may prove fruitless. When they slack off and appear to get discouraged, the major opens his wallet and gives each of them twenty *piasters*. They gratefully accept and continue lifting and pushing. Finally, one of them takes command and directs the others to fetch a log and roll a large nearby stone over for use as a cantilever, a simple system that had never occurred to me. With the cantilever in place they are able to lift the jeep high enough to place other logs beneath the tires. With great relief, the major pulls free and drives back to base.

In the afternoon, Major Powers holds his daily staff meeting. First on his agenda for this afternoon is security. He wants to know how much security we need, how much is enough, and what, specifically, are we guarding against. I'm not much good at the staff meeting. I lose my confidence because I don't really know what is going on down here yet. I'm afraid of saying something dumb, so I let the others speak.

Joe Goodrich is first to speak, or at least tries to speak. The others seem to have it in for Joe. Apparently Joe is not around much anymore because he spends a lot of time in Qui Nhon, something about a missionary—"Mary Missionary," the others call her jokingly. Joe Goodrich listens, but obviously doesn't appreciate their remarks. All Joe wants to talk about is the civilian labor force. Me, I just sit quietly, wondering what this is all about.

Powers again takes over with his favorite subject: security at the quarry. He says there is definitely a security problem at the quarry that he wants to resolve, pointing at me. Apparently we lose land communications with the quarry every day because someone keeps cutting the communications wire between the quarry and the camp. Every day the como chief has to chase the breakdown. It is nearly a one-mile walk to check the wire, and Powers informs me it is cut in the same place every time. He then, as the others laugh, appoints me Sabotage Prevention Officer.

The quarry operation is discussed a great deal at the staff meeting—Powers arguing we should hire more civilians, while Fallon insists he can produce more crushed stone without civilian interference and the security risks associated with civilians. I sense they have had this discussion before as they argue back and forth about the limits of security and whether or not we should hire more civilians and what our responsibilities are to them. The consensus seems to be that we are responsible only for ourselves. We take care of ourselves. Civilian employees offer a security risk we don't need.

When the meeting breaks up, I walk back to the officers' tent with the other officers. That includes Powers, Swartz, and Goodrich, as well as the other two platoon leaders, Jim Edge and Bob Reed, whom I haven't seen much of because they operate on remote construction sites in Qui Nhon. Listening to them, I somehow sense my appointment as Sabotage Control Officer is some sort of joke. The others must know something I don't know, and I am determined to find out what it is. "I guess the old man finally found a job for me," I say, half expecting some smart comment back. And I get it.

As we walk into the tent, Rodney Swartz informs me Powers has another assignment for me. After all the officers are in the tent, Rodney reaches into his briefcase and pulls out a set of official company orders. "Let's see, Lieutenant Jeffries. You are the Vector Control Officer."

"What is a Vector Control Officer?" I ask.

Rodney pulls another piece of paper from his briefcase. "Let's see. This is a notice that all pets are to be inoculated at the Qui Nhon Medical Center."

"So?"

Major Powers lifts his head up over the bamboo partition that separates his quarters from the rest of the officers. "That is the job of the vector control officer."

I slouch down, disgusted, into my chair while the others laugh.

"We must have more animals than any other unit in Vietnam." Powers says. "There are several dogs in the area and I understand the quarry has some chickens. They also have some pigs over there."

I modestly suggest that it should be the responsibility of the respective own-ers to have their pets inoculated, but Powers disagrees. He orders me to arrange for a truck, hand deliver and personally see to it that all pets are inoculated. I presume he is joking when the others laugh.

Rodney continues to pull orders from his briefcase. "You are also the Rodent Control Officer."

"I am?"

"Yes, you are."

"So what?"

"So, we have mice in the tent."

The major again pokes his head over the bamboo partition. "You know, there is considerable room for improvement in our rodent control program."

Joe Goodrich laughs. "Listen, Dave, Rodney has been catching the mice in here. Don't let him shove that job off on you."

Rodney then screams at the top of his lungs, "I'm not the Rodent Control Officer and I'm not catching any more mice for you guys."

But he is. Rodney doesn't know it yet, but I am afraid of mice—deathly afraid of mice. He finds that out after picking up two wire mousetraps, each with a swing door which closes automatically when the mouse touches the bait. When he tosses one onto my cot and tells me my duties start as now, I pick it up and throw it back at him, hitting him squarely on the back.

I explain to him that I am not capable of serving as the Rodent Control Officer, but that I will gladly serve as Sabotage Prevention Officer.

Determined to find out who is cutting the communications line to the quarry, I direct Roscoe to get the jeep ready for a recon trip. When he asks me where we are going, I tell him we are going to look for a communications break in the land-line. Somebody keeps cutting the line and we are going to get to the bottom of this. Roscoe tells me not to worry about that, saying everything is OK. Even so, I insist that Roscoe drive me over there to see what is going on. He drives me to the back of the quarry, to a quiet little pond where several of our men swim nude with some local girls. They have tapped into the communication line with loud speakers for background music. *The generality of man seeks that which is good.*

CHAPTER 9

Rodney Swartz is getting short-tempered. With only a few weeks left in the country, his main goal now is to avoid danger, stay comfortable, and leave on time. When he leaves, assuming he does, that will leave me as Executive Officer again because I am the ranking officer of the four other lieutenants. By this time the rest of us have been promoted to first lieutenant and we all feel pretty good about that. I can't speak for the others, but what I don't feel good about is my mission here in Peaceful Valley and Qui Nhon. Jim Edger and Bob Reed and Joe Goodrich are apparently happy with their assignments on local construction sites. Fallon is happy at the rock quarry. Swartz enjoys swinging his weight around as Executive Officer. And me, I guess I want Rodney Swartz to break me in as his replacement, even though I consider that an insult. Rodney feels it is his duty to break me in before he leaves.

My main concern is security, or the apparent lack of security. From what I see, we simply put too much faith and trust in the local civilians. After all, we don't know any of these people. We freely let a few civilians drift into the quarry each day and then chase them out at night. I frequently express my concerns to Rodney, but he insists I am overly concerned and that everything is all right. Finally, I tell him if I am to take over his job as Executive Officer I must become as comfortable as he is with our interpersonal relations with the civilians. After all, to me, if one civilian cannot be trusted, then none of them can be trusted.

Rodney doesn't trust everybody either. In fact, I don't think he trusts anybody other than himself. What he does do is make things easy. Rodney Swartz is firmly committed to doing things the easy way, and for some unknown reason, seems bound and determined to train me to do the same. Simply stated, train me to find out what makes others tick, and then tick in time with them. I tell Rodney that is really not my thing to find out what makes others tick, especially those whose language I can't speak, but he insists that it is my obligation to humanity. Rodney insists that he be allowed to teach me how to size up the local civilians where they live, in Qui Nhon, and to learn how to trust them.

While I think that to be totally impossible, I really don't have anything else to do anyway, so I agree to spend one day with Rodney in Qui Nhon to let him show me how to live the good life. Maybe I can learn something.

We get off to a late morning start. I would have liked to have left earlier to observe people going to work, but we don't get up very early in Canh Van Valley. Rodney drives his jeep and I ride in the passenger's seat. Turning north on Route 1, we are surprised to see a lot of people on the road for this time of day. Most are walking, many ride bicycles, and some ride in three wheeled Lambrettas. Those walking are dressed in peasant clothing—cut off loose fitting plain colored clothing and open sandals. Those riding bicycles are dressed the same, but they also wear conical hats strapped to the chin. Those riding in Lambrettas are a bit more formally attired in long pants, sport shirts and dresses.

God knows where all of these people are going this time of day. Some in the Lambrettas must be going to market, because they carry crates of live chickens and fresh vegetables on top of the roof. One Lambretta even carries a small pig. Occasionally we see a bus, usually packed with riders and caged chickens and pigeons. These people must eat a lot of chicken. The pigeons, from what I understand, are only for the wealthy. Pigeon heads are a delicacy.

Rodney jokes that the pigeons are probably headed to Fallon's Bar. I haven't figured that out yet, but I plan to do so before day's end. I also hope to find out more about Mary Missionary, or to determine once and for all if these guys are pulling my leg. I think they must be, because nothing about Fallon's Bar and

Mary Missionary makes sense. But then it doesn't have to make sense, because this is non-fiction. Only fiction has to make sense.

Straight ahead on the right stands an old naked woman, holding a burlap bag at her side. As we pass by, the woman reaches into the bag, pulls out a handful of buffalo manure and throws it at us. Fortunately, she misses.

Further up along the road, on a high hill to the right, there is an old Buddhist temple, a real old one, of stone. Rodney and I decide to take closer looks, so he turns off onto a single lane dirt road, puts the jeep in low gear, and climbs to the top of the hill where we stop, get out and go inside. The room is empty except for a large masonry Buddha sitting on a high stone pedestal. Obviously, this temple is no longer in use, but it does leave us with a sense of respect. I tell Rodney I don't know much about the Buddhists, but that Joe Goodrich says they believe in reincarnation. Rodney says he believes that is right and that, depending on how good or bad people are, they might be reincarnated as a rich American or as a water buffalo. In any event, the temple instills confidence in the moral virtue of the Vietnamese people. There is no graffiti of any type anywhere on this temple. We find that remarkable.

From there Rodney drives me to Qui Nhon. He starts by showing me the people in Qui Nhon, people whom we can see in the streets, in the shops, in the restaurants and in the bars. The bars in Qui Nhon look all the same to me. I doubt there is much difference in any of them. A bar is a bar. From what I can tell, the main difference is in the signs.

"This is it," Swartz says as he pulls over and parks on a concrete sidewalk in front of a medium-sized single story white masonry building with a brightly-colored sign hanging above the doorway, which is screened off to prevent hand grenades from being tossed inside. The big red and yellow sign reads "Hong Cong Bar."

"Very appropriate," I say. "It's a catchy name—something with class." This is the bar Fallon brags about buying one-third interest in, but I don't believe him and I won't even mention it to Rodney.

"There's a guy in here with real cheap cigarette lighters," Rodney brags, "and hot watches."

Inside the bar, there is a four-piece band: two guitars, a bass, and a drummer. Near noontime, the place is crowded with GIs and a few Vietnamese. Teenage boys tend bar. Vietnamese girls stand around the dance floor with their arms folded, looking bored. The girls lining the wall look disinterested. I remark to Rodney how surprised I am the Vietnamese could afford such an expensive time on the town at midday. Rodney says they are all looking to sell something.

I tell Rodney the band is too loud for me and suggest we move further away to another table.

"Too tight," Rodney says. "The band is too tight."

"It's not too tight," I tell Rodney. "It's too loud." I motion to the guitar players to turn the volume down. They don't pay a bit of attention to me. But when Rodney makes the same signal, the band immediately obliges, even changing to a slow quiet song. They obviously know Rodney Swartz. I wonder if they also know Fallon.

"This is a classy bar," Rodney says proudly. "They even serve food."

Rodney convinces me to have lunch. I order steak, which arrives looking more like water buffalo, and Rodney orders pigeon heads, the sight of which nearly makes me sick. But the food is surprisingly good. I have to admit to Rodney that the Hong Cong Bar looks like a classy operation. I do, however, question Rodney about the young girls hanging around the dance floor. These girls don't in the least bit resemble the prostitutes at An Khe. These girls look like local girls—the sisters and the daughters of the men we hire to work in our camps for fifty *piasters* per day.

"There aren't any prostitutes in here," Rodney remarks. "They're only B-girls."

"How can you tell?"

"These are nice girls, taxi dancers. As long as you are buying drinks, they will be nice to you. They will even dance with you. But most of them in here don't go to bed with strangers." Rodney takes a big gulp of beer. "Of course that's not to say they wouldn't. Some of them probably would, if the price was right."

I sit with Rodney, looking at these young girls, wondering what the right price is, when who should walk in but Joe Goodrich. Joe has at his side a beautiful, tall, young American girl with long, sandy-blond hair, wearing a white full-length silken Vietnamese dress. The small-rimmed glasses she wears make her look like a librarian. Rodney and I both rise, inviting them to join us, but for some reason, they decline.

"That's Mary Missionary," Rodney says. "Goodrich won't let you get close to her."

"She looks like a really nice girl."

"She is a really nice girl. She lives at the Baptist Mission and teaches at the Mission School."

What can I say? What can I say about Mary Missionary? What can I say about someone I cannot speak to, but only observe? I can say she looks like a really nice girl. I can say she appears to be devoted to her cause. I can say she reverberates love and wouldn't hurt anyone. I can say she is trustworthy, loyal and honorable. I can say she represents Christianity at its best. That is what I can say about Mary Missionary, even though we have never spoken; it is perceived because of her pleasant demeanor.

The day ends with me being convinced that the Vietnamese people in Qui Nhon can, for the most part, be trusted, so long, that is, as we treat them with respect, which some of us do and some of us don't. With that in mind I look forward to tomorrow's staff meeting, which Powers has scheduled to discuss, among other things, civilian employees.

The next morning all the officers and NCOs gather to sit on folding chairs in the command tent while Powers sits behind his desk. Powers had scheduled the meeting to discuss quarry operations and arrangements for an impending inspection by a group of visiting general officers.

I am very anxious to speak because I am a candidate for civilian employee coordinator. I am now prepared to serve as coordinator for civilian employees and hope the major will appoint me to that position, even though I have very little experience. I do now feel that the civilian employee program is an important one, and the opportunity for employment with our company is an attractive one. It is a natural. We have set up here a manufacturing plant, a rock crusher. We produce a product. We can generate jobs.

And we can pay employees in cash. This is great. Civilian employees are needed at the quarry not only to help with the crusher, but to provide a real and true service to the country: employment. I now support the program and want to let Major Powers know that I want to be a part of it.

Once seated, we all sit quietly, waiting for Major Powers to open the meeting with some of his famous words of wisdom. But he doesn't. Instead he sits squarely behind his desk, studying a maintenance manual. Powers is intent. He doesn't even bother to look up when we start to politely cough; all of us, that is, except Fallon.

Fallon sits squarely on a wooden box at the side of Powers' desk, his arms resting on his knees and his head leaning forward. Fallon looks up at me. I point my finger at Fallon to let him know I am going to talk, but I don't get the chance to say anything because Fallon abruptly interrupts.

"The crusher is down," Fallon announces. "The drive shaft of the screening unit is broken."

Powers slams his fist onto his desk. "Why now?" he yells. "Why does the shaft have to break now?"

The rock crusher is broken down. It is not completely broken down, just partially broken down. We can still crush large boulders into small boulders, but we cannot fine crush or screen.

For us that is big time, really big time. The rock crusher is the only reason for us to be in Peaceful Valley. When the rock crusher breaks down, we break down. It doesn't work. We all agree it doesn't work, and *if it doesn't work, try and fix it.*

For us, this is a major crisis, because we are scheduled to soon be inspected for our capacity to perform our assigned mission. The generals are coming. "Generals don't like problems." Powers says, "Generals want to see things running smoothly. They won't accept a broken-down machine, and neither will I."

I interrupt to ask why. "What's so important about a broken-down rock crusher?"

Powers places his elbow on the desk and his head in his hand. He again stares at the maintenance manual. "I have been informed that the broken shaft is on national back order. That means it is not available. We will have to try and fix the machine ourselves."

I keep looking for positive signs of encouragement from the major, but he shakes his head in the negative. "We can't possibly repair the shaft before the inspection. We don't have the right tools. We will have to modify the operation."

I ask, "What is the worst the generals can do?"

"Fire me," Powers says, "and send you to Pleiku. Do you want to go to Pleiku?"

I pull up a chair and sit down next to Fallon and Powers. "No sir. I don't think so."

"Then we must modify this operation," Powers says, leaning back in his chair. "We will have to use more people and fewer machines."

"You mean a human machine?"

"Yes. That is exactly what I mean."

Fallon stands up and yells at the major. "We don't need any more local people. They just get in the way. They can't compete with a machine."

Powers argues back. "The idea behind this civilian labor force," he explains, "is that we are supposed to train these people in a skill."

"All they can do is squat down," Fallon roars. "Besides, there won't be anything for them to do expect sweep the crusher. You certainly don't expect them to sort rock by hand. Do you?"

"I don't see why not," Powers says. "The rough crusher part of the machine still works. All the people have to do is to pick out the various size pieces and put them on the appropriate pile."

Fallon shakes his head in the negative. "They can't do anything else. I certainly won't let them touch dynamite. We're liable to all get blown to smithereens." But Fallon does indicate they might be able to sort rock, if they are willing to work. It would be hard work, of course, and physically demanding. The civilians might not want to do it; and those who are willing to do it might not be physically able to produce a high quality product.

As a backup, Powers orders me to have the carpenters build a timber screening plant. We all try to explain to him that is impossible, but he refuses to listen. His mind is made up. If the shaft cannot be repaired in time for the inspection, then the generals will witness a piece of American ingenuity. We again advise Powers against his recommended course of action. A timber screening plant simply will not work and we don't have the time to try to design and build a metal one, which won't work either. But Powers is insistent. He wants a timber screening plant built in two days. He wants it built in two levels, with four-inch steel mesh on the upper level and two-inch steel mesh on the lower level. He wants the frame built of timber. He tells me he doesn't want a big complicated engineering design. All he wants me to do is build him a small screening unit onto which he can dump rock. The big rocks will roll off and the little rocks will fall through.

"Sir," I tell him, "this will never work. All this contraption of yours will do is to pile up with rock and collapse under its own weight."

Powers must know that, but he doesn't care. "You're the engineer. Build me a screening plant. And in the meantime hire a bunch of civilians and put them to work hand-sorting."

The first step in hiring civilians is to spread the word that jobs are available. That is done at Group by word of mouth, not much different than it was at home. We advertise. But here, because of possible Viet Cong interference, we must take specific precautions to insure that those whom we hire can be trusted. In order to accomplish that, we must arrange for interpreter services.

Official requests are made through channels, and within one day job notices are posted throughout Canh Van Valley and the town of Qui Nhon. In addition, we are assigned an interpreter to conduct the interviews—a South Vietnamese Army officer with security clearance. The interpreter assigned is a sergeant in the ARVN army. He is a stocky, muscular man in his mid-thirties. He has a full head of hair, is very good looking, extremely articulate, and speaks fluent English. That gives me confidence and a feeling of finally being in control.

On the morning of the interviews, over one hundred people show up, many more than we can use, let alone guard. The applicants for employment are lined up in single file. The line stretches from Powers' CP out the main entrance and down Route 1. Because of the great number of applicants, I nearly cancel the interviews. It looks to me like an undesirable situation to interview so many potential employees and then have to hire only a few and turn the others away. To make things worse, the company barber arrives—a local native dressed in western trousers and western shoes. The barber strides past the waiting line and arrogantly marches right into the compound. The Vietnamese Army Sergeant does not like the barber. He mumbles something to him as he passes and the barber mumbles something back. I suggest it is poor taste for the barber to show up before we start the interviews. The sergeant agrees that the barber should have stayed away this day. The barber makes too much money.

The employment interview procedure is really quite simple. A two-page printed form in both Vietnamese and English is to be filled out with the applicants name, spouse's name, all children, parents, and grandparents, place of birth, date of birth, all former places of residence and present place of residence.

The sergeant explains to the potential employees how to fill out the forms. He also explains a requirement that I was unaware of that each applicant must furnish a two-inch snapshot of themselves, along with a letter of recommendation from their village chief certifying that they are loyal citizens.

The sergeant actually conducts the interview and then briefs me as to what happened. It takes me a little time to learn what is happening, but I slowly catch on. First, Vietnamese names are composed of three elements: the first is the family name, the second is the middle name, and the third is the personal name.

Nyugen Van Nam is a thirty-five-year-old unemployed schoolteacher from Kontum Province. After a short discussion in Vietnamese, the sergeant informs me that this man is from an area that is now controlled by the VC. He has no friends or relatives in Qui Nhon. He is obviously well educated, and I gather from listening that he probably really is a schoolteacher. He also claims to have been a village chief in his former province and that he was forced to leave his wife and family behind when the VC came. I ask the sergeant to find out why he didn't bring his family with him. The man explains that his wife and children have always lived in that district. Being the village chief, he was forced to leave, but his wife chose to stay behind with her family.

The sergeant turns to me and says, "I doubt very much that this man will be able to get a letter of recommendation from the Qui Nhon authorities." The man mutters something and the sergeant explains further. "He says that if he worked here two weeks he will be able to afford the letter."

"What do you mean?" I ask.

"These things cost money."

"How much?"

"Five hundred *piasters* if the authorities know him, two thousand if they don't."

"Wait a minute," I say. "Do you mean to tell me that anybody can buy a letter of recommendation if they have enough money?"

"Yes. That is correct."

"Well to heck with it then," I say to the sergeant. "This man is hired."

The sergeant replies, "I recommend we don't hire this man without a letter of recommendation."

"But the letter isn't worth the paper it's written on."

"But the Viet Cong won't ask for one."

I am extremely angry and the sergeant knows that. He tells me there are thousands of refugees here. They all need work. Many of them have no friends or relatives. They need a letter to get work. If they get the letter, they get the work. And they get the letter only if they have money. The sergeant and I are extremely verbal, and extremely loud. It is upsetting for both of us. We both lose control in front of the civilian applicants, which is uncomfortable for us all. We apologize to each other and then agree not to make any more decisions until the interviews are over.

Ly Cam is next. He is an old man.

"This man doesn't know how old he is," the sergeant says.

"Ask him how old he thinks he is," I suggest.

The old man smiles and mumbles something to a boy at his side. The sergeant laughs and then interprets. "Too old."

"If he wants to work, we will have to have his age."

"The boy is his son. The man says he is too old to work, but his son wishes to make an application."

Ly Tien is next, age 14.

The sergeant quickly vetoes this application. "This boy is too young to work." And his father is too old. The old man has four other sons and three daughters. This boy is the youngest. The others have all left home. I ask the sergeant how they will survive if neither of them work. He says he doesn't know.

Nugo Duc Loi is age 24; place of birth: Darlac Province; military service: none.

"This man is a draft dodger," the sergeant declares while joking and laughing with the man.

I notice that the man has rotting teeth and mention that to the sergeant. "I wonder if the army would yank out his black beechnut teeth."

"No. That is too expensive."

"How long will it take for the army to catch up with him?"

"Maybe forever. Let's let him go."

"Why not hire him?" I ask.

"We can't hire a draft dodger. It's against the law. We would have to turn him in."

"So what will the authorities do, send him to the front?" I say. "He's already here."

"Lieutenant, this man might be a Viet Cong."

"Yes, he might be. Or maybe he will be. Or maybe he was. But he's here and he's willing to work, so let's use him."

Dinh Duc Loi is age 38. He has a wife and three children. His place of birth is Qui Nhon Province.

"This man can work," the sergeant declares. "He can get the required letter."

The sergeant says something to the man in Vietnamese. I presume he congratulates him for being hired. After he does, there is a commotion among the other civilians. Some of the civilians start mumbling something to the barber, who has been cutting hair nearby. The barber points his scissors at the sergeant and yells something. I sense a problem. Some of the other candidates for employment are uneasy; the sergeant knew the man he had just hired personally. The others do not approve of his choice. They think he should not have hired this man unless he was willing to take the others also. I tell the sergeant to make his decision and that I will back him up, whatever he decides.

But the arguments continue. The sergeant argues loudly with the barber for several minutes. Finally, nearly in tears, the sergeant says, "I don't know what the matter is. I don't know these people very well. Maybe I hired the wrong person."

His face wrinkles as the bitter argument continues. "The barber says I got a kickback, but I didn't get any kickback, Lieutenant." He folds his trembling hands and walks away, cursing. "Nobody trusts anyone anymore." He points his index finger at me. "If I got a kickback, do you think I would be wearing these stripes?" He wipes a tear from his eye. "Lieutenant, tell me what you want me to do. Decide what you want to do with these people and do it. Please just don't ask me for my advice."

Finally, after consulting with Major Powers, I hire everybody, all one hundred of them. I wish I had never bothered with the interviews. It would have been easier to take the first twenty people in line and tell the others they arrived too late to be considered. That would have been a lot easier. But I didn't. I hired all one hundred of them.

We put most of them to work in the quarry. Several speak broken English, so we make them chiefs. The chiefs don't have to work with their hands, but will be required to make the others work.

For the first couple of days things go pretty well. Some of the people even seem to enjoy sorting rocks. The workers make neat little piles. All of the rocks one inch and less go into one pile. All of the rocks between one inch and two inches go in another pile. All of the rocks between two inches and three inches go in a third pile, and so on. There really isn't enough final product to do us any good, but the people seem to enjoy working together and appear to be happy at end of the day when they receive their pay.

Surprisingly, there is no lack of funds for civilian employment and the major could have in fact hired more at the 75 *piasters* per day rate. In addition, at the major's discretion, ten percent of the employees could receive 85 *piasters* per day, ten-percent incentive pay. But the workers soon form a labor relation board and complain that everyone should receive either 75 *piasters* per day or 85 *piasters* per day. The ten-percent incentive pay is soon dropped.

Inspection day is approaching, and Major Powers has panicked because we haven't yet built his screening plant. Two nights before the inspection, four of us pull chairs up around a folding table in the officers' tent. We sit there—Goodrich, Swartz, Powers and me—wearing tee shirts and fatigue pants, designing the Big Screen. We decide the frame will be constructed of six by six posts. The major wants six by six posts, so the rest of us agree. The screens themselves will be relocated from the exiting screening unit of the crusher. Each screen is about two feet wide and six feet long. They will be nailed onto four by fours and laid into of the frame. We sketch the design on the back of an army map and record the bill of materials alongside the sketch. It is a very simple design. It is also very stupid. Not only will it not work, it will probably collapse within a few seconds of its initial loading. We all know that.

"Now," Major Powers says, "I want the generals to observe this demonstration in comfort. I want you to build an observation platform for them. Place the platform on a high hill so they will have a good view. I want them to remember what they are going to see."

Finally, we all understand. And we are all in complete agreement.

The major points to Rodney Swartz. "I want chairs in the tower, and a table. I want you to get cups from the officers' mess kit and serve lemonade to the generals. And I want a tablecloth."

Rodney agrees that is a good idea. "They probably don't care about the rock anyway." Rodney says. "They will be happy to be here because this is a safe place for an inspection."

Joe Goodrich and I also agree. Maybe this inspection trip is not all that important. Maybe all we have to do to keep them happy is to see that they have a good time.

"Gentlemen," the major says, "I encourage you to make this inspection trip as comfortable as possible for the generals. Please do. I hope they have a good time. But I assure you they will not leave here happy. They will not leave here happy because we cannot produce enough rock for them to convince others we are doing a good job."

"It's a shame, sir," Joe Goodrich says, "that these generals aren't in the market for working civilians. It's a shame."

We decide that the observation platform will be constructed of four-inch lumber, with a tin roof. We have none of the required building supplies on hand, so Swartz gives me a hundred and thirty dollars to purchase material on the local market. The money is in green backs, not *piasters*, so I will be able to purchase what I want at a lower price.

With the money in hand, Hayman grabs a deuce and a half and we head for downtown Qui Nhon. Joe Goodrich goes along with us. Joe insists he knows the best buys. We do not have to search far for building supplies because there is only one store in town. The building supply store has all the lumber we need, and a good selection of tin. We buy the lumber immediately and then move to the tin. All sheet metal is of the same size, but of different thicknesses. And it all carries the Korean seal. There are several price grades for sheet metal. Prices vary according to gauge and finish, the unfinished thinner gauge being the least expensive. We want to buy the cheaper grades, but those have already begun to rust. We can't imagine why the cheaper grades are even for sale, but there must be a market for cheaper grades because there is plenty of it available.

We buy six sheets of heavy gauge galvanized steel metal roofing and have it loaded onto the truck. I pay the bill and then inform Joe Goodrich that we have twenty dollars left. Normally, we would have returned the twenty dollars to Rodney Swartz, but not this time. Instead, we use it to buy vodka to spike the lemonade.

The Big Screen is finished in two days, just in time for the inspecting generals. We build it of six by six uprights with four by four bracing. We install the screens on top of it and place the unit near the discharge hopper of the rock-crushing unit. We then request permission from Major Powers to run a full test before the generals arrive.

Powers, of course, denies the request. "I don't care whether the thing works or not," he says. Powers has his twenty in. "You go finish the observation platform I told you to build. I want the people who see this demonstration to remember it."

That evening we build the observation platform. We provide an access stairs with handrail and cover the roof with tin. Inside, we place the table and chairs.

The following morning we cover the table with a tablecloth, pull the aluminum cups from the officers' mess kit and place them neatly on the table, one cup in front of each chair. The view from the platform is quite spectacular. The 360-degree panorama permits an unobstructed view of the entire quarry site, the rock face, the blasting area, the rock crusher, and the sorting area.

Powers has directed that all hundred civilian workers be on site and busily involved for the general inspection. That makes the site crowded, so crowded that not everyone can sort rocks. We have a couple dozen sledgehammers so Powers directs two dozen people to stay busy pounding large rocks into smaller rocks. It takes several whacks of the sledgehammer to have any effect, but the hand crushing system does work to an extent, qualitatively.

The rest of the civilian laborers sort rock from the discharge chute of the rock crusher. We can only load a small amount of shot rock into the receiving hopper at one time because that is all the laborers can keep up with. The laborers must stand back from the discharge and wait until it is safe to approach the pile of crushed stone. Then they slowly pick through the pile of crushed stone, transporting each piece to the appropriate sorting pile. It is a very slow and inefficient operation, but it keeps a lot of people busy.

Just before the inspecting party arrives, Rodney Swartz brings two large pitchers full of lemonade, generously spiked with vodka, and places them on the table atop the inspection platform. All of us know the lemonade is spiked except Powers, whom none of us tells because if he knew, he would be mortified.

The arriving inspection party consists of two general officers, a bird colonel, and two captains. Powers proudly leads them up to the top of the observation platform, gives them a glass of lemonade, and begins bragging about how proud he is that we employ so many civilian laborers. The inspecting officers listen rather intently, while helping themselves to several more glasses of lemonade, but they are not impressed with the operation. It is too inefficient. Not enough products are being produced to justify the effort. *The very things that please some pain others.*

Not to be outdone, Powers then directs the Big Screen be placed under the discharge chute. "This is American ingenuity," he says. Then the crusher is turned on and we all watch the falling boulders rip the big screen to pieces. Major Powers gets his show. The generals get their lemonade, and the generals' aides steal the cups.

CHAPTER 10

As a last resort, we *seek help*.

Powers orders Roscoe and me to fly the broken shaft to Saigon, find a machine shop, and have it fixed. We are to stay there until it is repaired, rebuilt, or we find a new one.

We leave Canh Van Valley at 0600 hours to catch a flight from Qui Nhon with our jeep and jeep trailer loaded with the broken shaft.

Roscoe drives to Qui Nhon Airfield where we find a lone C-130. It is the only cargo plane at the airport. We assume it is our flight. The rear cargo door is open and the cargo compartment is empty, so Roscoe pulls the jeep behind the plane in preparation to board, but the loading ramp is chocked with large timbers to prevent vehicles from boarding.

I am sure this must be our flight, so while Roscoe waits in the jeep I decide to get out and head to the passenger terminal to see if I can get boarding passes. I step from the jeep onto the loading ramp and then down onto a crushed stone runway covered with pierced metal planking. My ankles feel weak in low-quarter shoes after wearing heavy combat boots for so many months. My khakis are wrinkled, as if pulled at the spur of the moment from a laundry bag; I have not worn them in over eight months.

Approaching the passenger service terminal gives me a feeling that I should be purchasing a ticket to go home. This is primarily a civilian passenger terminal, which also happens to be used by the military. The terminal is a large metal hangar with civilian and military flight reservations set up at one end. The terminal is crowded with people—a few GIs but many civilians. Most of the civilians are young, in their teens and early twenties. The mixture is pretty much fifty-fifty male and female. The young men in the terminal look like military personnel in civilian clothing going on R&R. Most of the young women are dressed in white slacks, bright blouses, and the traditional cone-shaped hat.

I toss my B-4 bag onto the floor of the crowded passenger terminal, pull out a set of travel orders from it, and present those to one of the desk clerks. The clerk says there is a C-130 load of civilians leaving soon, and he must go see if there is enough room for our jeep. The clerk tells me he will have to check with the pilot before issuing a pass, and that in the meantime, I should be seated nearby. He directs me to go sit in a particular chair, a comfortable seat next to an attractive young Vietnamese girl.

The girl is very pretty. She is young, rather short and thin. She has a flawless complexion, long black hair that flows down her back, and penetrating Oriental eyes.

She sits in the chair with her legs crossed and smiles at me as I approach. When our eyes meet, I think to myself how beautiful she is. I cannot take my eyes off of her. I immediately walk to the empty chair next to her and sit down, then I turn to her and smile. She smiles back and then modestly turns her head away.

I ask her if she knows the time. She shakes her head and mutters something in Vietnamese. Obviously, she doesn't speak English. It is annoying not being able to communicate with her. I wonder to myself if she has a reservation on the C-130 to Saigon. I hope so, and think she must. I desperately want to talk to her, so I look around for an interpreter.

There right next to me, opposite the girl, is the adjutant general's office. I notice, and can clearly hear a young PFC talking to a lawyer. The PFC is apparently seeking permission to get married. The young lawyer at his side is gathering all the necessary information. "Are you sure you want to marry this girl?" the lawyer asked.

"Yes sir," the PFC replies. "We're in love."

The lawyer tactfully tries to discourage them. "I should first of all inform you that the American government normally will not approve of quickie marriages to foreigners. However, if you insist on trying I will fill out the necessary paperwork. I will need her birth certificate, citizenship papers, and a great deal of information on her family. In addition, she will need a physical."

"Sir, how long will that take?" the PFC asks.

"About six months."

I am still looking around for an interpreter when the ticket clerk motions to the civilians that their plane is ready and all of those desiring to board should now rise. The girl alongside of me stands, and when she does, I can see through her white slacks that she is wearing polka-dotted panties underneath. I can see the multi-colored polka dots through her thin silken slacks. I am determined to take this flight.

The clerk has not issued me any boarding passes, but even so, I follow the group of civilian passengers out of the terminal toward the C-130. The civilians present their boarding passes to the flight sergeant, who directs them to step into the plane. There are about a dozen civilians boarding this flight: three teenage boys, an old man and old woman, and the rest are young girls. The girl with the polka-dotted underwear stands near the front to the boarding line. She turns often and stares at me.

I am certain there will be enough room for us on this flight, so I motion for Roscoe to remove the chocks and drive the jeep and trailer up the rear cargo-loading ramp.

Roscoe starts up the loading ramp about the time I hand our travel orders to the flight sergeant and ask if he has room for a jeep and two passengers.

"Yes," the flight sergeant says, "but you don't want to ride on this plane. I have seven dead bodies on board and one of the rubber body bags is broken."

By this time the girl in the polka-dotted panties is already on the plane. "That won't bother us," I insist. "We need to get to Saigon as soon as possible."

The flight sergeant again warns us, "You and your sergeant better see if you can take the odor. I don't want any sick passengers."

I explain to Roscoe our predicament with the dead bodies and the broken body bag. He gets out of the jeep and we both walk up the rear of the loading ramp and into the open cargo section of the plane. The dead bodies are lashed against the side bulkheads. The civilians are seated next to the dead bodies and are holding their noses. Roscoe and I walk forward, toward the bodies, until the odor becomes unbearable.

"Cheap rubber," Roscoe says.

We turn and walk back out of the rear of the plane where Roscoe asks the flight sergeant if this plane goes straight to Saigon.

"No," the sergeant replies. "It stops at Cam Ranh Bay and then Saigon."

Roscoe is not as anxious to take this plane as I am. He doesn't like the idea of being with dead bodies and asks why I don't want to wait for another plane. I suggest a little broken rubber bag shouldn't bother him and remind him that this plane will at least get us out of Qui Nhon.

A dozen Vietnamese civilians are seated in the plane—eight on one side and four on the other. I tell Roscoe the time for us to go is now. If these people are willing to ride with dead bodies, we should be also. But Roscoe is not convinced.

The girl in the polka-dotted panties is seated in the last seat, near the rear of the plane. I point to her and shrug my shoulders. She unfastens her seat belt, stands, turns her back to us, bends over and sorts through her handbag.

Roscoe looks at the girl and the multi-colored polka-dotted panties showing through her white slacks. "Well, what the hell!" Roscoe agrees to take this plane. "We might never get another chance like this."

Roscoe pulls the jeep up the ramp into the open cargo area, where it is lashed down and secured by two airmen and the loadmaster. Then the loadmaster lowers two passenger chairs next to each other near the rear of the cargo area and directs Roscoe and me to sit down and tells us to keep our seat belts fastened during takeoff. Finally, Roscoe and I sit down and buckle our seat belts.

The girl in the polka-dotted panties is seated directly across from me on the other side of the plane. She is strapped to her seat. Her legs are together. Her hands are in her lap. I think she is the prettiest girl I have ever seen. She raises her right arm and places her hand over her heart. I assume she does that as a gesture of fear because she is afraid to fly. I notice that she wears a small Buddha over her heart. She stares at me, and I stare back.

The pilot starts the engines, one at a time, beginning in a soft whistle, then a loudening roar. The civilians begin to chatter. They look around at one another and laugh and giggle, joking with each other in Vietnamese. They point at each other, kidding around like this is the first flight for some. The boys point to the rubber bags, mocking the girls.

I look at the girl. She looks back at me and takes a deep breath and closes her eyes. I think she is afraid of flight. As the plane begins to taxi down the runway, the other passengers start talking and joking with the girl. They, too, sense she is afraid. The boys point and laugh, joking with her as the plane approaches the runway.

At the head of the runway the pilot pauses. The passengers quiet down and brace themselves in their seats. I lean back in my seat and grasp my seat belt with both hands, while continuing to stare at the girl.

She stares back. Her eyes are open wide and her hands are in her lap, fists clinched.

The pilot revs the engines. The plane rocks from side to side and then lurches forward speeding down the runway. At the moment of liftoff, the girl screams. She reaches up and clutches her blouse and leans forward in her chair.

Soon the plane gently lifts off and glides out over the South China Sea. The civilians talk wildly. The girl lowers her head into her lap and covers her face with her hands. The pilot makes a wide, sweeping movement over the beaches to gain altitude and then turns the aircraft in an arching movement back over the mainland. I turn to look out of a window to gaze at the dense green jungle below. But I can't. There are no windows in the cargo compartment.

Not long after takeoff, suddenly and without warning the plane begins to shake furiously. We begin to lose air speed and altitude. The civilians scream.

Roscoe turns to me. "Damn, sir," Roscoe moans.

"They can't do this to us," I say.

"Is this plane going to crash?"

"It sure feels like it," I reply as the ground rises rapidly. I feel a sudden sickness deep within my stomach.

By now, all of the civilians are screaming and yelling. I pay particular attention to the girl. She, too, is screaming and yelling and pounding her fist on her lap. Then she unbuckles her seat belt. She stands, runs across the plane and jumps onto my lap. She throws her arms around my neck and straddles my legs.

"Damn, sir," Roscoe yells. "We can't let this plane crash. We don't have any parachutes."

The cargo compartment is by now so noisy we can barely hear each other. The plane is shaking and vibrating, the civilian passengers are yelling and screaming, as is the girl who sits on my lap, bouncing up and down. Soon the pilot's voice comes over the intercom. "This is the captain speaking. Two minor problems have developed on the flight so far," he says apologetically. The pilot calmly continues. "This is nothing major," he says. "I can take care of it."

"Damn, sir!" Roscoe screams. "We've only been airborne five minutes."

Finally, to our great relief the shaking stops. The aircraft has been stabilized. Immediately, we all become calm and become quiet. The only noises we now hear are the engines.

The girl on my lap stops bouncing up and down, but her arms are still wrapped tightly around my neck. She lifts her head and looks me squarely in the eyes.

Roscoe turns to me and says, "Sir, you got a lapful."

The girl looks embarrassed. She smiles and places her fingers over her lips. She lifts herself from my lap, brushes herself off and returns to her seat on the opposite side of the plane, where she sits back down and re-buckles her seat belt.

Two airmen come into the cargo area and motion for me to come forward to the cockpit. The pilot wants to speak with me—alone. I enter the cockpit, where four crewmen are stationed: the pilot, co-pilot, navigator and engineer. The pilot motions for me to lean forward so he can be heard without having to yell over the roar of the engines. "The landing gear is jammed," the pilot says.

"That sounds serious," I reply.

"I have called ahead to Cam Ranh Bay and informed them that we may have to make a crash landing."

"Oh my God!"

"We will be all right," the pilot reassures me. "The ground crew at Cam Ranh Bay will prepare a bed of foam for us to land on. My main worry is those people back there in the cargo area. I want you to try and calm them down."

I return to Roscoe and explain the situation, reassuring him there is no danger. Roscoe seems to understand; he has seen C-130s crash-land in foam before and agrees the biggest problem will be the civilian passengers. Roscoe suggests it might be best to conceal from the passengers that there is going to be a crash landing. "They might panic and do something stupid," Roscoe says as he looks across the plane at the girl with the polka-dotted panties.

"We don't speak their language," I tell Roscoe. "The only way they would know we are going to make a crash landing is if we explain it to them in sign language, which we will not do. So just look calm."

It takes about an hour to reach Cam Ranh Bay. When we get there, the pilot circles the runway for several minutes. The delay seems like an eternity to Roscoe and me, so we go to the crew's cabin and peer out the window to examine the foam-covered runway where we are to land. Only half of the runway is covered with foam—the leading half. Roscoe mentions that he would feel better if the entire runway was covered, but that he guessed the landing distance would be less with no landing gear.

Calmly returning to our seats, we are able to keep the crash landing a secret from the other passengers. The approach is normal, and exceptionally gentle. The Vietnamese civilians are calm and quiet, totally unsuspecting. But the actual landing is a rough one.

It is a rough landing, even in a bed of foam. The bottom of the fuselage scrapes across the runway, sliding through the foam and creating a loud scraping noise and violent vibrations. During the landing, the aircraft turns sideways. The plane shifts and turns and slides off course, sliding off the runway into a drainage ditch alongside the runway, where it comes safely to rest.

The pilot was right. It was nothing major. No one was hurt.

The C-130 was badly damaged during the crash landing, so badly damaged that we have to schedule another flight.

Roscoe and I inspect the jeep and trailer. No damage seems to have been done to our equipment, so we immediately make plans for another flight to Saigon. Several C-130s are available, and it appears we should be able to catch a flight most any time.

Our problem seems to be getting our jeep and trailer out of the damaged plane. During the landing, the plane had skidded into the drainage ditch in such a position that the rear cargo doors are jammed shut and cannot be opened until the plane is pulled free. That could take three days.

I tell Roscoe that I am not particularly thrilled to have to spend the next three days in Cam Ranh Bay. He says he understands, and that perhaps I should catch an earlier flight to locate a machine shop and make advanced arrangement for repairing the shaft. Roscoe offers to remain here in Cam Ranh Bay until the jeep and trailer can be freed, and then fly to Saigon and meet me there later.

That sounds like a good idea to me, so I head to the Cam Ranh Bay passenger terminal to find a flight. Like the terminal at Qui Nhon, the Cam Ranh Bay terminal is basically a civilian terminal set up in one end of a metal hangar. By the time I arrive, most of the civilians from our flight from Qui Nhon are already there, waiting in line for new boarding passes—all, that is, except the girl in the polka-dotted panties.

The girl in the polka-dotted panties is off to the side, standing and talking with an Air Force lieutenant. The lieutenant speaks a little Vietnamese, enough to find out that the girl needs to get to Saigon as soon as possible.

The Air Force lieutenant is a pleasant fellow, and extremely handsome. He asks me what my problem is, and then takes the time to listen to my explanation of the crash landing and the broken shaft. "Listen," he says. "I'm flying as far as Vung Tau in a few minutes. Why don't you come fly with me to Vung Tau and then catch a shuttle to Saigon from there?"

I tell the lieutenant that sounds fine to me and ask him what kind of aircraft he is flying. He says he is flying a bird-dog reconnaissance plane and that it is just big enough for him, me, and the girl. He also tells me that Vung Tau is an R&R resort and that I will enjoy it there, and that he needs me to ride in the passenger seat of his bird-dog and hold onto the girl to see that she doesn't fall out.

It sounds like a good idea to me, so I return to the C-130 to get my rifle and a few personal belongings and to tell Roscoe that I have been offered a flight to Vung Tau and that I have definitely decided to proceed on to Saigon without him so I can make the advance arrangements to repair the shaft. I tell him to fly the jeep to Saigon himself and to call me at the Meyer Cord Hotel or leave a message at Saigon Engineer Headquarters when he arrives.

Roscoe agrees. He asks me if I know how I will get from Vung Tau to Saigon. I tell him no.

The plane to Vung Tau is a two-seated bird-dog, a fixed-wing observation plane with a single pilot seat in front of a single passenger. The seats are separated from each other in separate compartments. The pilot compartment is in the front of the plane. The passenger compartment is in the rear of the plane. There are doors to each compartment, but the tops of the compartments are open to the air.

The pilot opens the door to the rear passenger compartment and directs me to step inside. I climb up and sit down in a small padded seat and toss my personal belongings—shaving gear and clean socks—under the seat. The passenger compartment is so small and cramped that I am unable to lay my weapon on the floor and have to hold it upright between my legs.

The pilot then motions for the girl to get in. She climbs in around my rifle and sits down on my lap. She sits with her back tight against my chest and her legs spread apart so the rifle, upright between my legs, is upright between her legs, too.

After the pilot has secured us in the passenger compartment, he climbs into the pilot's compartment and begins pulling preflight maintenance. The first thing he does is turn the radio to a military band and open communication with the control tower. He then reaches under the pilot's seat and pulls out a clipboard. With the clipboard in hand, he follows a written procedure for pre-flight check. He pushes several switches, and then starts the engine.

The pilot says he doesn't like the sound of the engine; there will be a slight delay. He then communicates with the control tower, telling them that he thinks there is engine trouble and requests a mechanic. The controller in turn replies that there are no mechanics available today, and advises the lieutenant that if he plans to fly to Vung Tau today he will have to fix it himself. The pilot then climbs out of the plane, leaving the engine running.

In the meantime, the girl on my lap begins to squirm. She grasps the rifle between our legs, lifts herself up slightly, and then lowers herself back down again, twisting from side to side.

I stick my head out the right side of the plane and look for the pilot, who is working on the right side of the engine. The pilot has a screwdriver in his hand. He adjusts something and then moves to the left side.

I stick my head out the left side of the plane and look for the pilot, who is now working on the left side of the engine. The pilot has a screwdriver in his hand. He adjusts something, and then moves back to the right side.

He continues this procedure for several minutes while I sit with the girl squirming on my lap. The pilot finally returns to the cabin and tells me he thinks he can get us to Vung Tau, but he doesn't know if he will be able to get back. I joke with him that maybe he will have to spend the night in Vung Tau.

We taxi up to the runway, and after watching a couple of C-130s land, receive word from the control tower that the runway is clear. With that word, he positions the flaps of the plane and takes off. Within seconds after liftoff he reaches for the radio and turns off the military band and flips to Chinese rock and roll. I sit in the back seat, listening to music, while the girl with the polka-dotted panties bounces on my lap with my weapon between our legs.

The flight to Vung Tau is straight down the coast, and it is beautiful. Below to our left are the deep blue waters of the South China Sea. Below to our right are lush green jungles. Above is the clear pale blue sky. It is a gorgeous day, with not a cloud in the sky.

Vung Tau is a beach resort town on the South China Sea near the base of the Saigon River. The town begins along a bay near the mouth of the River and then wraps around a peninsula, and northward up the coast. It is a small town, long and narrow, about a mile along the beach and four or five blocks wide.

At the eastern end of town is an American R&R Center. The R&R Center is located in a group of beautiful old French chateaux along a sandy beach. At the other end of town, the west end, is the airstrip. Next to the airstrip, along the banks of the bay, is a small, marshalling area for landing craft, and a storage yard full of conex supply containers.

We approach Vung Tau from the west, flying over the bay to approach the airstrip from a southerly direction. During the landing approach, we see many supply ships lying in anchor in the South China Sea. It is hard to estimate how many ships there are here—many dozens, perhaps even a hundred. And on the shore, next to the airstrip, is a huge storage depot, stacked high with conex containers.

The pilot lands his bird-dog on the runway and then taxies up to an abandoned hangar next to the storage yard. With the engine still running, he turns around and motions for the girl and me to get out of the plane; which we do, with considerable difficulty. The pilot then cups his hands and yells to me that he is returning to Cam Ranh Bay. He yells that he is afraid to turn the engine off for fear he won't be able to get it started again. He then taxies the plane back out to the runway and takes off into the sky, leaving me alone with the girl.

I expect the girl to be shocked and panicked. After her erratic behavior on the flight from Qui Nhon to Cam Ranh Bay, I expect tears. But the girl is calm. She merely looks at me and softly says, "Saigon."

Although I don't speak her language, it is pretty obvious to me she doesn't want to stay in Vung Tau and expects me to take her to Saigon. I try and communicate with her. I point to a hangar at the far end of the runway, motioning that we should go there. I start walking toward the hangar, and then turn to see if she is following; she is not. Instead, she points toward the storage area loaded with conex storage containers and says, "Saigon."

The girl slowly walks toward the storage containers. I follow.

The storage yard is about the size of two football fields and crowded with stacks of freight. The girl and I walk together, between the rows of conex containers, toward the bay. There, along the banks of the bay, is a loading area—a sandy beach where three small landing craft are moored and being loaded or unloaded by a forklift truck. The forklift is stuck in the sand, axle-deep in water.

Near the beach is an elevated platform. The platform is about twenty feet high and covered with a metal roof. High upon the platform is a quartermaster captain. The captain is yelling instructions though a megaphone to his one-man unloading crew, a sergeant atop the forklift.

As we approach the platform, I look up into the late afternoon sun and yell to the captain, "It looks like you're sort of shorthanded."

The captain lowers the megaphone from his mouth but continues to stare off at the stranded forklift. "I told that stupid sergeant not to load at high tide. He was supposed to have loaded those ships three hours ago. So what happened when the tide came in and he hadn't finished? He turned his men loose for the afternoon and left the two of us here to finish the job, just him and me. I can't imagine what they were doing all afternoon. Now what am I going to do?" The captain lifts the megaphone back to his mouth and yells, "Sarr-gent!" and then he looks disgustingly down at me. "He'll never hear me," he says.

He lays the megaphone down. He cups his hands and yells again. "Sarr-gent." This time, the sergeant turns and waves.

The captain places one foot up onto the railing. He lifts his baseball cap with one hand and lowers his head into the other hand. "I just don't know how I am going to get it all done."

The beach is stacked high with supplies. I try to cheer him up. "Sir, it looks like you've unloaded a good bit already."

"Unloaded?" he says. "These supplies were unloaded here by mistake. I have spent two weeks unloading this stuff and now they tell me to load it up and send it to Saigon." The captain pulls a handkerchief from his rear pocket and wipes the sweat from his forehead. "I just don't know how I'm going to get it all done."

I feel sorry for the captain, but not sorry enough to forget my own problems. "Sir, I have a little problem myself."

"Yes, I can see you have," the captain says looking down at the girl.

I explain to the captain that I have to get to Saigon and I think the girl wants to go to Saigon too.

"Well," he says, "these three landing craft here are headed up the river tonight. I want them to stay here and get loaded up with supplies, but the seamen say they're headed up the river tonight. You might be able to get a ride from them. I wish I could load them now, but we have a bad tide."

The three small landing craft moored at the beach have their loading ramps extended on the sand. Leaving the girl with the captain, I approach one of the landing craft, motioning to the men on board that I want to talk to them.

These landing craft are small vessels with a crew of three: two seamen and a machinist. The junior seaman also serves as gunner. The ranking seaman, a non-commissioned officer, serves as the ship's captain. One of the crew members yells at me, asking if he can be of assistance.

I walk to his landing craft, intending to board, but I stop at the edge of the water, about ten feet short of the loading ramp. I explain to the seaman that I need a ride to Saigon and ask if I may go with him.

He confirms that the three ships will be pulling out for Saigon in a few minutes and that I am welcome to ride along, but that we will be traveling at night and will not dock until morning. He says there are only enough bunks on board for the seamen, so if I come along I will have to sleep on the deck.

I point to the girl and tell the seaman that I think she wants a ride too.

The seaman says it is probably against regulations to transport civilians in a landing craft, but he will check with his chief to see if they can accommodate her. After conferring with several other men, he informs me that they cannot accommodate her.

But I have come to know this girl well enough to trust her, and motion for her to come forward to meet the seamen anyway. She walks slowly toward them, her hands folded to her front, and with a smile of innocence on her face. She stands at the edge of the water, points upriver and says to the men on board, "Saigon."

It is late in the afternoon at the landing beach when the seamen finally agree to transport both of us up the river to Saigon. They tell me we are both welcome to ride with them, but they remind me we will not dock until morning and that we will have to sleep on the deck and ask if that is acceptable to both of us.

I try and explain that to the girl. She seems to understand, I think. Then we both wade into the water and board one of the ships.

The three landing craft back away from the shore at 1830 hours, just before sunset, turning upriver in formation, three abreast. Once at sea, the three ships tie broadside to one another, enabling one seaman to steer all three. The other seamen sweep and mop and hurl buckets of water onto the deck.

The machine gunners clean the machine guns. The gunner aboard my ship cleans his atop the wooden deck cabin which houses the steering controls and bunks. I jump up on top the cabin alongside of him. I take my shirt off and lie down beside him on the warm tar-paper roof and close my eyes. The girl climbs up also and lies down beside me.

We travel up the river toward the setting sun. The river is muddy and the distant shores quiet. There are no other ships in sight and no signs of life on the barren shores other than birds skimming the still water. The river gently narrows and branches into tributaries, and when darkness comes, the river seems to close to a narrow channel.

The trip up the river takes about three hours. The river becomes very dark, but channel buoys are visible in the moonlight. The crew proceeds up the river with great confidence. They have no concerns whatsoever for danger. It is a peaceful moonlit night under the stars.

The girl and I ride the entire way on the cabin roof, along with the machine gunner. I do not speak to the girl, but the gunner and I chat about the beauty of the river and of the moonlit night. We also talk about home and the war.

The machine gunner has seen no action. I tell him he is lucky, and he tells me he is thankful for that. He mentions that he is from Alaska and that he is perfectly at home on the sea and what excellent training this tour of duty is for him. Upon discharge, he hopes to own and sail a commercial fishing boat.

We speak of the girl, wondering who she is and where she is going. The gunner asks if I will shack up with her in Saigon.

I tell him no, I don't want to get involved with this girl. She is too nice. I might get interested in her, and I can't afford to do that. I have other commitments at home, more important commitments which I cannot jeopardize over an affair with a Vietnamese native.

The sky brightens into a dim aurora as we approach Saigon. The city is not well-lit at night, but lights do shine in parts of the city inland from the waterfront. People live here. A lot of people live here—a lot of people who need each other.

Then, there is the waterfront. The entire waterfront area is dark except for hundreds of individual candles bobbing from sampans in the harbor. Entire families live here aboard the sampans. They live here for the good of the families and friends, and for the good of the individuals. *The good of the individual cannot be secured independently of family or community.*

At night I sleep well aboard the landing craft, atop the roof, alongside of the girl and the gunner—my family for the night—and awake to the morning sun.

CHAPTER 11

I stand on the deck of the landing craft, watching the early morning sunrise over Saigon Harbor, where hundreds of sampans bob in the water as far as the eye can see.

There may even be a thousand of these handcrafted boats here, which serve as both home and workplace for many. In the morning, some hoist sails and lift anchor for daily fishing. Others remain in harbor, from where their residents commute to work in the city. These ships are all different sizes, ranging from small oar-powered crafts with partial shed covers to large, long, high crafts with spacious cabins and huge sails.

In many cases, entire families live aboard these sailing ships, some spending their entire lives here at sea. That is remarkable. Even though the climate here favors year-round dwelling, there are times of violent inclement weather, typhoons, and other events that can force residents to temporarily relocate to terra firma. But home at sea does offer several advantages, like the ability to move to another location at any time. Then, of course, aboard ship there are no property taxes.

Nearing the dock, we feel dwarfed by huge merchant ships berthed there. There are at least a dozen being unloaded by civilian longshoremen.

Our seamen pull the landing crafts up to a berthing facility reserved for small military vessels. They tie them securely to balusters, mounted at the edge of a wide concrete dock that is crowded with many people. The waterfront is bustling with activity, with many civilian workers unloading supplies and equipment onto small trucks or into nearby warehouses.

There are really a lot of people here, some unloading ships, some loading ships, some carrying heavy loads, some just walking alone or with families. But no matter what they are doing, they all move at a fast pace. I watch with admiration those who are working hard. I watch them sweat. I watch the muscles of their naked backs tighten to lift heavy loads.

I notice in particular one hard-working young family—a father and son, both shirtless, wearing only cutoff shorts and open sandals. These two arrive on foot at the waterfront early to search for salvage and see if they can locate any timber floating in the harbor. On this morning there is plenty of floating wood. The father spots floating pieces of lumber from his position on the dock, and then directs his son where to jump into the water to retrieve it. They wrap the boards with rope ties, strap the bundles of wood to their backs, and carry them from the waterfront into the city. I find that to be remarkable and admirable.

Once we are on the dock, I keep the girl near my side, holding her hand tightly. I don't think she knows where she is going, and I certainly don't know where I am going, so we might as well stay together, at least for a while. It doesn't take us long to clear the waterfront and walk into the city.

I am surprised upon entering the city to find it developed and built-up with high-rise buildings. Many office buildings, commercial buildings, and residential buildings are located there, some as tall as a ten to fifteen stories high. This is a completely different world from the rural areas where I have spent all my time so far. The cultural change is shocking.

The streets here are crowded, with many bicycles, rickshaws, European cars and small taxis. The sidewalks are crowded with pedestrians, most in this area dressed in western clothing. We walk on the sidewalks, the girl and I, not speaking, merely walking hand in hand. We do not communicate verbally. Nevertheless, there is an understanding between us, a silent trust. I wonder where she thinks she is going and what she expects of me. I presume she has family and friends here. I glance at many of those we pass, wondering if they might know her, knowing they do not.

With several million people, Saigon is crowded and congested, a world of busy people trying to survive. Almost everybody I see travels fast—almost everybody, that is, except the monks.

Everywhere I look there are young Buddhist monks, men who serve two years in the ministry. They are easily recognizable. They wear bright orange robes. Their heads are shaved. I wonder if they also have to serve in the military.

The streets are crowded with taxis and rickshaws, many taxis and many rickshaws. The taxis seem to constantly blow their horns. That is annoying. The rickshaws are much more pleasant and peaceful. The rickshaws are pulled mostly by middle-aged men—men who work all day, pulling wooden carts so others may ride in comfort. The girl and I need transportation, but I, for some reason, am reluctant to hail a rickshaw. Maybe it is because I fear the man pulling the cart. Or maybe I think he works too hard. It just doesn't seem right for a middle-aged man in bare feet to be pulling me around town in a cart, with a local girl at my side. Definitely not; we might get bombed.

Instead of a rickshaw, I hail a taxicab. The cab driver speaks perfect English. That gives me confidence. I tend to trust a man with whom I can communicate. I ask him to drive us to the Meyer Cord Hotel. The thought never occurs to me that he might actually drive us someplace else. I trust him; we can communicate.

The Meyer Cord Hotel is a four-story-high, reinforced concrete building, recently renovated to house transient officers. I know the girl can't stay here, but I hope at least to find someone here who can find her accommodations nearby, or find out where else she wants to go.

An MP stands guard at the hotel entrance. He is armed with a sawed-off shotgun and stands behind a sandbag barricade. I pay the taxi driver, get out of the taxi and walk alone toward the MP, leaving the girl waiting on the sidewalk. Although I am in uniform and think it unnecessary, the MP requests I show him my ID card before entering. I also present him with a copy of my travel orders, which he reads and then tells me I am welcome to enter and stay as long as I wish.

The girl then walks over and stands by my side. I am embarrassed. I look into her eyes with concern. She looks back like a loving kitten. I then turn and ask the MP if she can get a room here, knowing full well his answer. The guard says no. He won't even let the girl into the lobby.

Immediately, the girl senses rejection. She turns, walks back to the street and flags the nearest rickshaw. I follow her, and as she gets in, I place my left hand on the side of the rickshaw, still holding my rifle in my right hand, and stare at her. She slides to one side of the narrow seat, leaving just enough room for me to climb in beside her. We have known each other only a single day, but I love her already. I love her smile. I love her eyes. If she leaves now, I know I will never see her again.

Her rickshaw driver waits patiently for me to get in, which I don't. Still, I try to get her to stay. I try to ask her to wait, but I don't speak the language. I try to tell her I love her, but I don't speak the language. I try the best I know how. Finally, the rickshaw driver picks up the handle tongues and pulls away.

Dejected and alone, I turn and walk into the lobby of the Meyer Cord Hotel. The decor there cheers me up somewhat. The lobby is a rather spacious room, with a large crystal chandelier hanging from the ceiling, padded furniture along the walls, and a hardwood registration desk at the base of a wide, spiral staircase. After registering, the desk clerk hands me a key to a fourth-floor bedroom. Before going to my room, I ask the clerk if I have any messages. There is one message, from Roscoe, which says he has freed the jeep, caught a flight to Saigon, is at Saigon Engineer Headquarters, and that I should report there as soon as possible.

A bellhop then escorts me to my room—a large single bedroom with a large double bed with clean sheets and pillowcases, a toilet, and a shower. I immediately strip naked and take a hot shower. Then I flush the toilet three times. And then, just for fun, I flush it again.

Saigon Engineer Headquarters is located in an office complex not far from the Meyer Cord Hotel. It is housed in a long, single-story building with concrete floors, wooden clapboard siding and timber roof, covered with asphalt shingles. Outside, there are no flags or insignia, only a small bronze plaque near the main entrance identifying it as a United States Army Engineer Installation. Inside is a small lobby, flanked by two large rooms lined with desks. At half the desks sit officers—captains and majors—and at the rest sit high-ranking NCOs, all with manual typewriters. The rooms are crowded, covered with clouds of cigarette smoke, and quiet except for typewriter noise.

Most of the desks are piled high with paperwork, and everyone seems to be busy at their typewriters or talking on the phone. I ask around if anyone knows anything about a broken shaft from Qui Nhon, which seems kind of stupid. Like who cares? Even so, I expect to get immediate attention and am disappointed to find that nobody wants to be bothered. They are not interested in my problems; they are preoccupied with their own problems, whatever they are.

Finally, I am put in contact with a lieutenant colonel who is familiar with the situation at Qui Nhon. He says he met with Roscoe this morning and sent him to a local machine shop to see what could be done to repair the broken shaft. The colonel tells me they will try to fix it, but not to worry. *If it can't be fixed, something else will take its place.*

That evening I have dinner in the officers' club atop the Rex Hotel with an infantry lieutenant who just arrived in Saigon, he being the only person in the club wearing fatigues. He has flown in for a one-day buying expedition to purchase a battery-operated droplight for his platoon of tunnel rats. I am pleased that he invited me to join him for dinner. It is good to have somebody interesting to talk to.

The dining room is a large, open area that occupies about half of the top floor of the hotel. There are open windows on three sides of the room, crystal chandeliers overhead, and several dozen tables draped with white tablecloths. Along one side of the room is a long bar with a brass foot rail and brass trim.

The restaurant is about half-filled with patrons. The infantry lieutenant and I are seated at a table near the center of the room. Our waiter is neatly dressed in black slacks, black shoes, white shirt, a tie, and a bright red blazer.

The lieutenant and I order cocktails and then chat for a while, mostly small talk. The infantry officer is tightlipped, telling me only that he is a platoon leader with the First Infantry Division somewhere north of Saigon near the Iron Triangle. That sounds dangerous.

We are soon joined by a captain, a short heavyset adjutant with a crew cut, who is working out of USARV headquarters. The captain is dressed in wrinkled khakis. Unlike the lieutenant, the captain is an aggressive conversationalist.

"I'm in USARV personnel," the captain tells us. "I just got back from emergency leave. I was here only six weeks when I received word that my wife was ill. She just missed me. It was hard leaving her again. It was really hard."

The infantry lieutenant looks at him in disgust and smartly asks, "Is it still hard?"

The captain is rather arrogant. "I think it is unfair to leave my wife alone for a whole year. Sometimes I wonder if making the Army a career is worth it."

The infantry lieutenant leans back in his chair and says, "It might be, if you live long enough to retire."

The captain obviously resents that comment. "This is a terrible sacrifice to make for retirement, being away from home for lengthy periods of time. I'm selling my life away."

"Well," the infantry lieutenant says, "I'm sorry it was hard leaving your wife, captain. I hope you can adjust, and that she can adjust also. That's the price career officers pay."

"That's unfair," the captain says, turning toward me. "I'm married. I have a wife to care for and support. The lieutenant here is obviously single. He has only himself to think of."

The infantry lieutenant puts his hands under the table and leans forward across his plate. "I know it's hard for you, captain, but it's hard for me too.

While you sit behind a desk and think about your wife, I'm out in the field every day, many nights too. I'm out there where people are getting killed."

I place one elbow on the table and turn to the lieutenant, hoping to say something profound like from an old John Wayne movie. "You're out there every day where the action is. Who's winning this war?"

But the lieutenant doesn't get a chance to answer, because the captain immediately interrupts. "Air power is winning it."

The infantry lieutenant smirks, but doesn't argue.

"We will never win with just infantry," the captain rudely insists. "Air power is the only answer, a few highly trained individuals aiming machines of destruction at the heart of the enemy. Today's other officers are just managers. Otherwise winning this war is merely a matter of putting the right people in the right place at the right time."

"It seems like I've heard that someplace before," the lieutenant says.

The captain acknowledges that he has, too. "I'm in personnel, you know. I make personnel assignments and cut orders."

The infantry lieutenant lifts his head and quietly says, "We know. There are a lot of men out there in the jungle who would like to meet you in a dark alley."

"This is my job. You can call me a Saigon warrior if you want, but this is a job which has to be done and I am doing it." The captain senses that it is time for him to leave. "Well, it has been pleasant, but I have to get back to work." Then, turning to the lieutenant he remarks, "I have several hundred assignments to make."

After the captain has left the room, the lieutenant lifts a glass of water and makes a toast. "To the Saigon Warrior." He drinks the entire glass of water and then sets the empty glass back down on the table. "I would like to have him out with my platoon for one day. I really feel sorry for him and his poor lonely wife. This is the first night I have had off in weeks. I only wish I could have brought my men down here."

"That wouldn't work."

"I guess it wouldn't," the lieutenant says. "The minute the animals see civilization, they wouldn't be worth a damn in combat."

From our position atop the hotel we see distant flares and hear occasional artillery fire. "The war is not far away," I say.

"Oh, that yoyo captain thinks it's right here in Saigon. I'll take you out and show you where the war is. It's not here behind a desk. It's not here in Saigon. The war is out there in the villages and the rice paddies. It's out there where people wake up not knowing where breakfast is coming from, or the barrel of which gun they will have to look down next. The least these Saigon warriors can do is to have respect for those of us out there in the jungle."

I stare intently at the infantry lieutenant and say, "I will never understand why one man must die in a rice paddy while another eats steak in the officers' club."

"Neither will I," he says. "I'll bet most of these guys here in Saigon have air-conditioned apartments with flush toilets." The infantry lieutenant looks across the room and out the window at the Saigon skyline. "Out there we sweep an area and then leave it for the VC to move back in." He whispers, "That is stupid."

"Well," I tell him, "I'm not in the infantry, thank God."

The lieutenant continues. "Maybe, just maybe, that personnel captain is right. Maybe the infantry can't win. Frankly," he says, "I don't know what it is we are trying to do." He looks dejectedly down at the floor. "When I take my platoon out into the jungle, I am completely on my own. There are no generals. There are no colonels or majors. The captain is nearby, but I can only reach him by radio. The lives of my men rest on me, as do the lives of those with whom we come in contact. There is no greater responsibility than that…" The lieutenant takes one last drink. "…except maybe making personnel assignments."

After dinner we leave the main dining room and move off onto a large patio that overlooks the city. There is a stage there where the evening's entertainment is in progress, a heavyset platinum blond telling dirty jokes. I think, *What a miserable failure she must be to end up in a place like this.*

The following morning after sleeping late I am nearly scared out of my wits to find a middle-aged Vietnamese woman in my room. Pulling the sheets over my bare body, I look at her with a surprised look and am greatly relieved to discover that she is the maid. Without batting an eye, the woman sweeps the floor, empties the waste cans, and then leaves.

After dressing in my wrinkled khakis, I feel dirty, so I decide to go on the town and buy some civilian clothes. I walk down four flights of stairs and ask the desk clerk where to find a clothing store. He suggests I try the French District a few blocks away. I leave the hotel and cross the street, where I stand waiting for a taxi. I really want a rickshaw, but I am afraid someone might throw a grenade, so I walk the three blocks to the clothing store.

The clothing store is Indian owned. The owner is there, along with his wife and his son, a cute little boy with a big smile. The store is long and narrow, with rows of clothing hanging from racks along the walls. I browse for a while and then purchase a white shirt, a new set of underwear, and a pair of blue slacks. The owner comments that he has never seen a man with such a large waist.

I return to the hotel, change into civilian clothes, and then spend the rest of the afternoon walking and marveling at such an oasis of merchandise. The quality of goods offered in Saigon is a far cry from the junk at Qui Nhon and An Khe. Here there are numerous high-end jewelry and clothing stores with expensive prices—too expensive for the average native to afford.

I walk the streets near the hotel, and along the way I accidentally stumble into an antique shop that carries many fine heirlooms, oriental art, furniture and jewelry, mostly things I cannot afford but still find attractive. After looking around for a while I buy a few things to ship home: a small Buddhist prayer set, a small bronze elephant, a small inlaid pearl set of chopsticks, and a large bronze gong. The store owner gladly offers to crate them up and mail them home for me. I thank him and take him up on the offer. I don't know whether I will ever see these things again, but I like the owner and decide to trust him with the mail.

People here do, for the most part, seem trustworthy; perhaps it is in the Buddhist culture. One of the larger Buddhist temples in Saigon is nearby. I have passed it several times and have already examined closely the brightly painted, hand-carved figurines, which decorate the entrance-way. I decide to enter the temple. An eight-foot high gold leaf Buddha sits squarely in the center on a floor of inlaid ceramic tile. Around the walls are small bronze figurines, flanked by several small prayer rooms.

A Vietnamese woman enters. She is young and pretty, and is the spitting image of the girl in the polka-dotted panties, except this girl is neatly dressed in a western-style business suit and has her hair done up in a neat, tight, businesslike bun. After standing for a few minutes, looking up at the Buddha, she kneels to pray, and when she does, her dress stretches snugly across her hips. I think perhaps she is employed by the American government, maybe as a diplomat's aide or something like that.

I soon leave the temple to return to the Meyer Cord Hotel, where I take a short nap. I still have on my new set of civilian clothes, the first civilian clothes I have worn in many months. It feels great, like I should do something exciting. After having supper at a small restaurant in the French District, I cross the street and walk about a block when a blue Renault cab pulls up beside me.

The cab driver speaks broken English. "You want a girl?" The driver asks.

"What?" I reply.

"You want a girl? Very pretty girl."

I spend the next several days in Saigon alone, wandering the streets. Each day I check in with Saigon Engineer Headquarters for a status report on the broken shaft, but I continue to hear nothing. I haven't seen Roscoe since arriving here, and I really don't want to. There seems no need for us to get together to discuss the status of the broken shaft, and even less reason to discuss returning to Qui Nhon without it. I am in no hurry to return to Qui Nhon, and I am sure Roscoe isn't either.

The next two days I meander through the French district, ignoring any potential danger. The fact that I wear civilian clothes makes me feel closer to the local people and gives me a sense of belonging. I feel much more relaxed than when wearing military clothing. As soldiers, we have been trained to stay constantly alert in guerilla war. The mere presence of a uniform is an open invitation to get shot at. The presence of a weapon makes it even worse. Soldiers are marked men, but in civilian clothing we feel human again. That is a good feeling.

Eventually, I get up enough nerve to wander out of the French District into more adventuresome parts of the city. Downtown, the streets widen and become more crowded and congested with busy people and noisy vehicles. There are many street vendors selling Vietnamese food. I don't see any hot dogs, but I do hear a lot of traffic horns and see a lot of policemen. Policemen in white uniforms stand at nearly every corner of the downtown area, helping both vehicular and pedestrian traffic move smoothly.

Poorer sections of the city are nearby. I walk there, too. I walk to the poor sections, but not too far inside these undesirable areas where many refugees are crowded into dilapidated shanties and many others live in the streets. The plight of these poor refugees is painfully obvious. Many lack even the basic necessities of life—sanitary facilities, clean water, plentiful food, and shelter from the weather. I wonder how they survive. I wonder who takes care of them. God, I suppose. He must have a really big computer to keep track of all of this.

Sometimes I think living in the country is better than living in the city. I recall a man in Qui Nhon who early each morning pulls a cart into the mountains where he burns logs into charcoal, returning each night. He has most likely done that the whole of his life. Then too, there are people here in this city who each morning rise and hurry about from dawn to dusk. I doubt that they produce nearly as much as that man in Qui Nhon hauling charcoal, but they too have important things to do. They too must struggle to survive.

With darkness approaching, I once again go to the Rex Hotel for supper, this time to eat alone. After climbing six flights of stairs to reach the restaurant atop, but before entering I walk out onto the balcony to overlook the city. It is a beautiful view at sunset. There is so much to see and so much to do.

Looking several blocks away I see Tu Do Street. The busy street is clearly visible from the patio. It bustles with activity at night. Hundreds of civilians roam Tu Do Street, or "The Strip," as it is known in Baltimore. I see many GIs and many lighted bar signs. I climb back down the six flights of stairs and leave the Rex to go there.

Tu Do Street is a narrow street, and it is crowded. In many places people on the sidewalk areas are shoulder-to-shoulder, young people for the most part, young Vietnamese men, little boys and girls, and GIs dressed in fatigues, khakis or civilian clothes. After walking a short distance I find myself standing in front of a three-story brothel, complete with girls hanging out of the windows of dimly lit rooms, and teenage pimps soliciting at the main entrance. The girls wear tight western dresses, low-cut blouses, and heavy makeup. I stand and watch for a few moments as the men come and go while children play in the street. I stand and watch for a few moments, wondering how long it will be before these children will have their room in the brothel, and what this city afloat on American money has in store for them. But where else is there for them to go? Into the countryside controlled by the Viet Cong or the NVA? To Qui Nhon to work in the rock quarry for eighty cents a day? No. These kids will stay here and shine shoes for the rich GIs who treat them well.

Although I am hungry, it is still early, so I continue to walk the streets to watch the people. As I do so, I slow down my pace in order to more closely observe those who pass by. I pay particular attention to the GIs, many of whom are like me, alone, savoring a moment of peace and joy. I study each man I pass—first his height, then his color, then his complexion, and lastly the expression on his face.

Ahead on the street, amidst the crowds of people, a tall, slender man approaches. His head towers over the others, even in the dark. His height draws my attention. He is dressed in a tee shirt and fatigue trousers, but he wears no hat, and he looks familiar.

It is Roscoe.

"Well hello, sir," Roscoe says as we meet. "I been lookin' all over town for you. Where have you been?"

It is good to see Roscoe. We shake hands and laugh. "I've just been hanging around," I tell him. "Just hanging around."

Roscoe has been drinking, heavily, but he his coherent. "Did you get the word?" he asks.

"About the shaft?" I reply. "No. What happened? Did it get fixed?"

"No sir. It didn't get fixed. But we got the shaft anyway. We've been ordered to some godforsaken place near Pleiku—the whole damn company, you and me and them other rinky-dinks back in Qui Nhon."

I am shocked. I am shocked here on the back streets of the strip to hear the news. I have no intention of going to Pleiku. "It is a little late for them to send me to Pleiku," I say with disgust. "I go home in five weeks."

"Well, in the meantime you're going to Pleiku, you and me the rest of them rinky-dinks." Roscoe puts his arm on my shoulder and says, "Let's drink to that."

There are several bars nearby. I tell Roscoe I could certainly use a drink now and ask him to pick a bar.

"There are plenty of bars here," Roscoe says, pointing down the street. "One's the same as the other. It don't make no difference." Roscoe motions toward the bar with the biggest sign, a brightly-colored ten-foot wide sign, trimmed with flashing red lights that reads "All At One Time." "That one looks like a winner. Let's you and me go in there and get drunk."

There are only a few people in the narrow bar room, all GIs except for a few B Girls, all sitting at tables along one wall. Roscoe leads me past the tables and up to the far end of the bar where we sit down on high barstools. Roscoe tells the bartender he is a Special Forces sergeant and I am his lieutenant. He orders drinks and motions for two hostesses. Roscoe thinks that it is cool because he is drunk, but it makes me a bit uneasy. The hostesses sit down alongside of us, looking very uninterested. We sit there, the four of us, staring into the wall mirror that is hanging behind the bar. I feel silly, sitting there, not knowing what so say.

Roscoe looks at me, then at the girls and motions for them to leave. As soon as the girls leave, returning to the far end of the bar, the bartender brings us our drinks—four drinks. Roscoe immediately downs both of his. "Good booze," he says.

"Sergeant Roscoe, how many drinks have you had today?"

"Not as many as I'm going to have. We're going to Pleiku."

"I meant to ask you about that."

"We're actually going to someplace called Cheo Reo, about thirty miles south of Pleiku. It's an ARVN base camp with a small airport for C-130s."

"Oh, God, no!"

"And there's a new commanding officer, Major John Slaughter. Slaughter has been promoted to Major. Powers has been relieved."

"You're kidding."

"No sir, I am not. Powers was transferred back to Group Headquarters. And Lieutenant Swartz will soon be sent home to be discharged. Sir, you'll be the XO."

The bartender brings Roscoe another drink. I finish mine and order another, a double. I don't like the sound of John Slaughter at an ARVN base camp near Pleiku. That's too near Cambodia, too near the NVA Regulars.

"And there won't be no milk there," Roscoe says. "No milk and no ice. We'll have to drink hot beer." Roscoe smiles at me. "But you won't have to drink hot beer for long because you're goin' go home soon, you and Lieutenant Goodrich."

I look at Sergeant Roscoe and ask, "Do you remember the day we arrived in Qui Nhon?"

"Yes sir," Roscoe says, lifting his glass. "I remember it real well. There was a bunch of Vietnamese recruits up there."

"And now we're going to an ARVN base camp in some godforsaken place where these little recruits are supposed to protect us."

Roscoe laughs. "Hell," he says, "they can't even protect themselves."

"Maybe they won't have to. Maybe they'll bring Mary Missionary along to protect us."

"No way," Roscoe interrupts. "You're too idealistic. You can't have it both ways. You can't be a soldier and a missionary at the same time. Soldiers are trained to fight. Missionaries are trained to love."

"We pass out medals to soldiers. Why don't we pass out medals to missionaries?"

"Yes," Roscoe says in a soft voice. "And I remember the Alamo." His voice becomes louder. "And remember the Maine." Then he stands and yells. "And remember the shaft. Remember the broken shaft."

I grab Roscoe by the arm and attempt to pull him back down onto the barstool, but he is too drunk to handle. He motions to the girls at the far end of the bar for them to join us. "Get up!" he yells to them. "Get up. We're ready now."

The girls recognize his gestures, but ignore him. Roscoe then walks toward them, but he doesn't stop. He merely walks out of the bar and, I assume, goes back to his billet and goes to sleep. He is certainly too drunk to do anything else.

One of the girls walks over beside me, sets her drink on the table, gently presses her hand on my leg and rests her head in my shoulder. I sit, looking at her long flowing black hair, but notice only the sadness in her eyes. The bartender yells something to her and she casually slides her hand up my leg and threads it between the two lower buttons of my shirt.

I look into the mirror and say aloud, "I have to get out of here."

To my surprise, the girl speaks English. "Let's go to my place," she says. She gently takes me by the arm, lifts me off the stool and leads me toward the door. We leave the bar, arm-in-arm, and walk outside and a short way down the street to a door of a small white building. She opens the door of the building and leads me up one flight of stairs to a second door, which she opens with a key. Inside, the room is dark. I'm afraid to enter. I tell her I don't want to go in.

"What's the matter?" she asks. "Are you afraid of the dark?" She turns on the lights to a well-furnished, clean little apartment that looks like home. There are curtains at the windows and there is carpet on the floor. There is a sofa, an easy chair, and several other chairs. At one end of the room is a dining area with stove, refrigerator and a small dining room table. Clean dishes are stacked on a shelf above the sink and pots and pans hang from the kitchen wall.

She tells me to have a seat, so I sit down on the sofa. She walks to the kitchen and leans back against the sink. "Fifty dollars," she says. "I cost fifty dollars."

This girl is a tough professional. She is businesslike and efficient. She wastes no time. She identifies her market, displays her wares, and announces the price, but she is not what I am looking for. After falling in love with the innocent little girl in polka-dotted panties this professional leaves me cold. Her cold approach lacks innocence and sincerity. I do not want this girl and tell myself that I live by higher standards. *A man may be permitted one principle to any one engagement. And he must keep all others in their due place relative to this one.*

I rise from the sofa and ask, "Do you really think you're worth fifty dollars?"

She slams her fist down on the sink top and screams at me in Vietnamese. She grabs one of the plates from the shelf and throws it at me, hitting me squarely in the forehead. The blood starts to run heavily. I feel my head and then reach into my pocket for a handkerchief to stop the flow of blood. She screams again and reaches for another dish. I run toward the door and open it just as the second dish hits the side of the door, breaking and scattering pieces of broken china around the room. She throws one final article down the stairs at me, striking me in the back—a steel pot.

The next morning I meet Roscoe for breakfast at an open-air café in the French District. From there we proceed to Saigon Engineer Headquarter to pick up our flight orders and schedule a flight to Cheo Reo for the following day.

I spend the rest of the day trying to get rid of a nasty hangover. I go to the USO. The waitresses there are friendly and the atmosphere homey. Hundreds of magazines line the walls. I haven't seen a magazine in months. There are pool tables and musical instruments. In the late afternoon a rock and roll band rehearses on a small stage where movies are shown in the evening. The USO club is moral, and that in itself is refreshing. I wish I had found the USO sooner. They even sell beer.

Early the next morning Roscoe pulls my jeep and jeep trailer, less the shaft, aboard a C-130 headed for Pleiku, with a specially scheduled stop at someplace nearby called Cheo Reo.

CHAPTER 12

The landing strip at Cheo Reo is cut into a heavily vegetated highland plateau. There are no other planes there—no hangars, no buildings—just a bare military runway of pierced metal planking surrounded by rubber trees. It is short and tenuous for our C-130 to land on. The pilot approaches at a steep slope, slows the engines immediately upon touchdown, and brings the plane to an abrupt stop.

There, waiting for us, are John Slaughter and Joe Goodrich. Slaughter is driving his own jeep. Goodrich is in the passenger's seat. They both wear flak jackets and are accompanied by two machine gun jeeps, manned by ARVN infantry. Slaughter jumps from the jeep and walks toward us. On his shoulders are brand new polished gold leaves.

I salute him. "Congratulations, Major."

Slaughter returns my salute. After not having seen each other in several months, we give each other a warm handshake. It is really good to see him, and I think he is glad to see me too. We have spent a lot of time together, shared a lot of good times, and endured a lot of heartaches. I'm delighted to see that he has risen from the ashes as a major. I really like John Slaughter. We can confide in each other with our innermost secrets. There are few others I can say that about.

Slightly behind him, to the left, stands Joe Goodrich. Joe Goodrich is one of those I do not trust with my innermost secrets, although I admire him greatly. Joe points to the machine gun jeeps. "The major wants to try and train these people to be warriors."

Slaughter grits his teeth and turns to Goodrich. "And you?" he growls.

"Lovers," Joe growls back.

Slaughter then turns back to me. "I suppose you want to do both."

Looking around, I see several little straw shacks tucked into the green jungle terrain. The area appears quiet and peaceful. Except I know that nearby are the beginnings of a military base camp with a barbed wire perimeter. "No," I reply, "we can't do both. Something has to change."

Slaughter is excited. He explains that an ARVN combat brigade is to be stationed at Cheo Reo and that we are to build a base camp for it. "A whole shipload of brand new equipment has been delivered for you guys," he says. "It's being unloaded now at Qui Nhon: bulldozers, loaders and graders."

I am not at all excited. Reminding Slaughter that I have only a few days left in the country, I ask him if anything about this place is at all dangerous.

"You're not short yet," he tells me. "There's plenty of time. We brought a couple dozers with us and we are all ready to open up a borrow pit like the one you had at An Khe. You can set things up there."

"Major," I say to him. "Sir, with all due respect, I may not be your man."

"Oh, yes you are," he says as he gets back into his jeep, directing Roscoe and me to get into our jeep and follow him, which we reluctantly agree to do. We have to; this is his show. All we can do is try and be careful. *We can only choose how we act, not under what circumstances we must act.* "There are two ways to get where we are going. We are taking the dangerous route. Don't ever go this way by yourself."

"No sir," I reply. John Slaughter may still be John Slaughter, but now he is Major John Slaughter. Instead of acting like his old self, he tries to act like a major. That's OK with me. I still like him, just the same.

"Let's go," he says. "Keep your weapons loaded, and keep your legs inside the jeep. There may be mines."

Slaughter leads us out of the airfield, driving for a short distance down a smooth-surfaced dirt road and then onto a narrow, bumpy dirt road. There are no asphalt paved roads at Cheo Reo, only dirt roads. Although he drives too fast for the conditions, Roscoe stays with him, close behind in our jeep, until we arrive at what looks like the site of the new base camp. It is not a pretty picture. Armed ARVN guards stand in fortified bunkers, overlooking large open areas of cleared terrain bordering the jungle. Two bulldozers are being used to build a defensive berm as several squads of Vietnamese troops lay barbed wire.

Slaughter stops in front of the first bunker we come to. We get out of the jeeps and step up onto one of the firing positions where a 50-caliber machine gun stares across the open barbed wire perimeter. "We have this bunker here set up with grazing fire and another on down the berm about two hundred yards. The firing lines cross right over there in the woods." Slaughter looks down at the Spec 4 gunner and asks him to show him his fields of fire.

The gunner points to two small sticks, spaced eight feet apart and stuck in the ground about six feet in front of his weapon.

Slaughter nods approvingly. "You ever see a man hit by a 50?" he asks the man.

"No sir," the Spec 4 replies.

"Tear an arm off. This is one of the best weapons the army has, and we have four of them." Slaughter points across the bare stretch of ground which lies between us and the jungle. "It cost us two men to clear that piece of land: booby traps. That's why I ordered these flak jackets. We're playing a nasty game here."

I look down at the gunner and then back at Slaughter. "I'm impressed, Major."

Joe Goodrich now speaks up. "I'm not."

Slaughter places his arm on my shoulder and whispers into my ear, "Jeffries, you get in my jeep." He then tells Joe Goodrich to ride with Roscoe.

"Do I need a weapon?" I ask.

"Don't ever travel around here without it. Do you have a bulletproof vest?"

"No sir."

"Well, get one," he tells me. "I want every man in the company to have one."

Slaughter jumps into the driver's seat. He fastens each snap on his bullet-proof vest and zips the zipper all the way up. Then, with me riding shotgun, he drives off in a cloud of dust toward the far end of the compound.

"We have a lot of little people working here, too," he remarks as we pass a group of civilian laborers. "You know there are lots of jobs here for the little people. We put them to work."

Slaughter stops near a road junction where an ARVN platoon is laying a section of drainage pipe under the direction of an American sergeant supervisor. The sergeant in charge is standing on the road surface, alongside of a six-foot deep excavation. Slaughter gets out of his jeep and stands with his hands on his hips, looking down at several Vietnamese men who are sitting in the squatting position down in the trench.

"Now, Jefferies," Slaughter leans over and whispers, "here is a perfect example of how to not get a thing done. You watch me get this sergeant's tail. He's a good sergeant; he just needs a little guidance and direction. That is one of my jobs, you know, to give guidance and direction."

The sergeant motions for the people to stand up and go back to work.

Slaughter looks down in the trench and yells, "Now we're not all moving in the same direction." He takes one jump and lands firmly in the bottom of the hole. He slaps his hands together and smiles at the laborers. "All right, we're going to work," he says. He then motions for the sergeant to jump down in the trench with him. "You grab one end of the pipe and I'll grab the other end." Then he motions for the civilians to move up.

"Jeffries," he yells up while working. "You have to get in here and work with these little people and show them what to do."

I extend my hand to the sergeant. "David Jeffries."

"When he's done showing off," the sergeant says softly, "we'll go back to work."

Down in the trench the major roars, "How are you going to drain water downstream with the downstream end higher than the upstream end? Water won't flow up hill, Sergeant. Now you're going to have to do better than this. I want this job done by quitting time, and I want this road open again." The major points to the Vietnamese workers, "Start digging right here." He screams while signaling for them to go back to work. "That's it. Go ahead."

Finally, the sergeant jumps down in the trench with the major.

Slaughter appreciates that. "See? They don't understand, Sergeant," Major Slaughter explains. "You have to show them. You have to demonstrate what you want done, and you have to try and explain to them how to do it."

The sergeant mumbles that it is difficult because he doesn't speak their language. "Sir," the sergeant says, "these people were on a temporary break while I was figuring the difference in elevations between the two ends of the pipe."

"You have a lot to learn, young man." Slaughter shakes his head and grits his teeth. "You won't get anything done standing around. You have to get in and do it with them." Then, having gotten that off his chest, Slaughter climbs back out of the trench and bounces back into the jeep. "Let's go," he says as he shifts the jeep into four-wheel drive and floors the accelerator.

John turns the jeep in the opposite direction and drives out of the camp. "When you pass this point, you put your steel pot on and grab hold of your weapon." He reaches across me and grabs the stock of my rifle. "But don't chamber a round unless you intend to shoot somebody."

"No sir."

About a mile beyond the camp he pulls off onto a bumpy dirt road full of potholes. "Stick your head up and tell me if you see any mines."

"Mines?"

"A lieutenant lost his leg here a couple days ago, right down here in the middle of the road. That young lieutenant liked to ride with his leg dangling out the side of the jeep. It took it off right here." Slaughter strikes a line across his leg just below the knee and then looks ahead down the road. "You see any?"

"No sir, I don't reckon I do."

He again floors the jeep and drives ahead, bouncing over the potholes. "While you are here," he says, "you have to stay alert every minute. Some officers, all they think about is drinking beer and going to the officers' club. When you're on the road you look for mines and snipers. You know, if we all move in the same direction we can get an awful lot done."

He then slows to drive a short way through a wooded area and then into what looks like the beginnings of a borrow pit. "This is it," he says. "This is where I want you to open the borrow pit." The open site is about the size of a football field. It is heavily wooded on all four sides. "When the Big Deuce gets here we are going to move some dirt."

"Yes sir," I say, wishing he was still a captain instead of a major.

"We're all in the same army, aren't we?"

"Yes sir."

"And we're all fighting the same war?"

"Yes sir."

"And we're all moving in the same direction."

After returning to camp, Slaughter drives directly to the supply tent where he pulls up in front of an open tent flap and yells at a supply sergeant inside, "I want two hundred bulletproof vests."

The supply sergeant yells back, "Those are hard to come by for engineers."

"I didn't ask you how hard they are to come by. I said I want them. And I want them here in two days."

We eat supper—K-rations—and retire to the officers' club, a small GP tent set up near the doctor's quarters. Inside are several infantry lieutenants, a doctor and a chaplain. I remark to Slaughter that I am surprised to see all of these people. He replies that this is a special contingent from the 173rd Airborne who are here only until the rest of the ARVN Brigade arrives.

Slaughter sits down at a folding desk, reaches under a nearby table and pulls out a small leather pouch. "Play some liars' dice?" he asks.

"OK sir," I answer.

The doctor and the chaplain join us. The major, sitting at the head of the table, rubs his hands together and looks at the doctor. "One beer," he says, and then he places his hand on mine. "How about you?"

"I'll have a beer."

"Two beers, Doc," he says. "Loser buys."

"You must be expecting me to lose."

"Have you ever played this game before?"

"No sir."

"You'll lose."

We play liars' dice with the doctor and the chaplain for about a half an hour. The major is good at the game; he wins consistently. Occasionally, the doctor pokes fun at the major, claiming he is the only one of us who knows the game and is using that as an unfair advantage. The chaplain says little. He simply smiles, taking his losses in stride. During the game we also try to discuss business, the pending arrival of our men from Qui Nhon, and our new equipment. The major is concerned because until a new replacement arrives, Rodney Swartz is in command at Qui Nhon, and Slaughter is concerned that Rodney will drag his feet until his discharge orders arrive to avoid the trip west. I assure him that Rodney would never do a thing like that, and I offer to call Rodney to see how things are progressing and when he expects to arrive here. Slaughter is somewhat reluctant to let me make the call, but he finally agrees, with the stipulation that I tell Rodney that we need him right away and ask him to hurry as fast as possible. I agree to that and go immediately to the communications tent.

It takes me almost an hour to reach Qui Nhon on the field phone from the ARVN base at Cheo Reo. I sit in the Como shack, waiting for a free line. For the first half-hour I try every few minutes, talking with operators all over Vietnam. Eventually, I decide there is either a technical difficulty at Qui Nhon or the Qui Nhon trunk is overloaded.

I sit in the communications tent, tracing the maze of wires, wondering what they are all connected to. I run my hands over the wires. I hold the terminals between my fingers, wondering who I might be able to reach. Maybe I could reach the States.

So I try it. Following the procedure I have recently learned so far tonight, I call Thunder and then ask for Lightning, then Bien Hoa, then Long Bien, then Saigon, then Saigon LD. When I ask for a line to the States, the Saigon LD operator puts me through to Guam. I can do it. I can call home. I can call home from a little field phone in Cheo Reo, almost. The operator in Guam asks me for my priority. When I tell him "routine," he says he cannot put me through on a routine priority. I understand that, but it is amazing to me that I got as far as Guam. It amazes me how easy it is to call halfway around the world to talk to most anybody. All that is needed is the right priority code. It is so easy. And it is also ironic. I can communicate with practically anybody halfway around the world, but I can't communicate with the civilian people here in Vietnam. I can't communicate because I don't speak the language.

Finally, after many tries, I hear a familiar voice over the field phone. "Three-Sixty-Second orderly room, Sergeant Fallon speaking."

"This is Lieutenant Jefferies." I answer enthusiastically. "Is Lieutenant Swartz there?"

"Hey, Lieutenant! How are you?" Fallon asks. "It's good to hear your voice, sir. Where are you?"

"I'm in Cheo Reo. Let me talk to Lieutenant Swartz."

"Oh, sir. Is anybody shooting at you over there?"

"No, not yet." I answer. "Listen, it's hard to get through to you on this telephone. If you need to reach me you have to first call Saigon."

"Yeah."

"Then you call Lightning."

"Yeah."

"Then you call Thunder. And then…Oh, forget it! Don't call me. I'll call you."

"Lieutenant Swartz says he doesn't want to talk to you anyway. He doesn't want to talk to anybody except the man who will cut his travel orders to go home."

Joe Goodrich and I feel the same way; we want our travel orders to go home. That is our favorite topic of conversation: going home. The only difference between us—Joe Goodrich and me—is that I am ready to go home immediately. There is nothing to keep me here, nothing at all. But not Joe; Joe has found a friend. Joe has Mary Missionary.

It is incredible to me that Joe found her here. She is simply too young and pretty to be in Vietnam during war times like these. Her long blond hair, flawless complexion, and tall thin body are more suggestive of a model than a missionary. She looks like one of those girls you see in clothing ads in the Sunday newspaper. That may sound like blasphemy, but I don't intend it to be that; rather it should be taken as a compliment. This girl is a well-educated college graduate who obviously had her pick of jobs after graduation. She chose the missionary field. But how did she ever end up here? Who in their right mind would have sent her to a war-torn country like this?

In any event, she is here, and Joe Goodrich is in love with her and doesn't want to leave without her. Joe and I talk about that often, especially since Slaughter has been giving us reenlistment speeches. Slaughter has to do that—army protocol. Slaughter indicates he wants us to re-enlist, especially me. I don't think he really cares about Joe, but Joe gets the same speech as I do. While I decide definitely against it, Joe seeks more information. Joe wants to stay near Mary Missionary as long as she is here.

Joe finally makes an official request in writing, offering to extend his tour of duty for six months provided he is transferred to and stationed with Group Headquarters in Qui Nhon.

Within days the company arrives, except Rodney Swartz, who received his travel orders and went home. Slaughter is so intent on commencing work that he doesn't even allow the men time to settle in. He assigns a few men to pitch tents, then he orders the rest to unload the equipment and begin work.

He assigns each of the officers to particular worksites throughout the base camp area. He assigns me to the borrow pit. He wanted to assign Joe Goodrich there, but Joe's request for transfer to Group has been approved. The night before Joe leaves, the officers have a little sendoff for him—a chocolate cake specially prepared for him by the mess sergeant and a double ration of beer for the rest of us. In the morning I accompany Joe to the airstrip and see him off. I wish him well with his efforts for peaceful coexistence, and especially well with Mary Missionary.

Otherwise, the company works around the clock. I spend a lot of time during the day at the borrow pit, constantly reminding the men of Fitzgerald's deadly accident at An Khe. I warn them repeatedly not to take any unnecessary chances and to never fall asleep on the machines. I make it a point to visit the borrow pit several times during the day and twice each night just to remind them to take care of themselves. As far as I am concerned, that pile of dirt is not worth one single life.

Traveling to the pit is easy during the day. We feel secure. But at night it is a different matter. At night we have an uneasy feeling that the VC are watching us. The people here are not as friendly as those in Canh Van Valley and Qui Nhon. I view everyone here with suspicion, even the ARVN troops. Most of the people here are standoffish, often refusing to even look us in the eye. There is, for some reason, a feeling of contempt between us, a feeling I have not noticed elsewhere.

Each night, for the past few nights, several brief firefights have occurred along the perimeter near the haul road. We are concerned, but not overly so. We continue quarry operations as routine. Still, we add some security: one squad of ARVN at the pit and one squad along the haul road.

Each night, about midnight, I make an effort to get out of bed and drive to the quarry. The haul road is about a half mile long and unsecured, so I drive as fast as possible, park my jeep near the loading area, and simply watch.

Roscoe is in charge at the quarry. He has three bulldozers and two front-end loaders. The headlights of the bulldozers burn intently in the late night hours as the big machines strip gravel from the surface of the pit and push it into neat piles, where the front-end loaders scoop it up and load it into dump trucks to be hauled to various sites, to be used for road construction. One of the operators has formed a ledge onto which he constantly backs up. It is a sharp ledge from which he could easily catch a track and overturn the machine. I mention that to Roscoe, asking him to suspend operations there and move to another location until morning.

Roscoe indicates that he feels I am being overly cautious, but he agrees to my request. He then starts walking up the hill toward the dozer. It is a very steep hill. Roscoe uses his hands pushing down on his thighs to boost him along the narrow, poorly lit trail. A hedgerow borders one side of the trail—a thick hedgerow with prickly stickers.

Suddenly, without warning, there is a violent explosion. The noise is deafening, several decibels louder than the bulldozers.

Roscoe falls to the ground, yelling. "I been hit! I been hit!" He screams loudly enough for me to hear him, and he lies directly in front of a front loader's headlights so we can see him clearly.

I run to him as fast as I can.

"I been hit, sir." Roscoe is bleeding from the right forearm and right side. "I been hit."

Nearby is a squad of Vietnamese infantrymen, one of whom has a radio. I motion for him to call for help, which he does, calling for a med-evac helicopter. What do you know? We communicated!

I kneel down on one knee by Roscoe's side. "We are going to get you out of here." I try to aid and comfort Roscoe as much as possible. His arm bleeds heavily. I remove my shirt and tie it around Roscoe's arm as a tourniquet. Within minutes, a helicopter arrives and transports him to a base hospital in Pleiku.

In the morning we trace detonating wire a few hundred feet into a nearby village, where the villagers claim to know nothing. "How," I ask myself, "can a detonating wire be traced into a neighboring village without anybody in the village knowing anything about it?" No way! They know. They are all a part of it. They are all responsible.

The infantry wants to burn the village down. I agree. It's too late here for talk. Now is not the time for peaceful coexistence. It is too late for that; we have already failed at peaceful coexistence. We are here to fight a war, not win friends and influence people. That is what we are equipped for. That is what we are trained for. That is our job.

The following day, I decide to catch a chopper for the hospital at Pleiku to see Roscoe. That seems to be the least I can do. I wish I could do more. I wish I could go back to that eventful night and tell him not to walk that trail. But all I can do is to visit him at Pleiku.

The hospital in Pleiku looks pretty much like the one at An Khe—prefabricated Quonset huts. I enter the hospital and see several nurses and long rows of beds, full of patients. One of the nurses leads me to a ward with two rows of beds, one row on each side of the long narrow room. All the beds are full. Roscoe is on the left side, near the middle.

I walk past many other wounded men, to Roscoe. Roscoe sees me coming and smiles. He is all right. His wounds are minor. We chat a while, small talk mostly. He will obviously soon be able to return to Cheo Reo. But not everyone there is so lucky.

Next to Roscoe lies a black man. The man's arms are strung up in the air with rope. Both hands are missing, amputated just below the elbow. His face is covered with pock-marks and his whole body has a purple tinge.

Roscoe is luckier. Roscoe's wounds are superficial. He will be bandaged up and sent back to duty. He feels good about that. Roscoe is a career man. Now that he has a purple heart, promotions may come faster. We talk.

While we talk, a nurse walks over and pulls a sheet over the black man lying in the next bed, then two male nurses come and lift the bed—one at the foot and one at the head—and carry the bed out of the room. The man is dead.

It is the night before I am to leave. Slaughter has seen fit to make me, "officer of the day," which means I am on duty all night at the CP. About 0100 in the morning I get a call from the major.

"Slaughter here," he yells over the field phone. "I'm at Division headquarters and I have just been informed one of your trucks has hit a mine on the haul road and that your men have shut down operation."

"They did?" I ask.

"You're the OD. Did they?"

"I didn't hear anything about it."

"Well, they did. I want you to go retrieve the truck and get the men back to work."

"Yes sir," I say. I sit for a moment behind the desk. I swear silently and then pound my fist on the desk top, wondering what to do. Fallon! I decide to call Fallon. Fallon will know what to do.

I get Fallon out of bed. Fortunately, he is sober, but he is also unhappy about being awakened in the middle of the night. He is even unhappier when I tell him what Slaughter wants us to do, but he is sober and agrees to come with me. We also get Bennett and Hayman up and have them ride in a three-quarter ton maintenance truck in case we need it.

Fallon drives the jeep, steering with one hand and holding his rifle with the other. We ride with blackout lights to a secured bunker leading out of the camp. We stop there and turn off the engines.

I get out of the jeep, walk to the bunker and up to an American infantryman, standing there staring down the haul road through an infrared sniper scope.

"They're out there, Lieutenant," the infantryman says. "The NVA are out there."

"How far to the truck?" I ask.

"About a quarter of a mile. Your men shouldn't have left it."

"I know. But it is there and we have to go out there and get it and bring it back."

"If you wait until morning the VC will have booby trapped it."

I tell Bennett to go get a wrecker. I ask the infantryman to hand me the scope. Looking through the scope, I can clearly see the bombed-out truck. It looks like it is totaled.

Bennett returns with the wrecker and an operator for it. "I don't like the looks of this," Bennett says.

Fallon agrees with him. "No sir. Not one little bit."

Neither do I. After thinking about it of a moment, I turn to Fallon and say, "I don't want to go out there. This is my last day in country. I have travel orders. I'm too short."

"You'd be a damn fool to go out there tonight. One mine could blow that little old jeep to smithereens. You're leaving tomorrow. I'll take care of this," Fallon says, reaching into his hip pocket, pulling out a flask of whisky and taking a big long drink. "Courage," he says. "You want some?"

We drive to the edge of the perimeter where we wait, nervously wondering what to do. The wrecker is waiting behind us. Bennett is riding in the wrecker. I tell Bennett to get out and into my jeep. I then direct Hayman to ride in the wrecker.

Soon Slaughter arrives. As usual, he is driving his own jeep. "What's the holdup?"

"Sir, we had to get a wrecker."

"So now you have one. So what are you waiting for?"

"I'm going home tomorrow," I say, "and I don't plan to get killed tonight."
We cannot change the preconditions that influence our actions, but we can act to change the preconditions of time.

Slaughter watches while Fallon finishes off the flask, then Slaughter claps his hands and smiles at me. "You stay here with the old drunks," he says. Then he turns the headlights on high beams and stands up in his jeep, motioning for the wrecker to follow him.

I stand respectfully by the side of Slaughter's jeep, watching him as he slides back into the driver's seat. I look down into his wide-open eyes and his smiling face.

Slaughter races the engine. "We're all in the same army, aren't we?"

"Yes sir."

"And we're all fighting the same war?"

"Yes sir."

"And we're all moving in the same direction."

Slaughter waits for me to acknowledge his comment. But I don't. I don't say another word to him. I simply stand there, silently. For me, after all this time, after all I have been through, this is the clear high point of action. This is the climax. I'm going home.

Slaughter smiles broadly while he continues to wait for me to say something. When I don't, after a while he pulls his jeep off onto the shoulder and waves for the wrecker to move forward down the road toward the disabled truck. We watch the wrecker. It is a dark night. Even so, the outline is clearly visible, because the driver has the running lights turned on. The canvas cab cover has been removed so we can see the driver, and we can see Hayman riding shotgun. The wrecker makes a lot of noise and produces a lot of diesel exhaust smoke. The diesel smoke creates a lingering gasoline smell, like the smell of napalm in the morning. It smells like victory. But we are not alone.

Moving forward, the wrecker gets only a few hundred feet when the NVA open fire with a machine gun and several small arms from the nearby tree line. They blast the hell out of the wrecker. The fuel tank explodes with a violent eruption.

The driver jumps from the vehicle and falls to the ground. Hayman is thrown wildly into the air, his body ablaze with diesel fuel. In one brief moment we can see that the driver is seriously wounded; Hayman has been killed.

The rest of us leap from our vehicles, take up firing positions and return fire. But it is useless. The NVA quickly disappear; probably back into the tunnels they have been building for years. We lost some expensive equipment. Somebody got killed. Here it happens every day. Every day there is another killing. And when the killing is over, all is forgotten. We tell ourselves to forget it. Forget it. It is over.

The following day—my day to leave for home—is beautiful. I arrive at Tan Son Nuit Airport early in the afternoon. There must be several thousand men here—some arriving, and some leaving.

After presenting my travel orders to a clerk in the passenger terminal, I get in line and stand amidst a group of khaki uniformed troops waiting to board a 707 jet liner soon to land. We all carry flight bags and march at route step past temporary billets used to house incoming and outgoing troops, and then into a briefing room to receive customs instructions.

It is a short wait, perhaps three hours. Time passes quickly, because we get to wait inside a large service club with rows upon rows of tables and benches. The benches overflow with singing GIs, and the tables are cluttered with beer cans. At the front of the room is a large stage where a Vietnamese rock and roll band with twangy guitars plays loudly.

The hours pass quickly for me, where inside the club the band sings, "I want to go home. I want to go home. Oh—how I want—to go home." As the band plays, the rows of men hold their beer cans high into the air, swinging back and forth, singing loudly. "I want to go home. I want to go home. Oh—how I want—to go home."

The 707 touches down upon a distant runway and then slowly taxies up to the terminal, where it unloads a stream of new replacements. I look intently at each new replacement as he walks out of the plane, down the stairs of the boarding ramp, briefly wondering what their tour of duty has in store for them. For each, it will be different, depending on their assignment, and which cattle car they get on.

As for me, I was lucky. I didn't get hurt physically. Psychologically, however, I paid a heavy price, as did we all. Looking back, I like to think we did good. At least we tried to do good, and that is noble. Looking back, I like to think that we addressed the real conflicts. At least we tried to. But that was hard to do, because we didn't speak the language. All in all, I am proud. It was a noble conflict. We did the best we could under the circumstances. That is all anybody can do. That is all these replacements can do.

When the replacements have passed by and are out of sight, we move forward to board the plane. The engines have stopped. All we hear is music in the background as we climb the boarding ramp past the smiling stewardesses.

0-595-33294-3

Printed in the United States
110422LV00003B/200/A